The Sommersby Brides

Sisters, Scandals and Society Weddings

Three sisters caught in scandalous situations
find their love for each other stretched and tested.
Three men will give each sister
the happy-ever-after they deserve.

There's Lady Charlotte, who, as an
independent widow, never thinks to find love
again. Lady Juliet finds herself caught in a highly
compromising situation, and Lady Elizabeth's
pretend marriage becomes all too real.

Read Lady Charlotte's story in

One Week to Wed

Discover Lady Juliet's story in

"One Night Under the Mistletoe"

Part of the *Convenient Christmas Brides* anthology

And Lady Elizabeth finds her happy-ever-after in

His Three-Day Duchess

All available now

Author Note

When I created Lizzy as a secondary character in *An Unsuitable Duchess*, I never considered her future. But her attraction to Lord Andrew Pearce stuck with me, and over the course of the Secret Lives of the Ton series, I had fun having his family tease Andrew about her crush on him. When some of you asked me to write his story, I knew Lizzy would have to be in it and decided, sadly for her, that Andrew would fall in love with her sister. Now Lizzy gets to find true love. I adored writing about the Sommersby sisters. Charlotte, Lizzy and Juliet hold a special place in my heart. I hope you've come to care about them, too. If you'd like to find out what I'm working on next, head over to my website at lauriebenson.net.

LAURIE BENSON

His Three-Day Duchess

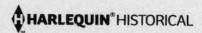

HARLEQUIN®HISTORICAL

Recycling programs for this product may not exist in your area.

ISBN-13: 978-1-335-63492-4

His Three-Day Duchess

Copyright © 2019 by Laurie Benson

All rights reserved. Except for use in any review, the reproduction or utilization of this work in whole or in part in any form by any electronic, mechanical or other means, now known or hereafter invented, including xerography, photocopying and recording, or in any information storage or retrieval system, is forbidden without the written permission of the publisher, Harlequin Enterprises Limited, 22 Adelaide St. West, 40th Floor, Toronto, Ontario M5H 4E3, Canada.

This is a work of fiction. Names, characters, places and incidents are either the product of the author's imagination or are used fictitiously, and any resemblance to actual persons, living or dead, business establishments, events or locales is entirely coincidental.

This edition published by arrangement with Harlequin Books S.A.

For questions and comments about the quality of this book, please contact us at CustomerService@Harlequin.com.

® and TM are trademarks of Harlequin Enterprises Limited or its corporate affiliates. Trademarks indicated with ® are registered in the United States Patent and Trademark Office, the Canadian Intellectual Property Office and in other countries.

Printed in U.S.A.

ɔr all the girls who weren't asked to the prom,
your best days are still to come.

Thank you to my insightful and patient editor,
Linda Fildew, and my team at Harlequin. This book
wouldn't have been possible without the love and
support of my family. Thanks for the care and feeding
of an author under deadline! Love you, guys! To
Anabelle, Lori, Mia, Jen, Marnee and my
H crew, thanks for your friendship and for making me
snort with laughter at the most unexpected times,
usually looking at my phone while I'm waiting in
line in a store. And thank you to my readers. Your
enthusiasm about my books means so much.

Laurie Benson is an award-winn'
author whose book *An Unexpecte*
featured Harlequin's 2017 Hero of the
by readers. She began her writing career
advertising copywriter. When she isn't at her
avoiding laundry, Laurie can be found browsing
antiques shops and going on long hikes with her
husband and two sons. Learn more about Laurie by
visiting her website at lauriebenson.net. You can also
find her on Twitter and Facebook.

Books by Laurie Benson

Harlequin Historical

The Sommersby Brides

One Week to Wed
Convenient Christmas Brides
"One Night Under the Mistletoe"
His Three-Day Duchess

Secret Lives of the Ton

An Unsuitable Duchess
An Uncommon Duke
An Unexpected Countess

Visit the Author Profile page at Harlequin.com.

Prologue

London—July, 1819

As she sat across the desk from her solicitor, it was beginning to feel as if Lizzy had been waiting all her life for Mr Simon Alexander. And as the newly widowed Duchess of Skeffington, she wasn't accustomed to waiting for anything or anyone. Her husband had died months ago and she had yet to meet Mr Alexander, her husband's heir or, as he would be referred to now, the Duke of Skeffington. His tardiness today at the reading of her late husband's will was doing nothing to help the annoyance she already felt towards a man she had never met.

'I'm sure he won't be much longer,' Mr Nesbit said, furrowing his grey brows and glancing at his pocket watch for what must have been the fifth time since she had arrived at his office at promptly one o'clock in the afternoon.

Lizzy toyed with her emerald necklace and didn't even try to hide her irritation. 'At least one of us is confident in that. You're certain he knows where we were to meet?'

'I was very specific in my letter. He knows.'

She glanced down the table to Rimsby, the impeccably dressed old man who had served as butler of Skeffington House here in London for as long as Lizzy had been married. This was a man who valued protocol and proper behaviour, and she imagined he was just as displeased with his new employer's tardiness as she was. Mrs Thacker, who was seated next to Rimsby, had an odd blush about her at the mention of the new Duke—a blush that in the twelve years that the woman had been her housekeeper, she had never seen brighten her normally sombre countenance.

'Do we still have to wait for him?' She directed her question to Lord Liverpool, the executor of her husband's estate, who at the moment was standing by the window looking out at the busy London street. 'We know he finally is in London after all these months. Can't we just begin and Mr Nesbit can give him a brief summary of what he missed when he arrives?'

He stepped away from the window and turned to face her. 'Skeffington was very insistent that the will was to be read only when everyone who benefited was present and Mr Alexander, as the new Duke, must be present.'

Beside her Mr Mix, her late husband's secretary, shifted in his chair. The leather gave a considerable creak, which was surprising in light of his small, wiry frame. The gentleman, who was about twenty years older than Lizzy's twenty-nine years, continued to sit silently, offering no indication on how he felt about the tardy behaviour of the new Duke. But as he had worked with her husband for all those years, she assumed he was accustomed to keeping his opinions to himself. He sat staring at his clasped hands on the table and she wondered once again why he had been content to be berated by her husband for so long. Certainly, there were other members of the House of Lords who would have welcomed his services. He could have put the Duke's company behind him long ago, unlike Lizzy who had been forced to endure it since she was seventeen.

'Do you know if Mr Alexander will be retaining your services, Mr Mix?' Lizzy asked him to pass the time.

'I do not. Since he just arrived here in London a few nights ago, we've not yet had the opportunity to meet.'

Now that Mr Alexander was finally in London, Mr Mix had to believe that the status of his job was precarious.

'I know how my husband relied on you. I'm sure the new Duke will, as well.' She tried to be reassuring when she noticed his right leg bouncing nervously under the table.

'That's very kind of you, Your Grace,' he replied, giving her what appeared to be a strained smile.

He wasn't the only one who was feeling the need to move. Lizzy wanted desperately to get up and walk about the room, but Lord Liverpool was already taking up that action. They didn't need to bump into one another as they waited for the tardy Duke to grace them with his presence. It appeared he had settled into his new station in life already and was going to be one of those gentlemen who strove to create a grand entrance by arriving late, reminding them all that he was a duke of England and they all would have to adjust to his schedule. She had witnessed behaviour like this before. Well, she was a duchess and had held her esteemed rank longer than he had!

She was just about to request a glass of sherry to still her agitation when one of Mr Nesbit's clerks appeared in the doorway and announced the Duke of Skeffington. Lizzy's stomach did an uncomfortable dip. It had been six months since she'd heard someone announce that name and she had to remind herself that her odious husband was dead. Now that his successor was in London, she would have to grow accustomed to hearing that name without that familiar feeling of dread.

Turning her head, she finally came face-to-face with her late husband's heir. The handsome gentleman standing tall in the doorway with the lean, athletic build was not what she had expected. He appeared to be only a few years older than she was and by the cut of his brown tailcoat and the state of his boots she could assume he was a man who dressed out of necessity instead of fashion—even though the cut of the coat did wonders to draw attention to his broad shoulders and the defined muscles in his arms. His dark eyes rimmed with thick dark lashes settled on Lizzy for a few additional heartbeats before he continued to survey the occupants in the room. For those extra moments that their eyes held, the room seemed to fade away.

Mr Nesbit came around the table, breaking the spell that had come over her, and shook the new Duke's hand. 'Your Grace, thank you for joining us. We were growing concerned that there might have been an accident.'

'No, there was no accident. As you can see, Nesbit, I am in one piece.'

And a very fine piece he was in with that jet-black hair, a lock of which was threatening to fall into his dark eyes. But when it was apparent he had no intention of apologising for keeping them waiting, it reaffirmed Lizzy's belief that only arrogant selfish men would hold the title of Duke of Skeffington.

'You have been keeping us waiting for over an hour.'

She hadn't intended to address him. She was at the end of her tether, waiting for confirmation that Skeffington had given her Stonehaven as her permanent residence. Six months was a long time to live without knowing what your future would hold—and it was all because of him. His laissez-faire attitude was irksome. It was the only explanation as to why she felt compelled to address him before Mr Nesbit had the opportunity to formally introduce them.

He turned to face her and Lizzy fought the urge to touch her hair to make sure it was still meticulously arranged.

'And you are?'

His accent gave away that he was from the north and, if she had to guess, she thought perhaps the Lincolnshire area.

'I'm Elizabeth, the Duchess of Skeffington,' she replied before Mr Nesbit could step in.

'You are his wife?' His deep smooth voice almost had a hint of surprise in it.

'If you are referring to your predecessor, then the answer is yes.'

He tilted his head slightly and appeared to be studying her more intently, and Lizzy forced her hands to remain lightly folded on her lap.

'You are not what I was expecting.'

'And I was expecting a gentleman who would arrive promptly to attend the reading of a will.'

'I had a matter that needed attending to first. You could have started reading it without me.'

It was taking considerable effort not to raise her voice. 'No, we couldn't. If we were able to do that we would have done so months ago when you were gallivanting wherever it was you've been.'

'Gallivanting?' There was a quirk to his slightly full lips.

'Yes, gallivanting. Now could we please finally have a reading of this will so we all can go forward with our lives? I'm assuming, Mr Nesbit, we are all here now and there is no one else we need to wait for?'

'There is no one else mentioned in the will. Everyone is present.'

He introduced the new Duke, who Lizzy was having a hard time thinking of as Skeffington, to Lord Liverpool and Mr Mix. The man nodded a greeting to Rimsby and Mrs Thacker, before taking a seat beside Lizzy at the table.

Sitting this close to him was far more distracting than it should be. Lizzy skirted a glance at him with the intention of studying him a bit more, but when he turned his head and caught her eye, she quickly shifted her gaze and prayed she wouldn't start blushing.

Lizzy settled into her seat and redirected her attention to Mr Nesbit. Now she would finally find out which of the four Skeffington estates would be hers and she could begin setting up her own independent household where she would never have to live with another man again. She had been praying it was Stonehaven in Dorset. It had been her private sanctuary outside London throughout her marriage and, most of all, it was the only Skeffington residence that felt like home to her. Her husband knew it was the one property, aside from the London town house, that she had spent the most amount of time in over the years and, since it wasn't his ducal seat, it was logical that he would bequeath it to her to live in. Although, knowing her husband, he could be unpredictable at times.

Placing her hands under the table, Lizzy crossed her fingers as Mr Nesbit read the particulars of the introduction to the will. Skeffington's snuffbox collection would go to Mr Mix, the chess set in their London drawing room was to go to Rimsby since they played the game together quite often, and a painting that belonged to Skeffington's first wife was given to Mrs Thacker, who had been her lady's maid when the woman was alive.

Finally, Mr Nesbit glanced at Lizzy. He wiped his brow with a white handkerchief before he continued to read from the will. 'And for my wife, Elizabeth, since she failed to produce any heirs during our marriage, I bequeath to her the sum of eight thousand pounds.'

The amount given to her floated past without any knowledge of what it was. All Lizzy was able to focus on was the fact that the wretched man was publicly shaming her for her inability to conceive a child with him. As if it were all her fault that he had no direct heirs to take over the ducal seat. As if all the people sitting in the room couldn't tell they had no children together and she had failed in her duty to bear him an heir. The presence of Mr Alexander was a clear reminder. The nails of her right hand were digging painfully into her palm as she tried her hardest to appear unaffected by her late husband's intentional barb.

But then the words Mr Nesbit had read came back to her and she shook her head, convinced she hadn't heard correctly. 'That can't be right. I was to have twenty thousand pounds as per my marriage agreement.'

Mr Nesbit wiped his sweaty brow once more and shifted his gaze between Lizzy and the paper in his hand. 'That was if you bore him an heir.'

'I was never told that. My father agreed to that?'

'Apparently he did, Your Grace. It was in the marriage agreement. I have a copy in my files if you would care to see it.'

'My father told me I was to get twenty thousand upon my husband's death.'

'That is correct. If there was a child. If you did not produce any children, then you were to receive eight thousand pounds, the amount of your dowry upon your marriage to him.'

There was a sharp familiar ache in her chest. How could her father have not thought to tell her about that clause in the agreement? How could he possibly think that was fair? They had to have agreed upon this at Skeffington's urging, but now she had additional proof that her father was only interested in furthering his own connections through her marriage and would agree to anything to make sure he had the privilege of having a family connection to a duke.

She was the Duchess of Skeffington! How was she supposed to live on less than ten thousand? She employed an extensive staff, had three carriages, hosted the most extravagant balls and wore the finest clothes. Eight thousand pounds would never do. She had a reputation to maintain. Her only consolation was that hopefully she would be able to live in Stonehaven and retain the income from that estate which would help pay for her expenses.

Mr Nesbit caught her eye and looked as if he expected her to throw her chair across the room. 'There is more, Your Grace.'

'Yes, well, I imagine there is. But I think we all can agree that if he references my childless state again there is no need to read it. It will just be redundant.'

He cleared his throat and adjusted his glasses. 'She also is to have the use of Clivemoore House until she dies or remarries.'

Dear God, no. The remainder of her life would now be spent in a house of his choosing, in a remote area of the country far away from her sisters and her aunt and where she had no friends. Even in death, that horrid man was going to make her life miserable.

She prayed that this time she truly had not heard Mr Nesbit correctly.

It was obvious to Simon, as he sat next to the woman who had been married to the old Duke of Skeffington, that she was someone who was very much taken with the finer things in life. She sat beside him with her thick black hair meticulously styled, the emeralds she wore about her long, slender neck and matching earrings were very expensive and he knew her capped-sleeve black gown with the thin band of fine white lace grazing the swell of her shapely breasts must be in the latest London style.

When he had entered the room and she cast a critical gaze at his wardrobe, he knew every rumour he had heard last night about the haughty Duchess of Skeffington had to be true. What he hadn't expected to find was an attractive woman who was only slightly younger than himself. It was apparent she was a fortune hunter who had married the Duke of Skeffington because he was a wealthy old man and she had probably assumed he would die shortly after they were married. The eight thousand pounds was a substantial amount of money in his view and could set her up with very sound investments. And yet by the furrow of her brow he saw she was not pleased.

She rubbed her lips together and narrowed her eyes. 'Would you repeat that please, Mr Nesbit? Not all of it. Just the last part.'

'Certainly.' The poor man gave a small cough and shifted his gaze nervously between the papers lying in front of him and the widow across from him. 'The will states you are to live in Clivemoore House.'

'Clivemoore House.' There was a cool impersonal tone to her voice.

'Yes, madam.'

'Not Stonehaven?'

'No, madam, Clivemoore House.'

She pursed her lips together as if she were holding herself back from saying something. 'And there is no mention of the London residence?'

'No, madam.'

Her gloved hands, which had been under the table, moved to her stomach. 'I see.'

Well, Simon didn't see. She was getting a house to live in for the rest of her life—rent-free. What difference did it make which house it was? He had spent the majority of his childhood living in other people's houses. And there were countless nights that he would lie awake and pray that one day he would have a home of his own. Those were the wishes of a small boy who had not yet seen the world. He thought those feelings were long gone, until he realised that now those prayers had been answered.

And from the sound of it he didn't have just one house. He had a few. How many houses did he own? As the new Duke, he should probably find that out.

'What other properties are there, Mr Nesbit?' he asked.

'Skeffington House in London, Stonehaven in Dorset, and your ducal seat, Harrowhurst Castle in Somerset.'

'Sound structures?'

'As far as I've heard they are. Although it probably would be best for you to visit them and speak with your stewards.'

He owned property in England now. The last time he'd had a permanent home here, he was nine. Now he owned houses that he could stay in indefinitely and no relative would be telling him he had to leave them after a year. Although he trusted Mr Nesbit's words, Simon knew it would not feel real until he'd stepped foot inside them.

Within minutes, the reading of the will was over and they all stood to make their way to the front entrance hall to leave.

'Your predecessor was a member in good standing at White's Gentleman's Club here in London,' Lord Liverpool said while shaking Simon's hand goodbye. 'I am sure I can introduce you to the right people and sponsor your membership.'

'That is kind of you, sir, but I have no intention of joining White's.'

'Why ever not?' the Duchess asked, even though it was none of her concern.

He turned and looked into her brown eyes. 'Because I don't intend to remain in England long. And if I join any club at all, it will be the Travellers Club.'

She opened her mouth as if she was about to say something, but Lord Liverpool cut her off. 'With all due respect, Your Grace, a man in your position needs to remain here to fulfil his duties and needs to think carefully about the clubs he will join. It is not a decision to take lightly. The men you surround yourself with will help you shape policy in Parliament.'

'I have no intention of shaping policy in Parliament. I intend to return to Sicily once I've got a good grasp of my holdings. I will be managing my estates and my investments from abroad.'

Lord Liverpool turned pale. 'With all due respect, the men who have held your seat have been some of the most powerful politicians in the history of this country. There are men who look to the opinion of the Duke of Skeffington to guide their choices in legislature.'

'Well, they can look to someone else now—someone who will be attending Parliament. I have other things to concern myself with.'

'Such as?' the Duchess asked.

Didn't the woman standing near them have better things to do? She had just been given a house. Shouldn't she be hurrying out to start packing?

'Such as things that do not concern you, madam,' Simon replied.

She gave a slight huff. She actually huffed at him before taking a step back and going to Mrs Thacker and Rimsby, probably to complain that some mere mister now had the title of Duke of Skeffington.

'I do hope you and I can discuss your participation in Parliament further at your convenience,' Lord Liverpool said, distracting Simon away from noticing how a few tendrils of her black hair brushed against the exposed skin of her pale neck.

It was apparent that Lord Liverpool would not let this matter rest. Simon had met men like this before. He would let him have his say and then he would continue doing what he wanted to anyway. It didn't matter. He would not be in England long enough to have repeated visits by the Prime Minister. *The Prime Minister of Great Britain.* If all this wasn't so annoyingly disruptive to his current excavation, he might have found it more amusing. As it was, he just wanted all of these details associated with his new title settled.

Lord Liverpool held out his hand and Simon clasped it firmly. 'Until we meet again, Your Grace.'

Not having people address him by the name he had used his entire life was beginning to grate on his nerves. 'Until we meet again, Lord Liverpool.'

Mr Mix, who Simon understood to be the old Duke's secretary and had been managing the ducal properties since the old Duke had passed, went hurrying by on his way to the front door. He was the one man who Simon needed to speak with to settle all the details about his new title and estates. If anyone knew the condition that his estates were in, it would be Mr Mix. He would also know where the ledger books were kept so that Simon could finally see how much of a wealthy man he was. When he returned to England, Lord Liverpool had informed him by post that all debts had been settled and that there were funds remaining. The only question was, how substantial was the size of the fortune sitting in his bank account and just how profitable were those estates.

'Mr Mix,' Simon called out, walking towards the door to catch the small, thin man before he disappeared out into the midday sunshine.

The man stopped before stepping outside. He bowed respectfully, but his eyes kept darting towards the door as if he had somewhere to run off to.

Simon held out his hand. 'I've been looking forward to meeting you, Mr Mix. I understand you served as secretary for my predecessor?'

There was a slight hesitation before Mr Mix took his hand and gave it a firm shake. 'That's correct, Your Grace.'

'Please, call me Simon. I'd like to arrange a meeting with you. I realise that you and I have no contract for employment, but I thought we might discuss the state of the old Duke's affairs and perhaps we can come to an agreement for the future. And you need to come to my house to collect those snuffboxes the Duke has given you.'

Mr Mix offered him a polite smile that did not reach his eyes. 'Of course, when should I call on you?'

'If you have no appointments tomorrow, I think the

morning would be best. I'm staying at the Pulteney Hotel on Piccadilly. I imagine we have many things to go over together.'

'I imagine we do. Very well, Your Grace. I will see you then.' He tipped his hat in a respectful manner and walked out the door.

Simon put on his own hat and turned to leave when the clear voice of the Duchess rang out in the entrance hall, stopping him in his tracks. He closed his eyes and gave a slight shake of his head before he turned around.

They were the only two people left in the unadorned hall and they stood only a few feet away from each other. She was close to his height, which was tall for a woman, and up close he could see her delicate features were rather scrunched up, as if she was trying to determine what to say to him.

'Sir, I wish to have a word with you in private.' She swallowed and looked back at the doorway that led to Mr Nesbit's office as if she was concerned the man would come out and find them together. 'Thank you for allowing me to remain in Skeffington House until the end of January. My man of affairs, Mr Sherman, notified me of your acceptance of our request this morning.'

'My pleasure. I shall not be in England long so you may take the time you need to move to your new residence. Good day.'

He turned toward the door again, but once more her voice stopped him.

'I have a proposition for you.' The last statement was spoken in almost a whisper.

A proposition by a pretty woman—even one who

was as trying as the Duchess of Skeffington—was something to consider. Simon turned back towards her and wondered what she could possibly want from him. 'Go on.'

She cleared her throat. 'I was wondering...that is to say...would you consider...?'

'I am not one to couch my comments to please the world, Duchess. I do not get the impression you do either. What is it you want?'

'I want Stonehaven.' She said it clearly, although she was twisting the handle of her reticule as she made the statement. 'That is to say, I would like to know if you would be willing to exchange Clivemoore for it?'

He hadn't had the time to review each of his houses. How could he possibly give up one before he knew anything about it? And if the Duchess of Skeffington wanted that one so badly, it had to be worth something.

'Why do you want the house?'

'Sentimental reasons.'

'You and your husband spent lovely weeks there and it holds good memories?'

'No. I simply prefer that property above the others. If you are leaving England as you say you are, then it should not matter to you which house I get.'

There had to be more to it than that. He had met fortune hunters like her before in his life. Hell, he had been tossed aside by a few. If he had to wager, he would put money on the notion that Stonehaven provided more of an income than Clivemoore.

'Ah, but your husband had a reason not to put you there. I am simply adhering to his wishes.'

'And what about my wishes? I'm still alive. He is dead.'

Without meaning to, he let out a low laugh. Her very direct nature was comical.

'Yes, well, it's quite obvious you are still alive and the reason I am here is because your husband is dead... How did he die, by the way? I never thought to enquire before now.'

'A chicken bone...he choked on a chicken bone one night at dinner.'

'You're sure it wasn't poison?'

'Poison? Of course I'm sure it wasn't poison.' A look of comprehension crossed her face before she put her hands on her hips. 'Are you insinuating I poisoned my husband?'

'You do seem very interested in that house. And as you stated, you're alive and he's dead.' Simon tried to say it with a straight face, but he wasn't successful.

'You are an odious man, Mr Alexander.'

'That may be true, but I am an odious man in possession of...what was the name of the estate again? Oh, yes, Rockhaven.'

'Stonehaven,' she corrected him through her teeth.

'I don't see a difference,' he replied simply to annoy her. 'Stones and rocks are the same thing. Perhaps I'll change the name.'

The Duchess began to tug her purple-silk glove up. Her emerald and gold bracelet caught his eye as the sunlight glinted off it from the fanlight over the door.

'I see you have no intention of taking my request seriously. I do believe we have nothing more to say to one another. I bid you a good day and wish you horrible weather on your journey back to whatever country has the misfortune of hosting you in the future.'

She raised her chin and sailed past him towards the front door and, thankfully, out of his life for ever.

Chapter One

Dorset—five months later

Since she was seventeen, Stonehaven had been a refuge for Lizzy from her horrible marriage. It was the one place she knew she could periodically escape to where she would be free of her husband's temper and critical remarks. And for the last twelve years she had spent Christmas there with just her sisters and her Aunt Clara. It had been their tradition—the one time of year she was surrounded by the only people who loved her.

Now both of her sisters were married and spending Christmas at the country estate of the Duke of Winterbourne. She had lasted three days on that estate. Long enough to see her sister Juliet married and to endure watching the loving looks her sister Charlotte was receiving from her new husband, Lord Andrew Pearce, the younger brother of the Duke of Winterbourne. That visit was a painful reminder that she would not be sharing the same type of future as her sisters. She was not one of those women who were destined to find love. The reality of her situation stung and she knew she needed the comfort and familiarity of Stonehaven. And she was not going to let something as tedious as her late husband's will stop her from being there.

As her shiny black-lacquered carriage with the Skeffington crest rolled along the snow-covered road past pale stone houses with smoking chimneys, Lizzy peered out the window and realised how much she had missed the local landscape.

Across from her, signs of apprehension creased Aunt Clara's brow once more. 'Perhaps you should have sent a note to Mrs Moggs and notified her that we would be arriving. I can't imagine that she has ordered the kind of food we are accustomed to having during the holiday for just herself and the staff.'

Lizzy let the black curtain fall from her hand and she met her aunt's troubled gaze. The staff would be aware that the house was now in the possession of her late husband's heir and that he had not given her licence to use it. There was no telling what kind of reaction she would receive if they knew she was arriving in advance. Hopefully, the element of surprise would be to her advantage.

'I'm sure we will have to make certain adjustments and our rooms will not be freshly aired and ready when we arrive, but I assure you I can have Mrs Moggs send someone into town and pick up anything we need to enjoy our usual Twelfth Night celebrations.' It wouldn't feel the same without her sisters, but she was grateful her aunt had said she didn't want Lizzy to spend the holiday alone at Stonehaven and asked to accompany her.

'And you are certain he will not be there?'

'For the third time, the last I heard, Mr Alexander is still abroad. All will be well, I assure you. He will never even know we took up residence for a fortnight.'

'You are going to be placing those servants in an awkward position. We still could finish the holiday in my home in Bath. It is not too far away.'

'We have spent Christmas at Stonehaven for years. Fear not, I will take all the blame should the new Duke find out we were in residence. He can chastise me all he wants when he sends me a letter.' Lizzy pushed the curtain aside once more and tried to determine where they were. 'We have just passed the church in the village. It won't be long now.'

The large Georgian house came into view after they rounded a rather narrow bend in the road. The late afternoon sun was making the pale rectangular stones appear more orange than beige. As Lizzy looked down to tie the string of her reticule, she missed noting there was smoke curling out of a number of chimneys, visible against the clear blue sky—more chimneys than were necessary for the number of servants residing in the house.

The carriage rocked to a stop and the step was lowered. In the past, a footman had always been stationed in the entrance hall awaiting their arrival. This year, when so much of her life had changed, with the death of her husband and the marriages of both her sisters, the closed black door was making her feel like a stranger in the one place she had felt the most at home. She raised her chin and marched to the front door with her boots crunching in the snow, determined to push her feelings of sadness and unease out of her mind.

The door opened just as she grabbed the ring of

the doorknocker and she almost fell forward with the movement of the large wooden door. She might have landed on the polished marble floor if it wasn't for the quick grasp of her former butler, who was staring down at her with a startled expression that probably matched her own.

As if he had just realised he was holding his former employer in his arms, Simpkins quickly dropped his hands and took a step back. 'Your Grace!' It was an exclamation as much as a question and he glanced back to the corridor behind him that led to the private rooms of the house.

'Hello, Simpkins. You are looking well.' Or as well as a man could who looked as if he had seen a ghost.

'Thank you, madam. I… I… I wasn't expecting you.'

'I imagine you were not,' Lizzy said, untying her bonnet. 'But as you can see, my aunt and I have decided to spend our Twelfth Night celebration here at Stonehaven.'

'You have?'

'Yes. I realise I should have sent word that we were coming so that you and Mrs Moggs could have the house and staff in order. However, I just decided yesterday that there was no sense breaking this tradition since we have spent our holidays here since I became the Duchess.'

She handed her bonnet to Simpkins, who took it reluctantly, and then went to work quickly on the buttons of her black pelisse. If she could manage to plough through getting settled here, remaining for a fortnight should be easy. Before he had a chance to say anything, Lizzy continued. 'Now, it has been a rather tiring journey and it's rather cold out. Please see that a tea tray is brought to us in the Gold Drawing Room. We will wait there while you instruct a footman to remove the furniture covers and start a fire in the hearth. And I'll need to speak with Mrs Moggs. While there are only two of us staying here this year, I would like to plan a menu out with her for our stay.'

His eyes widened as Aunt Clara draped her cloak over his arm that was now serving as a coat rack for Lizzy's pelisse. 'Your stay? That is to say—'

'I understand you were not prepared for our arrival. I realise it will take time to make the house ready for us. Do not fret. We are patient women and are prepared to endure a cold room and some discomfort until everything is arranged.'

But as she walked towards the back corridor she suddenly caught the distinct smell of meat roasting and turned a questioning eye to her former butler. His wide eyes shifted from her to an area past her shoulder.

'How very kind of you to inform Simpkins that you are willing to endure some discomfort, but I think it bears noting that he is no longer your butler, but mine.'

Blast it! The man was supposed to be in Sicily. Why was he not in Sicily?

Lizzy turned to face him and was taken aback at the sight of Mr Alexander wearing an unbuttoned blue-quilted banyan, black trousers, shiny black shoes, a black waistcoat and a crisp white shirt. He was missing his cravat, and his smooth neck and the slight dusting of hair near the opening of his shirt had her transfixed. It was proving impossible to look away and it wasn't until he cleared his throat that she met him in the eye.

'Simpkins had no idea my aunt and I were coming here.' Thank heavens it was stated without the slightest crack in her voice.

'I think that is quite obvious.' He walked to Simpkins and motioned with his hands for the outer garments the butler was still holding. 'I'll take those and see to these unexpected visitors.' After he took the pelisse and cloak from the man, he turned back to Lizzy. 'It was kind of you to drop in on your way to wherever it is you are going, but as you can see from my attire, I'm not receiving callers at this time.'

At the mention of his attire, it occurred to Lizzy that Mr Alexander was the only man outside her late husband that she had seen in such a state of undress and he looked far better in his banyan than the old Duke had ever looked in his.

'Duchess, did you hear me?'

'I heard you,' she replied, shifting her gaze away from his exposed neck once again and up to his eyes. 'We weren't exactly calling on you. Not in a formal way.'

'Well, I am not receiving callers in an informal way either. Now, be so kind as to take your things. Good day, ladies.'

Lizzy wasn't going to be so easily swayed from remaining at Stonehaven. If there was a way she could get him to leave the estate and agree to allow her to stay for the holiday, it would save what was left of a very trying year.

'Forgive me,' she said, giving him a bright smile. 'I have not had the opportunity to introduce you to my aunt. This is Mrs Sommersby,' she said, gesturing to Aunt Clara. 'We have spent the holidays together since I was a child—and the last twelve of them we have spent here.'

He gave Aunt Clara a respectful bow. 'I am charmed,' he replied rather smoothly, earning him a smile from her aunt.

But when he turned back to Lizzy, his polite demeanour was put aside. He stepped up to her and held out her pelisse. 'Well, now you can say that you have spent some time here this year, as well. I was kind enough to agree that you could stay in my London residence until the end of January since I had no need for it. I will not be granting you permission to stay in any of *my* other homes, including this one.'

The emphasis was not lost on her and she felt her demeanour souring. 'I heard you were somewhere in Sicily.'

'As you can see, I have returned. I needed to be back here by Christmas.'

'Why?'

'You ask a lot of questions for someone who was caught trying to take up residence in a house that does not belong to you.'

'It should have belonged to me. This should have been my house.' The anger at her late husband was resurfacing.

'But it's not, though, is it? It is my house and because of that you have no right to order my servants about or to stay here without an invitation. And based on all those trunks that are being unloaded in the drive, it appears you were planning on staying here for quite some time.'

'A fortnight…just a fortnight.'

His eyes widened. 'All those trunks are for a fortnight?'

'There are two of us and our maids who have been travelling in my aunt's carriage.'

'That is still a substantial number of trunks for a fortnight.'

'We are not coming from home and one can never have too many dresses when travelling. There are times you find yourself in unusual situations and you need to be prepared with the perfect ensemble.'

'I see. Well, this certainly is an unusual situation. I've never had to throw a woman out of my house before.'

His house? This was more her house than his! She had decorated it. She'd had the gardens restored. This was her sanctuary. It held no meaning to him. She raised her chin. 'You wouldn't throw me out.'

'Not if you leave peacefully,' he said slowly. 'If you resist, you will leave me no choice.' He took a step towards her. Now she was even closer to the exposed skin of that neck of his. The very masculine force of his presence made her insides do a funny flip.

How could he not feel a bit of sympathy for her? She placed her hands on her hips, preparing to argue to make him understand.

Aunt Clara stepped in front of Lizzy and looked up at Mr Alexander. 'Perhaps you would be so kind, Your Grace, as to allow us to please remain a bit longer to warm our bones and imbibe a cup of tea to warm our souls. Certainly you can see it's a rather blustery day to be rolling through the countryside.'

There was a hesitation on his part before he gave

Aunt Clara a polite smile. 'Then one might have been advised not to venture out on such a day as this.'

How could he refuse a polite request from her aunt? Lizzy could see the woman was oozing every ounce of sweetness she possessed. Certainly, this man was cold-hearted and callous if he intended to throw them out into the cold.

She needed to take matters into her own hands. She was a duchess! Lizzy stepped from behind her aunt and tipped up her chin. 'After the long journey we have had, you truly expect us to continue on our way without so much as a warm cup of tea? Why, we have travelled all the way from—'

He held up his hand, indicating he had no desire for her to continue. With a sigh, he let his gaze move between the two women. 'If I agree to arrange tea for you, will you agree to leave peacefully when you are finished?'

Lizzy pushed back her shoulders. 'Peacefully? Sir, we have not arrived at this door with pitchforks in hand.'

'No, just enough clothing to set up every woman in this village quite nicely for the next few years.'

She stared into his dark brown eyes to make her point plain. 'Sir, I find the more I am in your presence the less I enjoy your company. It will be my pleasure to place miles between us once we are finished with our tea.'

And if she could find a way with her aunt's help to make him create that distance between them by his wanting to leave Stonehaven first, it would be all the better.

Chapter Two

Simon led them to what the servants called the Gold Drawing Room, holding the pelisse and cloak of the two women trailing behind him. He wasn't about to risk having the garments stashed away by a footman. Their presence on a sofa in the room where the ladies were to have their tea would be a sharp reminder they would have to leave soon. He was well aware it wasn't a very proper thing to do, but it would be effective.

Upon crossing the threshold, he heard an audible gasp behind him. He held in his satisfied smile and hoped it was the Duchess, and not her aunt, who had uttered it. Shocking her into realising this was no longer her home was his purpose for bringing them to this particular room to have their tea. It wasn't because he had felt compelled to honour her request to his butler when she barged into his home.

'What did you do to the Gold Drawing Room?' Her astonishment was apparent in her voice.

He turned to find her scanning the room with wide eyes as her aunt settled herself on the pale green sofa by the fire.

'I changed it,' he stated plainly.

'I see that. Why? Why would you do that?'

'Because this happens to be one of my favourite rooms in the house and I prefer the classical style.'

'It is mine, as well, or it was before you altered it.'

'I enjoy the view of the gardens and spend a considerable amount of time in here when I'm in residence. I'm thinking of having it converted to my study.'

'Your study?' she choked.

'Yes. I haven't had the opportunity to have the furniture moved in yet, but I was able to change the mouldings to the Grecian style and had the walls painted blue to match the colour of the Aegean Sea.' There was no need for him to explain to her why he had altered the design of a room in a house that was his. In his annoyance with himself, he walked to the sofa near the door and unceremoniously dropped their outer garments on it. 'I'll go arrange for your tea.'

The sooner he got them out of the house, the better it would be for him. Elizabeth, the Duchess of Skeffington, had a nosy nature and her close proximity to the Blue Drawing Room was not what he needed. Before he went in search of a servant, he would make certain the door to that room was locked. But before he was able to leave, she stopped him with her voice.

'Why would you change it?' Her tone was soft and he wasn't certain if the question was rhetorical. 'It was perfectly lovely the way it was. What was so objectionable to you that you felt the need to alter it as you have?'

He turned to find her with a furrowed brow, skimming her finger along the top of the new marble mantel that was supported by two replica statues of classical women clad in sandals and sleeveless gowns.

'There was nothing objectionable with how the room was decorated. However, this style is more to my liking.'

'I liked the way it had been decorated.'

There was a slight hint of sadness in her voice and he almost felt sorry for her until she opened her mouth again.

'I realise this style is currently in fashion, but it will not last. People will grow weary of the classical look and then this room will be woefully outdated. It might be already, for all we know. The previous design of the room would have made it quite simple to redecorate by replacing the paint colours or hanging paper on the walls. But this,' she said, gesturing around the room, 'this will now require considerable renovation to keep it up to date.' She uttered the last sentence on a dramatic sigh and her expression was one of false pity.

'Then I am fortunate I am not one to allow the whims of fashion to dictate my taste and will not be renovating this room. The next Duke of Skeffington can concern himself with that task.' He took a step closer and folded his arms. 'And I'll have you know Mr Robert Adam would be very pleased with this room.'

'Mr Adam died in 1792.'

'But many fashionable houses still retain his mark. Shall I name the ones that do?' He had furnished some of those patrons with a number of antiquities to complement the architectural elements of their rooms. He knew them by heart.

She held up her hand to stop him. 'I do not need you to list them. There are also many fashionable homes that

do not support his classical style. Such as Stonehaven…
before you barged in and altered its refined character
with these reproductions.'

Should he even bother to inform her that the small
gold statue of Mars she had just picked up off the mantel was not a reproduction and was over two thousand
years old?

In what he believed to be an attempt to check for a
maker's mark, she eyed the bottom of the statue. 'Perhaps the woman you marry will not be fond of this
style. What then?'

'Perhaps I'll know the woman is the one I *should*
marry because she will confess how much she adores
this room.'

'I believe you will remain a bachelor, sir, for a very
long time.' She placed the statue back on the mantel.

'Oh, I'm sure I can find a number of women who
would want to be the Duchess of Skeffington regardless of my partiality to the classical style. It's well
known that there are certain women in Britain whose
aim it is to marry a man for his money and his prestigious title.' He arched his brow and tilted his head.

It was apparent from the way she narrowed her big
brown eyes at him that she was aware he was referring to her marriage to the old Duke. He knew women
like her and, since he had become the latest Duke of
Skeffington, he had been introduced to too many for
his liking here in England. Women had shunned his
advances in the past, sighting his unimpressive fortune and lack of title. He had little use for such women
like these now.

She raked a critical gaze over him. 'How lucky
for you that you now have the title of Duke. You will

need that title of yours and your fortune if you hope to entice a woman to marry you. Your lack of charm certainly is not to your advantage.'

'Perhaps we can have that tea now,' Mrs Sommersby called out pleasantly from where she was patiently sitting on the sofa near the fireplace.

Why had he allowed the Duchess to distract him from leaving the room? It had only delayed her departure from his home.

'Did someone mention tea?'

Simon turned away from the annoying Duchess to find his friend and business associate Adam Finley lounging against the door frame, openly assessing her with his eyes.

'I thought I heard voices,' Adam continued as he walked into the room.

Simon stepped between Adam and his female intruders. It was no wonder that his friend had become curious about what was taking Simon so long to fetch the small marble statue that he suggested would appeal to Lord Bollingbrooke. He only had to go into the Blue Drawing Room where it was stored, which was a few doors away from his study where the men had been meeting.

The last thing he wanted was to have Adam anywhere near these women. Worlds were colliding and this could be a disaster. While Mrs Sommersby appeared pleasant enough, the Duchess was everything that wasn't. Her only redeeming quality was that she smelled nice when you were standing close to her. She was opinionated, nosy, and much too condescending for his taste. Not to mention that she measured a man's worth by what was in his bank account. And while he could manage her probing questions with deflection, Adam's mercurial nature made it hard to predict how he would react to her inquisition.

It was probably best to quickly introduce them and then leave the ladies to wait for their tea by themselves, since Adam had already walked around him and was making his way to the Duchess.

'Your Grace,' Simon addressed the woman who was openly eyeing Adam with an inquisitive brow, 'may I introduce my friend, Mr Finley. Mr Finley, this is Elizabeth, the Duchess of Skeffington.'

The surprised look on Adam's face was quickly replaced with a sly smile before he executed a bow. 'Your Grace, your beauty has exceeded my expectations.'

She shifted her gaze from Adam to Simon and then back to Adam. 'I assume this means that His Grace has been speaking of me or you would hold no expectations of me at all.'

Adam gave Simon an amused glance before showing off his charming smile to the Duchess. 'Only in passing, I assure you, but he certainly did not do you justice when he described you.'

Of course he had. What more was there to say about her when Adam enquired after the reading of the will? She was rather tall for a woman, with dark hair and dark eyes. And she seemed to possess a sense of entitlement that grated on him. Simon thought he had been rather generous in his description.

The Duchess, however, was eyeing him as if he was something she had brought in on the bottom of her shoe from the stables.

'Adam,' he said, with a hint of chastisement as he pulled his friend away from the Duchess and over to her companion. 'Mrs Sommersby, allow me to introduce you to Mr Finley. This is Mrs Sommersby, the Duchess's aunt.'

'It is a pleasure, Mrs Sommersby,' Adam said with a bow as his attention became fixed on the woman's cameo bracelet. 'That is a stunning piece of jewellery. If I may be so bold, I believe I recall a bracelet similar to that one in Rundell, Bridge and Rundell not too long ago.'

'I bought this recently at that very shop,' she said, appearing pleasantly surprised by Adam's admiration for her bracelet. 'Do you go there often, Mr Finley? I must say I am astonished you remember it.'

'That cameo is quite memorable with the details and the cut.'

'Are you fond of jewellery, Mr Finley?' the Duchess asked, approaching his side and looking down at the bracelet in question.

'It is one of my many interests.' Adam shifted his gaze away from the expensive-looking bracelet and gave a wolflike smile to the Duchess.

Her lips parted and she moved her hand to her chest. Whether she planned it or not she was now covering the emerald necklace she wore which decorated her neck. Simon needed to get Adam away from these women. He couldn't bear to watch him try to flirt with the Duchess and wasn't completely certain Adam wouldn't try to convince the women that he could arrange to sell their jewellery and fetch them a decent price. The unpredictable comments that could flow from both Adam and the Duchess were not a good combination.

'I believe you ladies were in need of tea.'

'Yes, I believe we mentioned that a time or two,' Mrs Sommersby replied.

'Well, Mr Finley and I will leave you now and I will arrange for it.'

Adam practically pouted at him. 'We are not staying for tea?'

'We are not. We have matters to discuss and had been interrupted.' He shot a pointed glance at the Duchess.

'But I enjoy a good cup of tea in the afternoon.'

'You can enjoy a cup of tea in my study.' He turned to the ladies on the sofa. 'I bid you both a fine journey to your next destination. I'm certain you won't mind if I do not show you out myself when you are finished with your tea.'

'They are leaving?' Adam asked over his shoulder as Simon practically dragged him towards the door.

'They are.'

'But didn't they just arrive?'

'This is a very short call.'

'I see.' Adam extricated himself from Simon's hold and walked back towards the ladies. 'It was a pleasure to make your acquaintance. I hope I have the opportunity to spend time with you both in the future. Perhaps I will see you here again.'

'I hope not,' Simon muttered, walking out of the room.

After a few minutes of what Simon believed to be bowing his farewells to the ladies, Adam sauntered into the hall where Simon was waiting for him.

'She likes me,' Adam said with an arrogant smile.

'You think every woman likes you.'

He gave a careless shrug. 'They all do. I speak their

language.' Adam followed him down the corridor towards Simon's study.

'And what language is that?'

'The language of luxury goods—of fine jewellery and fashionable attire.'

'I wasn't aware you considered yourself an expert on women's fashions.'

'You pulled me away from them before I had the opportunity to compliment the Duchess on the Brussels lace on her gown.'

'She can thank me the next time I see her if, in fact, I ever see her again. I can only hope that I don't.' Simon rolled his eyes as they walked into his study and he pulled the tapestry bell pull to call for a servant to arrange tea.

'You didn't mention she was a prime article.'

'The Duchess? She is not that attractive.'

'If one doesn't like females with rich dark hair, fine features, radiant smooth skin, expressive large eyes and tempting curves, then I assume that's true. I, on the other hand, find her stunning.'

'You were in her presence all of five minutes. I assure you, she's a vixen.'

'You're exaggerating. I didn't find her at all shrewish.'

'She barely said anything to you.'

'Which means she was speechless because she was captivated by my charms. I tend to have that effect on women.' He tugged on the cuff of his deep grey tailcoat.

'You flatter yourself. You render them mute because they're shocked that a man as transparent as you believes he has charm.'

'I could have had an opportunity to prove you wrong, but you dragged me away from her and prevented us from enjoying a lovely cup of tea by the fire on this cold day.'

'Since when do you enjoy sipping tea by the fire in the afternoon?'

'Since there was an opportunity to have it with that delectable creature.'

'Truly, she is not that attractive.'

'Then you won't mind if I return to the ladies, seeing as you have no designs on her.'

Adam started to walk back out of the study door, but Simon placed a hand on his chest to stop him.

'I thought you wanted to leave soon to begin your journey to Portsmouth?'

'Portsmouth is not far. I can postpone my departure for a little while longer. What is one more night in this idyllic home of yours?'

'The ladies are not staying. They are leaving after they have their tea.'

'Then why are they here?'

'Just the thought of explaining it leaves me exhausted.'

A footman walked in and Simon arranged a tea tray to be delivered to the ladies, saving him from having to elaborate more about the persistent Duchess of Skeffington. He knew she wanted this house and he knew it had to be because of the income it would bring her. He had lived his life moving from relative to relative when he was a boy until his father arranged for him to join the navy when Simon was fifteen. Houses were just places to store your things and rest your head. He had never lived in one long enough to grow attached to any of them. The Duchess didn't appear to be the sentimental type—however, it was apparent she enjoyed her wealth. It had to be the income that drew her to Stonehaven. Perhaps she assumed, if she stayed here long enough, he would just give her the house.

This estate was within a few hours' drive to the port town of Portsmouth. Now he could ship the treasures he uncovered directly to this house. It saved in travel time and money, and this remote location kept his business hidden from potential thieves. He would never give up Stonehaven. Using this house was beneficial to his business.

'Before we were interrupted, you expressed interest in seeing the statue I uncovered which will certainly pay Lord Bollingbrooke back for his investment in the excavation,' Simon said to Adam. 'Wait here. I'll go and fetch it.'

'That's what you said the last time you left this room.'

'If I am longer than ten minutes, you can always ring for tea to enjoy by this fire.' He gave his friend a teasing look.

'Tea by the fire isn't quite the same without a tempting woman at your side.'

But it would be much more relaxing without the Duchess of Skeffington there to get Simon's pulse racing with the agitation she had a habit of causing him. Luckily, she would be gone from this house soon and his life would return to the quiet and boring state it had been in here in England before he noticed her carriage pull up in his drive.

Or so he thought.

Chapter Three

Lizzy sat beside her aunt, staring into the blue Wedgwood teacup that was part of the set she had purchased shortly after her marriage, and was holding back her tears. He had changed her favourite room—the room she had spent many hours in entertaining family and friends. It was a room that she had taken great pains to decorate to her exact taste. She recalled trying four different paint colours before she settled on the soft white paint that complemented the gold crown mouldings that had once outlined the room. Those four walls held so many good memories of so many wonderful visits.

Now that the room didn't even look the same, all of that was gone with the careless direction of Mr Simon Alexander. It was hard for her to think of him in terms of the Duke of Skeffington since physically he was so very different from her late husband, although he, too, could be infuriating, but in a completely different way.

'Try drinking your tea before it gets cold,' Aunt Clara suggested gently, patting her hand. 'You will not find the answer to your troubles staring into that cup. A good cup of tea can help with many things, but I believe it works only when you drink it.'

Lizzy placed the cup and saucer on the table beside her. 'It has lost its appeal seeing it in these cups.'

'They are lovely cups. I recall going with you to buy them in London. I've always been partial to Wedgwood.'

'They are his cups now.' She didn't even try to hide the despondent tone of her voice.

Not being able to look at the tea set any longer, Lizzy shifted her gaze to scan the new crown moulding that was painted a pale cream colour that matched the marble fireplace. What else had he decided to change? She got up and walked to the large windows that overlooked the back gardens. In the summer, they were breathtaking with a combination of manicured topiaries, water fountains and beds of roses. Now they were frozen in snow.

'The house feels different,' she said, staring bleakly out at the garden where she had spent many days enjoying peace and solitude in the sunshine.

Aunt Clara came up beside her and took her hand. 'I know it is painful for you to adjust to all that has changed.'

'My pain is all because of Mr Alexander. He changed this house. If he'd had the decency to remain in Sicily, he would have had no time to alter Stonehaven and this would still feel like home.' It was his entire fault.

'I'm not just referring to the changes in this house, Lizzy. In the past year you have become a widow. For months you had no notion of where you would be living. Your financial circumstances, while respectable, are not as grand as they once were. Charlotte is married to the man you wanted to marry and now Juliet is also married and in love. That is a lot of change in such a short time.'

'What do my sisters' marriages have to do with any of this?'

'When Andrew married Charlotte it was very difficult for you. You couldn't even go to their wedding and you refused to discuss your feelings with me or Juliet. You kept pushing us away when we would mention it. I know you now are speaking with Charlotte, but it has been six months since their wedding. I think it's time we talked about it.'

'They are married. I have come to accept that. What is there to say?'

'Why did you have your heart set on Andrew? When Skeffington died, you said he was the only man who you could love and would make you happy. Why?'

'It doesn't matter why. He loves Charlotte and she loves him.'

It was obvious from her aunt's expression that that explanation was not sufficient and she wasn't going to let the matter rest until Lizzy bared more of her pain. She had come to accept her fate—she could talk about it a bit more now.

'I understand that some people are meant to find love in this world and there are those of us who are not. Not everyone marries a man and finds a lifetime of happiness with him. Charlotte is fortunate she found love twice. I suppose when Lord Andrew married her, it reminded me that my future does not include a man who will love me. I thought he had cared for me, but I was wrong. He never had any feelings for me. I created that illusion in my head. I suppose believing in that for the past twelve years helped me through living in a loveless marriage. I could pretend there was a man out there in the world who was wishing I was his. But none of it was real. I know that now. I don't blame Charlotte for what happened. He was never really mine. I want her to be happy and she is with him. But, in truth, I can't help but wonder why her fate was to find two men to love her and my fate doesn't include even one.'

'Don't say that. You are still young. You have many years ahead of you to meet a man who will love you.'

'If there is one thing I've learned in life, it is that there is something about me that does not endear me to men. I don't have striking green eyes like Charlotte, or her sweet disposition, and I'm not lively and spirited like Juliet. I am just me. There is nothing remarkable about me. Even before Skeffington bargained with Father for my hand, suitors were not sending me flowers or filling up my dance card. And as a widow, I know that I may not be able to have children. Heavens, how Skeffington would remind me of that fact while he was alive and even reduced my fortune and income because of it. I was not a desirable debutante and I will never be a desirable widow.'

'Lizzy, you have a lot to offer a man.'

'I will not marry some man just because he is in need of my money. If I cannot marry for love, then I will not marry at all. And we both know I am not the type of woman a man falls in love with. I'm just not.'

Aunt Clara placed her arm around Lizzy's shoulders and the soft familiar scent of her rose perfume drifted on the air. 'I was not referring to your money, Elizabeth.'

'Everything is different now. The place that I considered home is no longer mine, nor its contents. That cup isn't mine even though I was the one to pick it out for this house.'

'Life isn't always fair.'

'It rarely is when you're a woman.'

For months, she had been telling herself that everything would be fine. That she would find a way to get back some of what she felt was hers, like the use of this house. But now, standing in her favourite room at Stonehaven, with its new marble chimney piece and mouldings, she now saw that the world had gone on without her for these past few months and there was no going back to the way things were. It was too late for that. Nothing in her life would ever be the same. She was a creature of habit and moving forward through all this change was terrifying.

'Thank you for coming here with me. You have been nothing but kind and patient. You knew this was going to happen, didn't you? If not Mr Alexander changing the house, then some other things would be different.'

'I suspected the servants would bar you from entering. I had hoped to save you from that humiliation. That's why I suggested we go to my home in Bath instead. I love you, Elizabeth, and I don't want to see you hurt. Living with Skeffington was punishment enough for one lifetime.'

Lizzy turned and scanned the room once more. He had done an admirable job. The reproductions in the room were of very high quality. You would almost think they were made a very long time ago. If this room were in anyone else's home, she would have said that she liked it. But not here. Not in Stonehaven.

'Let's finish our tea,' Lizzy said with a sigh. 'I only wish we didn't have to have it in my Wedgwood cups.'

They walked back to the sofa and settled in.

'I think you are right,' Lizzy said after taking a long, slow sip from her cup. 'I think we should go to Bath. There is nothing left for me here.' She was proud of herself for being able to hold back the catch in her throat.

'You will find your place, Elizabeth. All is not lost. You were able to make a home for yourself here in Stonehaven. You will find a way to do that at Clivemoore.'

It certainly didn't feel as if she would be able to do that at the moment. She had spent only a few weeks at Clivemoore while she was married and she had found the old house rather dark and gloomy. It wasn't the kind of place that inspired happy thoughts. It certainly hadn't felt like home. And it was a far journey from Clivemoore down to London or to Aunt Clara in Bath. She had never bothered to learn much about the gentry in the area. Would she even have things in common with any of them?

'I've spoken with Sherman, my man of affairs, and instructed him that I'd like to use the money that I inherited to purchase a small town house in London and use the income from Clivemoore to support me.'

'Why is this the first I am hearing of it?'

'I'll tell you more about it on our way to Bath. I'd like to take a short look around to see what else he has changed before we leave. I can think of no reason

I will ever be invited to return. I only wish the last time I had seen this place hadn't been in the middle of winter with all the snow on the ground. I would have loved to walk one final time through the gardens when everything was in bloom.'

Her only solace was that she wouldn't be seeing Mr Alexander again.

Chapter Four

Lizzy walked through the public rooms of Stonehaven with a heavy heart. She would miss this place. Peeking into them felt as if she were saying goodbye to an old friend. Short of chaining herself to the banister of the main staircase, she couldn't think of one thing to do that would make Mr Alexander understand how much she wanted to live here.

She had considered asking to sit down with him to have a rational conversation to once more suggest they switch houses, but she knew he would view her need to live here as somewhat irrational. He was a man. If she discussed her desire to reside close to her family and friends it would sound like sentimental drivel to him and she was not about to let him know how truly alone she was feeling since her sisters had got married. She was a duchess. Sharing her feelings with him was beneath her position.

As she walked along the corridor of the first floor of the house past the rooms that held so many memories, all was quiet and still. It was as if the structure was waiting to be filled with the sounds of laughter and excited chatter. Those were the sounds that had reverberated around these walls when Lizzy was there with her sisters and Aunt Clara.

When she entered the library, she sat on the window seat that her younger sister, Juliet, would often curl up on to read on rainy days during the years she lived with Lizzy after their parents had died of consumption. In the breakfast room, she ran her fingers along the round table where she would often share meals with Aunt Clara and Juliet. In the silence of the room, she could still hear her aunt's voice explaining the virtues of a strong cup of tea to start the day. And when she entered the conservatory, she still felt the pain in her heart from the time she held her older sister, Charlotte, in grief as she told Lizzy that she received word that her husband, Jonathan, had died during the Battle of Waterloo. They were everyday memories and some life-changing ones, as well, but they were the times that reminded her that in her horrible marriage without love she wasn't completely alone. There were people who loved her and cared about her and valued her. Now she would no longer walk these halls and enter these rooms to be reminded of that.

She trudged further down the corridor and stopped at the closed door of the Duke's study. Her husband had very rarely spent any time at Stonehaven. He would customarily visit the house twice a year to meet with his steward and inspect the house and grounds for himself. When he was in residence the door to his study would always be closed. All other times, the door to the room was left open. Even though she knew that Mr Alexander was probably inside with Mr Finley, the sight of the closed door made her muscles tighten as if she was anticipating Skeffington throwing it open and berating her for some minor faux pas. She could still picture his wrinkled lips, his yellowed teeth and the spittle that would form in the corners of his mouth when he would yell. The only consolation to leaving Stonehaven and finding a new house in London was that she would never have to look at that door or be inside that room again.

The next room was the Blue Drawing Room. When she tried to turn the door handle and go inside, she was surprised to find the room was locked. Why would he bother locking it? There was nothing of real value inside. Did he fear she would steal a deck of playing cards on her way out of the house? Or perhaps he believed she was inordinately fond of the Meissen dogs that lined the carved cream-coloured mantel of the fireplace?

The man really was a mystery. All that she knew about him was what she had been told by Lord Liverpool and Mr Nesbit. After Skeffington had died, they had informed her that his nephew, who was his presumptive heir, had also died two months prior in a riding accident. The ducal seat was to go to a distant cousin of her late husband and it had taken great pains to finally track Mr Simon Alexander down somewhere in Sicily. She didn't know why he had been there, or how long he had been staying there. No one really seemed to know.

What she did know was that he had not returned to England for almost six months after Skeffington had died and the delay meant that for almost six months she was a woman without a home—until the will was read and she learned the remainder of her life would be lived out in the far north of England, away from everything that was familiar to her.

When she reached the armoury, she was relieved to discover it had remained unchanged. As she walked inside, she immediately recalled the sound of Juliet's laughter the summer they decided to take fencing lessons with Monsieur LeBatt. Skeffington had decided to spend that summer at his ancestral home and there was no chance that he would be venturing down to Dorset in the heat. It felt like a form of rebellion to take the lessons and she found they helped to release some of the anger she felt towards her husband and towards her deceased parents who had arranged the marriage.

The four suits of armour that had belonged to Skeffington's ancestors still stood sentry in the corners of the red room, gleaming in the late afternoon sun that was streaming in through the long windows. Ancient broadswords and ceremonial swords were hung on the great expanse of wall opposite the fireplace and the small swords that Monsieur LeBatt had used to teach her to fence were hung on the wall between the windows. There was no telling the last time a fire had burned in the hearth and when she took one of the small swords off the wall, the metal grip was cool in her hand through her silk glove.

The weight of the weapon felt familiar and, with a swish of the blade, Lizzy saluted the imaginary image of her old fencing master. He had taught her so much that summer and she tried to recall why she had not taken lessons with him the following year. She did remember Monsieur LeBatt telling her on one particular afternoon that she had quick instincts, which made her a formidable opponent. She liked to believe he was telling her the truth and not simply flattering her because she was paying him to teach her. False flattery was one of the things she liked least about possessing her prestigious title.

She lifted the blade straight out to her right side and lowered her knees a few inches. Placing her left hand up in the air at a ninety-degree angle from her body and turning her head towards the blade, she lunged to her right. The stretch of her thigh muscles felt heavenly after spending a good portion of the day in her carriage and she let out an unladylike groan.

The movement had somehow also relieved some of the tension in her shoulders that she hadn't been aware was there and she tilted her neck from side to side to stretch it, as well. Rolling her shoulders, she adjusted her grip, then resumed her position and lunged again. This time she bounced off her soles as she lunged, taking a leap forward before retreating back to her original stance. The narrowness of the cut of this particular gown was somewhat restrictive and prevented her from lunging as far as she wanted. Needing a deep stretch of her legs, she picked up the skirt of her gown with her left hand so the hem was above her knees and once more she bounced off her soles and lunged towards the window.

A choking sound came from behind her and she spun around, sword in hand, and instinctively pointed the blade directly at the figure of the Duke standing in the doorway. His surprised expression must have matched her own because she felt her eyes widen and she immediately let go of her skirt. The downward swoop of the fine woollen fabric of her grey travelling gown pushed her cotton petticoat and chemise against her legs. For a moment, she feared she would trip if she took a step forward.

'How long have you been standing there?' she demanded, wanting to run out of the room from the embarrassment of knowing he had seen her legs.

'Long enough to hear you utter an impressive grunt and appear to wish to attack the curtains.'

Thank God he hadn't mentioned her legs. 'I was not attacking the curtains.'

'It wouldn't bother me if you were.' His gaze shifted to the red-velvet curtains behind her. 'I don't really care for them.'

'These curtains were quite expensive and complement this room perfectly. The colour speaks of past battles and is a testament to the men who fought them. *Your* ancestors, I might add.'

'I should have known the design of this room was your idea,' he said, glancing around the room before striding towards her with his open banyan billowing out behind him, revealing an impressive chest, which was covered up by his blue waistcoat.

Once more that bare neck of his caught her eye and his commanding presence made the large room feel smaller. Lizzy shifted in her stance before she unconsciously tightened her grip on the handle of the sword and steadied her hand.

He walked right up to the tip of the blade so it was pointing at his heart, all the while looking into her eyes as if to challenge her. 'This room is a bit too theatrical for my taste.'

She narrowed her gaze on him. 'Are you insinuating I'm theatrical?'

'I have seen curtains just like those in the opera houses in Italy,' he replied offhandedly.

He had ignored her question. She hated it when people ignored her. She was the Duchess of Skeffington. 'You didn't answer my question. Are you calling me theatrical?'

'That might be one word to describe you. I suppose *dramatic* is a more accurate word.' With the tip of his finger he slowly guided the blade of the sword away from his chest.

'And the other words you think describe me?' she asked, lowering the small sword to her side, annoyed that he had the ability to fluster her so much that she had forgotten she had been aiming a weapon at him.

'I don't think you really want me to say what the other words are.'

'If I didn't want you to tell me, I wouldn't have asked.'

He walked to the wall between the windows and selected a sword, testing the grip in his very masculine-looking hand. Without gloves, she could see he did not have the hands of a man who led a pampered life. They weren't smooth and pale like many of the men of the *ton* whose hands resembled a larger version of those of a child. His hands were tanned, like the colour of the gardeners' skins when they worked outside in the summer. The pronounced veins on the top of his hand seemed to pump while he adjusted his grip—and she took note of a narrow scar about two inches in length near his wrist. Lizzy didn't think she had ever paid this much attention to a man's hand before now.

He waved the blade in the air towards the window and the setting sun glinted off the metal. With his eye, he appeared to check the straightness of the blade. 'I suppose another word I would use to describe you is *wilful.*'

Lizzy pushed her shoulders back and raised her chin. 'That doesn't sound like a compliment.'

'It wasn't meant to be,' he replied with his back to her as he selected another sword.

'Are you ever civil, Mr Alexander?'

Calling him Skeffington just felt wrong. He was not her late husband—far from it. She could have referred to him as Duke, but at this moment she had no wish to remind him they shared their elevated status. At this moment, she wanted to remind him that she was a duchess and had been given the title long before he ever stepped foot into Mr Nesbit's law office.

'Mr Alexander, is it?' A small smile tugged at his lips, as if he found her amusing.

Kittens were amusing. Small children were amusing. She was a duchess. She was not amusing!

'That was the name you were given, is it not?' she replied sharply.

'It is and I had gone by that name for thirty-five years until people began to call me by my new one. It has been a while since anyone has called me Mr Alexander.'

If she thought it would have pleased him in some odd way to refer to him by his original name, she would have called him Skeffington instead. 'Why do you consider me wilful?'

He turned back to her with a different sword in his hand. 'You truly are asking me that question? You? The woman who wanted to switch houses with me and, when I refused, came to the house she wanted anyway and proceeded to enter—uninvited, I might add—and order my servants around.' He brought the handle of the sword to his eye and looked down the length of the blade, once more appearing to see how straight it was. Then his eyes met hers. 'I would say that was wilful. What would you call it?'

A warm rush was rising up her neck and into her cheeks. 'I don't know what I would call it. *Resourceful*, maybe.'

'*Rude*...you could also call it rude.'

'I have never been called rude in my life.'

'Maybe not openly, but I suspect it has been whispered about you behind your back.'

'Of all the nerve!' Lizzy tightened her grip on the sword's handle that she was holding down by her side.

He lowered his sword and cocked his head, looking her in the eye. 'Why are you still here? I was very generous to allow you and your aunt to take tea before continuing on your journey to harass another homeowner somewhere in the country. I agreed to allow you to stay with the understanding that when you were finished, you would go on your merry way and leave this house. Imagine my surprise when I showed Mr Finley to the door and was asked by *my* butler if he should have *my* housekeeper arrange for rooms for you and Mrs Sommersby to stay the night.'

She felt a small weight lift from her chest at the idea she might have another day to walk the halls of this house she had long thought of as her home. 'And what did you tell him?'

'That it wasn't necessary to have rooms arranged for the both of you since I would make sure you left shortly. I did, however, tell him to make certain your servants were fed so they had something warm in their bellies for the journey ahead. Your servants should not have to suffer because their mistress had made a foolish decision.'

'I don't make foolish decisions.' Not any that she would admit to him at least.

He arched his brow and did not appear convinced. 'You arrived on my doorstep in the middle of winter, from who knows how far away, assuming I would not be here and you and your aunt would be granted use of my house by my staff. That sounds foolish to me.'

'It was a risk worth taking. My aunt resides in Bath. It is not too far a journey from here. If we had been unable to stay, we would simply have continued on to her home. Haven't you ever tried something just to see if it was possible?'

'More times than I'd care to admit. Is that what you were doing in coming here today? You were just trying to see if you could indeed stay here for a while. What is it about this house that makes you want it so badly?'

She couldn't confess the complete truth to him. It would make her sound pathetic and needy. Let him believe whatever he wanted. Maybe there was still a way to convince him that he would be happier in the dark and sombre designs of Clivemoore House. Its dark colours would suit his grumpy disposition.

Chapter Five

Simon was well aware his mouth had dropped open and his breeches had tightened when he saw the Duchess of Skeffington raise her skirts and unknowingly give him the chance to admire her very shapely long legs from the open doorway of the armoury. He didn't want to admire anything about her. She was a haughty, materialistic woman who could agitate him like no other. But there was no denying she had legs that went on for ever and, for just an instant, he imagined skimming his hands up them.

Then she turned and pointed that sword of hers at him and he was reminded that she had the type of temperament that made it distinctly possible that she could turn that metal sword to ice simply by holding it.

In the late afternoon light that was now casting her face in a warm glow, he watched her attempt to gather the right words to explain to him why she couldn't give up Stonehaven. He suspected she was trying to think of something to say that didn't reveal that she wanted the higher income Stonehaven would bring to her over Clivemoore. He waited for her to offer some sentimental tale, like she had spent her honeymoon here, but she remained silent. Shortly after the old Duke's will was read, he met with the man's secretary, Mr Mix, and was informed of the profitability of each of the estates. Surprisingly, Clivemoore was the least profitable, bringing in eight thousand pounds per year. Stonehaven brought in ten thousand.

Simon was not about to give that income and this house to the Duchess. The Blue Drawing Room currently stored items that had come over on the ship with him from France and, although he would barely be spending any time at Stonehaven, the estate provided him with a tidy income that he could use to support both the house and some of his future excavations.

He couldn't imagine why she had wandered into the armoury. Had she left something here that she wanted back? He understood that the contents of all the houses were his and she had no right to take any of the items with her to Clivemoore unless he granted her permission. He had no attachment to any of the things that were owned by his predecessor. He felt no sense of fondness for the family who had deserted his father when he married Simon's French Huguenot mother. If the Duchess were honest with him about what she was looking for in the house, he might be inclined to give it to her, but she was not getting Stonehaven. It was the one thing he was grateful he had inherited with this damned title that placed too much attention on him and disrupted his plans.

She toyed with her emerald necklace. 'Surely you must know by now that I was responsible for redecorating a number of rooms in this house. I simply like it here. It suits me.'

'You say this house suits you,' he said, 'but as you can see, I am slowly going to be redecorating it to suit my taste. This house will not look the way you will fondly remember it when I am through with it.'

There was a slight twitch to her eye, letting him know that his statement had affected her.

'You're enjoying this, aren't you? You are enjoying taunting me with the fact that the one thing I want, I cannot have.'

'Is this truly the only thing in this world that you cannot have?'

There was a hesitation and he could tell her thoughts had wandered to something else—probably the grand ducal seat in Somerset that was the most profitable and prestigious of the Skeffington estates that could never be used as a Dowager House. But he knew by the set of her posture that she wasn't about to share her thoughts with him. At least she was not a hysterical female. He would give her that. Some women would have pleaded and cried to try to sway his decision. He had the impression the Duchess would have preferred to walk for days in the desert without water before she shed one tear in front of him.

'This house means a great deal to me as you can see,' she said, looking away towards the windows, 'however, I will not have you taunt me about it. You will be very happy to hear I will be leaving now. I find I cannot stand to be in your presence much longer.'

She walked over towards the window and lifted her small sword to hang it back up on the wall. Knowing that she was about to leave should have made him happy. And yet...

'How is it that you know how to hold a sword such

as that one?' he asked, trying to understand even an insignificant thing about her.

She appeared somewhat startled by the change in conversation. 'I took fencing lessons here years ago.'

'Are you any good?'

'I've been told I am.'

'By whom?'

She raised her chin. 'By Monsieur LeBatt, my fencing master.'

He hadn't heard of the man, but he'd been out of the country most of his life. In all likelihood Monsieur LeBatt had given her the compliment to ensure she continued to pay him for his instruction.

Their eyes held for several heartbeats, neither one seeming in a hurry to look away. There was something between them. He could not name it, but he did know that whatever it was, it had not been settled yet, and in his gut he didn't believe it had anything to do with the house.

'I believe you put that sword away prematurely,' he said, feeling the edges of his mouth curl up with the idea that popped into his head. He had a way to ensure that the issue of who got to live in Stonehaven was settled once and for all. He didn't want her showing up on his doorstep to be a regular occurrence. The only question was, would Elizabeth, the Duchess of Skeffington, be up for the challenge?

Her brows furrowed. 'I don't understand. You do not wish me to return the sword to the wall?'

He walked over to her so they were only a few feet apart. Standing this close to her, he could make out faint freckles on her nose. He had never noticed them before. It must have been a play of the light. 'I have a proposition for you.'

'What kind of proposition?' she asked with a dubious expression.

'Fear not. I am not interested in your virtue.'

A flash of what might have been anger flickered in her large brown eyes, which didn't make any sense. Did she want him to seduce her?

The waning sunlight bounced off the blade of the sword he held down against his side. 'What do you say we make a wager for this house?'

Her expression changed to one of interest, although it appeared she might be holding her emotions in check and trying to suppress some form of excitement that now danced in her eyes. 'I'm listening.'

He stalked around her, taking open measure of her form just to irk her. She moved in a circle with him so they remained face-to-face. Perhaps Adam was right. She could be considered attractive with her fine features and her big doe-like eyes.

Simon wet his top lip with the tip of his tongue. 'I was wondering if you would care to duel for it?'

'You expect me to shoot you for this house?' Her astonishment was evident in her tone.

'No, nothing that drastic. I was wondering if you would care to have a duel with the small swords—that is, if you are confident enough in your fencing skills.'

A slow smile lifted the corners of her mouth. 'How should we determine the winner?'

'The first one to touch the other with the tip of the blade?'

Her eyes darkened and she pressed her lips together in a firm line. 'How about the first one to draw blood?'

Simon had found a keen sense of satisfaction in shocking her with his proposal, but her suggestion had shocked him in return and it must have been evident from his expression. Who knew Elizabeth, the Duchess of Skeffington, shared his adventurous side?

'Drawing first blood is an absolute,' she explained. 'No one can deny when it happens.'

'Are you saying you think I will cheat if we duel my way?'

'I am saying there is no room for contradictory reports. Blood is blood. There will be no denying when it is shed.'

'How much blood are we talking about?'

'Not much. Only a scratch. Do you think you can manage to prick me?'

Simon had no idea if she was aware of how her question could be taken and that notion made him let out a low laugh, which seemed to ignite fire in her eyes.

'Oh, I think I can manage to prick you quite well,' he replied through his smile.

She huffed at him and spun on her heels to retrieve the same sword she had been holding when he had caught her lunging at the curtains.

'You agree, then,' he called out.

As she turned to face him, she pointed the tip of her blade at his chest. 'It will be my pleasure.'

He had learned swordplay on naval ships and had become quite adept over the years. Wearing his banyan would never do if he intended to show her what a great swordsman he was. As he walked towards the wall of broadswords, he shook himself out of it and laid it down on the sofa that was positioned against the wall. When he turned around and began rolling up his sleeves, he caught the eye of the Duchess, frozen in place staring at him.

He was well aware that he should not be in her presence in just his shirtsleeves and his waistcoat, but they had agreed to a duel. That was highly improper, as well, and she hadn't hesitated to agree to that.

He walked towards her, his breath catching in his throat when she began biting the tips of each of her fingers to slip her hands out of her lavender-silk gloves. The very act conjured up the erotic image of her stripping out of that gown.

'You might want to keep them on,' he managed to say without his voice cracking. 'They will offer your hands a bit of protection.'

'I will take that risk.' She turned and tossed them to the base of a window where they landed in the puddle of a red-velvet curtain.

He stalked her like a lion eyeing its prey. In his entire life he had never fought a woman. It went against the very core of who he was. Yet knowing that all of her attention was going to be focused on him was making his blood rush through his body. There was a determination and a confidence about her manner that he actually found strangely attractive. This was not a woman who would fold up into a ball when the cards were stacked against her. This was a woman who was willing to meet life's challenges head-on. And as much as he didn't like her, he could respect that part of who she was.

He stopped about ten feet away from her and saluted her with a swish of his blade. 'If you'd care to raise your skirts again to improve your footwork, please feel free to do so, I will not be scandalised.' It was unfair of him to try to upend her composure, but he wanted to try.

Unfortunately, it appeared he had missed his mark.

'That's very kind of you. I will consider your suggestion should our match require it.' With that, she saluted him in return with a sly smile.

The prolonged anticipation was almost unbearable, until she raised her blade and pointed it straight out towards him. This was the part of a match where you learned so much about your opponent. Were they the type to charge forward first or were they the type to wait for you to attack? As he watched her closely for any type of reaction, he raised the tip of his blade so it was inches from hers. He could tell that she was taking measure of him just as much as he was taking measure of her.

He circled the tip of his blade around hers, waiting to see if she would take the bait. She remained as still as a coiled cobra about to bite. Her chest was rising and falling as if she had just finished a bout of rather vigorous sex. It was the only thing that was giving away what effect the duel was having on her.

'We could be at this all night if one of us doesn't make the first move,' he said.

Since neither of them had bothered to light any of the candles, he decided to move things along before the two of them found themselves in a darkened room barely able to see each other. He gave a slight tap to the tip of her sword, which she deflected easily. The beginnings of a smile tipped the corners of her mouth as she circled her blade around his in what he had never considered before to be an erotic action.

Annoyed with himself for the direction his thoughts were taking, he flicked her blade away from his, sending out a clink of metal against metal.

'So you can circle mine, but I cannot circle yours,' she said with a full smile. 'You like to be in control.'

'And you do not?' he replied with their blades now circling each other.

'I do, but I am willing to let you lead for now. I am not in a rush to finish.' Her actions, however, did not match her words and she lunged forward as best she could in that gown and he had to jump back so she didn't reach his chest with her blade.

They both moved forward this time, crossing swords in the air as they both deftly parried the attack. He came at her with a riposte, but she hit his sword away. They moved in a circle, the blades clashing against each other, first up in the air and then blocking each other's strikes with their blades pointing down to the floor.

Simon knew if he lunged too far he could impale her. The trick was lunging just far enough to create a scratch. But where on her body would be the easiest to hit? If he was to look for exposed skin, there was her face, which he would never touch. She had a long and graceful neck that was a bit tempting, but if he accidently hit a vein she would bleed out. That didn't leave many more places to scratch. He would hate to scar the smooth skin by her breasts, but that would be a logical place—unless he was able to flick the tip of his sword over the guard by her hand.

The Duchess decided to take matters into her own hands and picked her skirts up with her left hand and lunged forward, slicing the top brass button off his waistcoat. He had jumped back before her blade could do any further damage and stared at her in shock. She laughed and saluted him with her sword while she waited for him to see if the tip of her blade had punctured his skin underneath.

She hadn't drawn his blood yet, but it was obvious she was determined to try and was enjoying herself while she was doing it. This woman was definitely no simpering miss and now he knew that she would not hesitate to strike him.

She lunged again and he deflected her blade by wrapping his around hers and moving it to the side. With a light flick of his wrist he made a three-inch slice into the long billowy sleeve of her gown. Her eyes widened before she checked the rip and showed him that he hadn't scratched her skin.

'It only seemed fair,' he said, raising his blade and pointing it towards her chest.

'I would think your button is easier to repair than my sleeve.' She knocked his blade away with hers.

'So you went for my button with the intent to show me your skill. I would think you would have just wanted to draw blood.'

'What fun is there in that when I can do this first?' She gave a slice to the sleeve of his white shirt without touching his skin.

Her gumption and skill made him laugh. 'Now who is taunting whom?'

They went after each other this time with obvious intent and the clanging of their swords reverberated about the room. They were both smiling broadly, giving away their obvious enjoyment even though they were both breathing hard from the exertion.

A lock of her black hair had come free as they moved about the room and he had the unexpected urge to tuck it behind her ear. If he tried, she probably would have aimed for his heart. There was a fierce determination about her now that made her a formidable opponent.

Their swords crossed between them and as they moved in a circle, the metal blades pushed against each other. Simon knew what he needed to do to end this. He wasn't sure why he was having a hard time bringing himself to just do it.

When they broke apart he clenched his jaw while he circled the blade of his sword around hers and lunged forward, giving an expert flick of his wrist. The tip of his blade arched over the handle of her sword and brushed across the skin near her right wrist, drawing blood. She let out a cry and looked down at her hand as if it weren't her own.

Knowing he had caused her pain shifted something inside him. Immediately he dropped his sword and took her short sword gently from her delicate fingers. He held her warm hand in his and smeared her blood with his thumb while he cleared a path to see the wound. She snatched her hand out of his as if he had burned her as well as cut her skin.

Chapter Six

Lizzy hadn't felt a man's touch on her bare skin in so long that when Mr Alexander grabbed her hand, she was frozen with shock. The heat from his hand travelled up her arm, making it tingle, and it was impossible to focus on anything else. She had felt the blade of his small sword slice her skin. Even though the cut wasn't deep it still should have hurt, but all she could focus on was the comforting warmth of his thumb, gently stroking back and forth over her skin.

The slow movement of his finger should not have affected her. *He* should not have affected her. Never in all her life had the smallest touch of a man sent her body aflame. She pulled her hand out of his quickly, afraid that he could tell how her body was reacting to him. The air had seemed to leave the room and she couldn't get her heart to stop pounding in her chest, even though their match was over.

'You're shaking,' he said, guiding her gently by the elbow to the sofa.

'I'm fine,' she replied, not wanting him to think she was about to swoon. She'd never had patience for women who swooned, but she took a seat on the sofa as a precaution.

'Shall I get you some wine to steady your nerves?'

She shook her head. 'No, I am fine, truly I am. There is no need to fuss over me. I was just surprised by your strike. I've never seen anyone handle a sword like that.'

He sat beside her and rolled his sleeves down, covering his forearms that she had been trying her best not to stare at. 'It is a trick I learned a long time ago,' he explained, 'and I assure you I am not fussing. I simply don't want you to slide off the sofa and on to the floor when you faint. It would be difficult to explain to Mrs Moggs when I ask her for the smelling salts.'

The ease of manner in which he was addressing her had her heartbeat slowing to a steady rhythm and it was gradually becoming easier to take deep breaths. But then he took out a white handkerchief from the pocket of his waistcoat and carefully blotted her blood, sending her pulse racing once again.

As he studied her wrist, he appeared to be searching for something to say. For a moment, it looked as if he were clenching and unclenching his jaw. 'It doesn't appear deep. Does it hurt?'

He looked up at her. Never before had she seen such concern for her well-being reflected in a man's eyes. No other man had tended to her the way this man was. Heaven knew Skeffington would not have cared to do so. If she were lying on the floor injured, he probably would have chastised her for getting in people's way.

Even her own father had never once treated her as if she were more than a means to achieve something greater. By arranging her marriage to Skeffington, he had received a political ally with one of the most influential men in Britain and the prestige of saying he was the father of a duchess. Her feelings on the matter were not to be considered.

There only was one other time that a man had shown some concern for her. It was during her first ball after Lord Andrew Pearce, who was now married to her sister Charlotte, had asked her to dance. On the way to the dance floor an older gentleman was in a hurry to leave the room and had bumped into Lizzy hard enough that she stumbled back. When the man didn't bother to apologise to her or to enquire if she was all right, Lord Andrew took him to task. For years, Lizzy held Lord Andrew in the highest regard for what she viewed as a gallant gesture. No other man had ever cared about her feelings before or since.

Until now—until Simon Alexander took her gently by the hand and tended to her wound. Her heart did an odd flip in her chest. It was the same sensation she remembered years ago on that ballroom floor. It was the same sensation she would get whenever she saw Lord Andrew after that night. She held back a groan at her foolish nature. Had she learned nothing this past year since Lord Andrew had fallen in love with Charlotte? She now knew his kind act was just a polite gesture that he had probably forgotten about moments after it happened. One kind act did not mean that a man had designs on you.

It would be foolish of her to think that this man was tending to her cut because he was attracted to her. She was not the kind of woman that attracted men of her age. And she had lived twenty-nine years—long enough to know that there was something about her that did not elicit tender feelings in men of any age. Oh, she knew that men were capable of those feelings. She had seen enough couples in love to believe it was possible. It just wasn't possible for her. And the only reason he was being this kind was because he was probably feeling guilty for making her bleed.

Lizzy shook her head and pulled her hand out of his. This time it was with a gentle slide. Her eyes were drawn to his wrist and her gaze settled on the thin white scar that she had seen earlier when he was selecting a sword.

'Your scar is in the same spot as the cut on my wrist. Did it come from a duel?' she asked, motioning with her head to his hand.

He bent his wrist, making the scar more pronounced. 'It did. My opponent was interested in leaving me with a lasting remembrance of our match. When you have that happen to you once and the wound is deep enough to leave a scar, you learn rather quickly how to do it back.'

Their eyes met and his eyes appeared to darken even more with every heartbeat.

Suddenly, he stood rather abruptly. 'You should see that your wound is taken care of.'

'I can tend to it myself. As I said, it is not deep.'

'Nevertheless, you probably want to clean it and use my handkerchief to put pressure on the cut. It will help it to stop the bleeding quicker.'

'You seem to know something about caring for my cut.'

'I travel a lot,' he said, for the first time giving her the smallest hint about himself while he stood a few feet from the sofa. 'When you travel, you need to be prepared for the unexpected and any inconveniences.'

She looked over to the swords lying on the floor where he had left them to force her mind to stop thinking about how kind he was being to her. The sun was dipping further in the sky and the armoury was lit with a yellow glow. The temperature outside must have been dropping because frost was forming on the windowpanes. This would be the last time she would experience a sunset from inside Stonehaven. Her time here had come to an end.

'I will not bother you about Stonehaven any longer,' she said, looking up at him from where she was sitting. 'My aunt and I will leave as soon as I tend to my wrist.' She stood and refused to let him see how much losing Stonehaven tore at her heart, but they had made a wager and she would not go back on her word.

His gaze settled on her wrist. 'You may stay until morning.'

'I don't understand. Why are you asking me to stay?'

'It's a moonless night, not the ideal condition for travelling once the sun goes down. I'll have Mrs Moggs arrange rooms for you and your aunt.' His attention shifted to the slice in the fabric of her sleeve that he had made with his sword.

He had to be feeling guilty about cutting her gown and her wrist. There was no other explanation.

'I'm certain dinner will be ready shortly,' he continued. 'I'll leave you and your aunt to enjoy it together. I have matters to attend to in my study for the remainder of the evening. In the morning, after breakfast, I expect you to honour our agreement and leave.' He arched his brow and waited for her acknowledgement.

It was more than she had expected of him. At least she would be able to spend one last night inside her home. She would take what he was offering. She would take this last night in Stonehaven and then leave for Bath with her aunt in the morning.

Lizzy nodded her agreement. 'Forgive me for getting blood on your handkerchief.' She held it out to him.

He stared down at the white cloth with streaks of her blood. 'If it weren't for me, you wouldn't be bleeding at all. You should keep it. Continue to put pressure on the cut.' And with just a slight hesitation, he picked up his banyan and walked out the door.

Chapter Seven

When Lizzy went back into the Gold Drawing Room, Aunt Clara jumped up from the sofa and the colour drained from her face. 'Elizabeth, my God, what has happened to you?' She rushed over and ran her hands down Lizzy's arms, and stared at the cut in her sleeve and then at the handkerchief wrapped around her wrist.

Lizzy hadn't considered what she must have looked like after her rather vigorous fencing match, but from the expression on Aunt Clara's face, it could not have been good.

'Did His Grace do this to you because we haven't yet left this house? There are some, knowing what we have done, who would say it was within his rights to punish you in some way, but to treat you so…' She wrapped Lizzy in her arms for a tight hug, squeezing her ribs before releasing her. 'Did he…?' She lowered her voice to a faint whisper and raised her small frame on to her toes to place her mouth by Lizzy's ear. 'Did he violate you in any way, Elizabeth?' she asked so quietly that Lizzy could barely hear her. 'If he did, I assure you we will find a way to enact some revenge where it would be impossible for him to know that we were behind the horrible deed.'

'Aunt!'

'Believe me, Elizabeth. I will find a way.'

'No. No. It is not what you think.' She took a step back, trying to push the heart-melting image of Simon Alexander sitting beside her and tending to her wound out of her mind. 'I am fine,' she said reassuringly to the second person that day.

Aunt Clara gestured to the rip in Lizzy's sleeve. 'But your dress…'

Lizzy let out a breath. 'It is not what you think. I am fine.'

Her aunt eyed her in that familiar way she had that let Lizzy know she was trying to determine if her niece was lying. 'You are certain.'

'I am. Honestly, I am quite well.'

In the light from the candles that were now placed about the room and the glow from the fireplace, Lizzy could see her reassuring words had put the colour back in her aunt's face.

Aunt Clara placed her hand on Lizzy's back and guided her towards the sofa. 'Come and tell me what happened.'

They sat in unison and Lizzy attempted to smooth the wrinkles out of her dress.

'I know you and His Grace do not like one another.' Aunt Clara glanced down to the handkerchief wrapped around Lizzy's injured wrist. 'And I know that he was not pleased to see us here. He made that very plain. I can't help but think that the state of your appearance and his feelings towards you have something in common.'

How could she explain that her time with the new Duke had left her confused about how she felt about him?

Aunt Clara motioned to Lizzy's sleeve that had been sliced open. 'Why don't you begin by telling me how that happened?'

He had ruined one of her most expensive travelling dresses. She should be angry with him for that and yet she found herself smiling. The match had been exhilarating and the fact that he had treated her as a worthy opponent and not a fragile flower while they crossed swords made her sit a bit taller.

'It is an amusing story, really.' She chewed on her lip and glanced sideways at Aunt Clara. While Lizzy found it amusing, her aunt might find it scandalous— and Aunt Clara wasn't easily scandalised. 'As I walked through the house one last time, I went into the various rooms—'

'You walked in on His Grace while he was having sexual congress with a woman. It all makes sense now.' Her aunt nodded sagely as if she understood completely.

'What? No... Why would you think that?' Lizzy sputtered.

'He is an attractive man. It's not a horrible image. Except for the part when the woman he was with, believing you were meeting His Grace for a liaison, attacked you and ripped your dress in a fit of jealous rage.'

Lizzy's head snapped back. 'Did you drink a bottle of sherry while I was gone?'

'I imagine women place themselves in his path, especially now with his new fortune and title, and probably do fight over him, even if not physically. It is not such a fantastical assumption.'

The idea that women might be trying to attach themselves to Mr Alexander was not something Lizzy wanted to think about. The notion of him with other women left a bad taste in her mouth.

'If you will allow me to finish my story, my dear aunt, you will know how I came to be in such a state.'

'Very well, I won't stop you. Go on.'

Lizzy opened her mouth to continue with her explanation when her aunt interrupted her once more.

'I do have one question before you begin.'

Lizzy rubbed her brow. 'What is it?' she asked on a sigh.

'Is His Grace involved in the story at all?'

'He is.'

'And is he wearing his banyan in this tale?'

'That is two questions and he was not wearing it the entire time.'

Aunt Clara smiled and wiggled in her seat, the curled tendrils of her auburn hair bobbing with the movement. 'I might like your explanation after all. Go on, then. Tell me what happened.'

Lizzy let out a breath and waited to make sure her aunt had nothing else to say.

'Go on. I'll not interrupt you this time.'

She moved closer to her aunt so they were inches apart and lowered her voice, even though the door was closed. 'As I was saying, I was walking through the house…through the *public* rooms on this floor…and I reached the armoury and went inside. While I was in there, His Grace came in—'

'What was he wearing?'

'You're interrupting me.'

'Yes, well, none of us is perfect. We all have our foibles. So, is he in his banyan or out of it when he walks in on you unexpectedly?'

'He is in his banyan,' Lizzy replied flatly.

'Excellent!'

'Why are you so interested in what he was wearing?'

'Elizabeth, do you know the last time I saw a man in a banyan? It was when your uncle was still alive and while I loved your uncle very much, he did not look as dashing in his banyan as His Grace looks in his. I know you despise the man, but even you must admit he is lovely to watch with his dark good looks and brooding manner.'

It was good to be reminded that she did, in fact, despise him. Their last few minutes together were an anomaly. He had caused her unnecessary hardship by taking months to reach England so they could settle her husband's estate. He had refused to switch homes with her when it shouldn't even matter to him what house he had in England since he planned to run back to the Continent every chance he got. And he hadn't treated her with the deference she deserved as the Duchess of Skeffington.

But she hated to admit that she might despise him a little less at that moment, even though Stonehaven was his.

'Now, go on,' Aunt Clara said, breaking into her thoughts. 'You were standing in the armoury and His Grace strode into the room wearing his banyan and smelling of bay rum.'

'He doesn't smell of bay rum.'

'In my version he does. What happened next?'

'Well, he insulted my taste in decorating. Told me I was theatrical and said I was wilful.' She eyed her aunt for some sort of indignation on her part, but she didn't see any, which was rather insulting. 'Do you find me theatrical and wilful?'

'If I say I do not, will you go on with the story? I want to find out what happens to his banyan.'

'Aunt Clara!'

'Oh, very well.' She patted Lizzy's thigh reassuringly. 'You are everything that is not theatrical and wilful.' She looked away and Lizzy could see her roll her eyes.

'I can't believe you think that of me.'

'I can't believe it is taking you so long to tell this story. It is a good thing I had the servants light some candles in this room while you were gone because had they not, we would be sitting in the dark by now and we still haven't reached the part where I get to find out why His Grace was wearing his banyan only part of the time.'

The conversation Lizzy had had with him was coming back to her now that the haze of his touch had completely lifted. 'He also accused me of being rude,' she stated with a huff.

Aunt Clara looked away. 'Imagine that.'

'You are my aunt. You should be insulted for me and yet I almost have the impression you agree with him.'

Her impression of him had softened when he expressed true concern for her well-being, but now she was remembering why she had such a low opinion of him in the first place. How had she so easily forgotten what an odious man he really was?

'Lizzy, as I stated earlier, none of us is perfect. It doesn't mean I love you any less. Are there any other traits of yours that he mentioned so we can list them all in a row now and get back to your story?'

'I believe those were the only ones,' Lizzy said through her teeth. 'Although I believe rudeness must run in my family.'

'Yes, well, we can't choose our family, now can we, my dear?' Aunt Clara replied with a teasing smile.

'I will tell you what happened next, even though I don't believe you deserve to know.'

The smile on her aunt's face brightened with anticipation in the glow from the fireplace.

'I told him about the fencing lessons that I had taken here and he proposed we have a duel. The winner would get Stonehaven.'

For the first time since Lizzy walked into the room, Aunt Clara appeared speechless.

'It seemed like a good idea at the time,' Lizzy rushed on.

'What part of that seemed like a good idea? The idea that you cross swords with a man whose skills are probably far above your own? Or the idea that you were allowing a man who you do not know well at all—and who obviously does not like you—to attack you with a sharp object?'

'There are times when luck can win over skill,' she tried to explain.

Her aunt looked once more at her bandaged hand. 'And did it this time?'

'No, he won. But he did take his banyan off while

we were fencing.' Lizzy knew she was blushing just by simply recalling him with his rolled-up shirtsleeves.

Aunt Clara let out a laugh. 'And did he look as good as I imagine?'

Lizzy's face was growing warmer. 'He might have.'

'I thought he might,' Aunt Clara said with a big smile. 'I'm surprised I didn't hear the two of you shouting at each other.'

'There wasn't any shouting. Neither one of us had a need to raise our voices.' Which was odd, considering she was in a room for an extended period of time with the man who seemed to be able to put her in bad humour when he was in her presence. 'We had agreed to fight until the first draw of blood. Eventually, he cut my wrist with the tip of his blade and won our match and this house.' She held up her hand that still had his handkerchief wrapped around it. 'The sleeve of my dress is the other casualty.'

'Is it a deep cut?'

'No, I'm sure I can take this off now.'

There was a small part of her that didn't want to unwrap his handkerchief. It was her only reminder that for a short while the self-centred man had shown her care and concern and it wasn't all a dream. Reluctantly she unwrapped her hand and placed the cloth inside the pocket of her gown. The cut had already stopped bleeding and, as she looked at the fine straight line, she couldn't help thinking again how it matched his.

She must have been staring at the cut for far too long because her aunt politely cleared her throat and Lizzy looked up at her.

'I asked you how things ended between you and His Grace.'

'We were cordial. Which in itself was…odd. And I let him know that I would be honouring our wager. Stonehaven is his and I will not be coming back.' It was just as well since she knew whenever she saw him she would be picturing him without his cravat.

Aunt Clara reached out and gave her uninjured hand a gentle squeeze. 'I'm sorry. I know how much this house means to you. I know that it was all you ever wanted from Skeffington and you waited for so long to find out it wouldn't be yours.'

'This has always felt like home to me.'

'I know, but maybe it's time to set up another home and you will create wonderful memories there?'

'Perhaps.'

But those memories wouldn't be the same. Any time that she spent with her sisters now for an extended period would include their doting husbands, of which she had none. She was now the lone Sommersby sister. The one who didn't have a loving husband. Things would never be what they once were when she had gathered together here with them. It was much too depressing at the moment to consider.

How she wished it was earlier in the day and she could take Aunt Clara into the village and visit the shops. A new pair of gloves might make her feel a little bit better. She liked new gloves. And they would cover up her cut. And perhaps she would have found a charming new bonnet. And some lovely embroidered stockings…

'You know you can always live with me. It will be quiet at home now that Juliet has moved out and married Montague. Maybe staying with me will feel a bit like home since we are family.'

She returned the squeeze to her aunt's hand and gave it a soft pat. At least there were a few people in the world who genuinely cared about her. 'That is very kind of you, but I have been the Duchess of Skeffington for too long to live as a guest in your home for ever. I know myself. I need my own home to manage and my own staff. I want to have all the rooms decorated just so to my liking. I want to plan more dinner parties and balls and garden parties. I know I can't live in as grand a house as I'd like to and entertain as I did with the money Skeffington left me and the income from Clivemoore, but I will not have people believing I am penniless and at the mercy of living with my aunt. I'm sorry. I do truly appreciate the kind gesture. But in my world perception is everything.'

'You really do enjoy being at the pinnacle of the social ladder?' her aunt said, watching her closely.

'It is all I've known for so long. And it is a long and hard climb back up when you fall.' She had witnessed it happen to others. It is not something she ever wanted to experience herself. Without her title and fortune, she would be nothing. There would be no advantage to being her friend and the friends she had now would abandon her.

Thankfully, she had noticed some of the smaller town houses in Mayfair were owned by a number of dowager duchesses. She would just inform her friends that she, too, had decided to find something snug and cosy for her London residence. She knew she would never be happy living so far up north in gloomy Clivemoore away from her family and had decided she would live year-round in London so she would never have to worry about what her friends thought of *that* house.

'I have been discussing my options with Mr Sherman on where I can live. He had assured me that with the money Skeffington left me I can purchase a suitable London residence and live off the annual income I get from Clivemoore. I won't be able to live as extravagantly as I had been, but it would still be a very respectable existence. So far there haven't been many to my liking, but there is one that I have had my eye on. It is Lady Wallingford's home on Mount Street. Lord and Lady Helmford live on that street, as does Lord Baxter and the Dowager Duchess of Hedgmont. Mr Sherman has heard a rumour that Lady Wallingford needs to sell it to settle her gambling debts and may agree to an offer below the value of the property. He has been watching it closely for me. She has exceptional taste and we believe it will not remain on the market for very long once people become aware that it is for sale.'

'Then I hope he is able to purchase it for you.' Aunt Clara stood up and smiled down at Lizzy. 'Well, in the meantime, what do you say to being my guest at least for the remainder of the holiday? It will be a slow journey to travel to Bath tonight, but maybe we can stop at the Linley Arms, which is nearby. I am certain our coachmen will appreciate not having to travel too far in one day.'

Lizzy grabbed her aunt's hand. 'I almost forgot. His Grace has invited us to spend the night here. He was going to arrange to have rooms ready for us and dinner served to us in the dining room—although he won't be joining us.' A sense of melancholy washed over her with the thought that she would not be seeing him again that evening. It was a foolish sentiment since she wouldn't be seeing him at all after she left tomorrow. She hadn't seen him for months after the reading of the will and that hadn't bothered her at all. In fact, she had been rather glad that she hadn't run into him and that she had heard he was spending all of his time in Sicily. This brief time today in his presence should not alter her feelings about him.

'I don't understand,' Aunt Clara said, interrupting her musings. 'He wanted us out of this house the minute we arrived.'

'I believe he offered us this reprieve out of guilt for injuring me during our match. Which is nonsensical since we had agreed to duel until one of us drew first blood.'

'You believe guilt to be his reason?' Aunt Clara sounded sceptical.

'Of course. What other reason could there be?' She hooked her arm through her aunt's and mustered up a smile. 'Let's find Mrs Moggs and see what part of the house he has relegated us to. One can only hope it is not the servants' quarters,' she said with a wry smile.

Chapter Eight

Simon should've had a restful night. He usually did. He was the type of man who could fall asleep anywhere the moment he laid his head down. It was a trait that had come in handy over the years since he very rarely knew where he would be sleeping from one month to the next, even as a child.

The tester bed in the Duke's bedchamber in Stonehaven, with its well-stuffed mattress and plush linens, was the epitome of comfort and yet he found himself waking up a number of times during the night with thoughts of the woman who he assumed was curled up in the Duchess's bed on the other side of his bedchamber wall.

Elizabeth, the Duchess of Skeffington, was not a woman who he particularly liked. He wasn't wrong when he told her she was wilful, rude and dramatic. She was also one of the haughtiest women he had ever met and, over the course of his lifetime as a man without privilege, he had been subjected to the scorn of quite a few.

When he noticed her shiny black carriage with the

ducal crest roll up to the house from the window of his study, he had felt a headache coming on. A few days earlier, a letter had arrived that was addressed to her and at the time he thought it might simply have been sent by someone who was unaware that she no longer was in possession of Stonehaven. The letter was still on his desk since he hadn't yet decided if he wanted to take the time to send it to her in London.

However, when he stepped into his entrance hall and saw her ordering his butler about and making her own arrangements to occupy his house, he knew the letter addressed to her at Stonehaven was no accident and she had planned to spend time here regardless of the fact that it was not her home. He had been so taken aback by the audacity of her arrival that he had to remind himself that he could not physically pick her up and throw her out—which was what he had really wanted to do. Spending most of his life with people who didn't care about him had taught him at a young age to stand up for himself.

It was during their fencing match that his reaction to her started to shift. The view of her long legs might have been the catalyst. The sight of them, bared to his eyes only, reminded him that in addition to being a shrew, Elizabeth was also a tempting beauty. And her playful enthusiasm while they crossed swords showed him an unguarded side of her that he would never have believed existed. That enchanting combination was in such a sharp contrast to his experiences up to that point that for a time, when they sat together on the sofa after their match had ended, he had forgotten why he disliked her so much—until he remembered that she wanted Stonehaven for its substantial income and she was willing to risk getting injured to acquire it. He was foolish for feeling guilty about injuring her, which had prompted him to offer her a room for the night.

And as the dark hours wore on, he continued to wake up with thoughts of her. She was a woman who enjoyed reminding him that she had been his social superior up until just recently. She was a woman who didn't leave his house when he had asked her to. And she was also a woman who had looked up at him with soft brown eyes when he tended to her wrist—a wrist that sent waves of desire coursing through his body when he held it.

He was too smart to let desire overrule his instincts about people. However, there was no need to make fighting that desire harder than it had to be and a number of times he cursed himself for asking Mrs Moggs to place the Duchess in the bedchamber next to his. It seemed like the right decision at the time. It had been her room while her husband was alive and he had a feeling she would stay in there even if his housekeeper had taken her to any of the other bedchambers in the house.

From the moment he lay down, it had become impossible to stop picturing her snuggled in her bed with her long legs wrapped around her white sheets just on the other side of his wall. He wondered how often she had spent nights with the old Duke in the bed he was lying on. There was a portrait of the man in each of the residences and Simon knew how old he had been. Just the thought of the young Duchess lying under his predecessor made his stomach roll. She had probably used that feminine beauty of hers to snag the old man. It never ceased to amaze him what some people would do for money and a title.

* * *

By morning Simon debated if he should have his usual breakfast tray sent up to his room or if he should venture downstairs to join the ladies at the table. While he hadn't been raised in the finest of homes, the various relatives who had taken him in after his mother died were of the gentry and all had instilled good manners in him. He found he didn't like the idea of the Duchess leaving Stonehaven believing him ill-mannered, so when the sun came up he got dressed and prepared himself to deal with her one last time.

Even though he could barely open his eyes from his lack of sleep, when he walked into the breakfast room his gaze landed on the woman who had unknowingly kept him up most of the night. She sat alone at the table, buttering her toast in her fashionable lavender gown with sunlight bouncing off the gold settings of her emerald earrings.

She looked up at him as she lowered the toast to her plate and wiped her hands on her napkin. 'Good morning.' She addressed him with a polite smile before shooting a glance at one of the footmen who immediately came over to her side of the table.

'Please see that a fresh pot of coffee is made for His Grace. This one has been out too long and it probably has cooled.'

Before he could stop the footman, the man nodded and removed the silver coffeepot from the table and walked out of the room. It didn't matter to Simon if his coffee wasn't hot. He had woken up on ships and in the desert, in boarding houses and in tents. Just having coffee available could be a luxury at times.

He wasn't particular if the coffee was hot or if it had cooled down.

Taking a seat across from her, he felt his brow wrinkle. 'How did you know I drank coffee in the morning?'

'I assumed it was either coffee or ale, but just to be certain I asked the footmen when I walked into the room. They informed me you had been having coffee in your bedchamber at eight each morning since you arrived. I wasn't certain if you would be coming downstairs today, but I thought to plan ahead in the event you did.'

'You arranged coffee for me?'

A faint blush spread up her neck. 'I suppose it was done in habit from hosting so many guests here over the years. There is bacon on the sideboard. I understand you seem to enjoy that in the morning. I took the liberty of having Cook make up some of my favourite bread, as well. It's quite good if you'd care to try some.' She gestured towards the sideboard.

If he were sitting across from anyone else and they had made their own arrangements with his cook without his permission, he might have been taken aback by the bold gesture. But he was beginning to discover that any actions on the part of the Duchess were of no surprise.

He was about to get up to fix himself a plate of food, when she delicately cleared her throat. The other footman who was stationed by the door approached the table. 'Please make a plate of bread and bacon for His Grace and be generous with the amount of meat you put on it.' She turned her attention to Simon. 'Do you have a certain preference on the type of slices you would like him to select?'

Simon just shook his head and watched his footman remove his plate from the table and walk off to the sideboard. *Did she always feel the need to control everything in her life?*

'I am capable of getting my own food.'

'I'm sure you are, but why would you want to when there are servants to do it for you?'

He was about to reply, but she kept talking.

'I've hosted enough house parties over the years to know how much men like yourself enjoy a hearty helping of meat in the morning.'

'Men like myself? What kind of a man am I?' He had insulted her several times yesterday in his description of her. He braced himself for how she would respond.

'You are a man who spends a considerable amount of time outside. Men like you usually prefer to fortify themselves in the morning with something hearty before they head outside to enjoy their physical pursuits.'

'And how do you know I am a man who enjoys the outside and physical pursuits?'

'The golden colour of your skin tells me that you have spent a considerable amount of time outside in the sun yourself while you've been away. I just assumed you might be venturing outside here, as well, even though there is snow on the ground and it is rather cold here in England.'

It was surprising that she had studied him that closely and he silently berated himself for feeling flattered that she paid such close attention to him. The assumptions she made about him were completely accurate. Simon was a man who didn't like to be in one place for too long and each day, since he had arrived back in England, he felt the need to get out of the house. There was nothing quite like inhaling fresh air and moving one's body. It didn't matter if it was cold out. Being inside for too long a period of time made him restless.

'Do you always pay such close attention to people?'

Her gaze dropped to his throat before she picked up her knife and reached for the butter dish. 'When you've served as a hostess to the *ton* for twelve years, you acquire a knack for anticipating what your guests need.'

'But I am not your guest.' He looked past her shoulders and to the windows, afraid of what she might see in his eyes. He was an ass for thinking her gesture meant she might have been attracted to him, as well. She would always think of him as some undeserving distant relation who should never have inherited her late husband's title. He knew many members of the *ton* thought that, as well.

As he kept his attention on the snowy landscape outside, he missed the blush that spread all the way to her cheeks.

The footman came back to the table and placed the plate in front of Simon. Just as he was about to pick up his fork, the other footman arrived and poured his coffee. The steam from the cup swirled in the air. He took a slow sip and savoured the feeling of the warm, smooth liquid sliding down his throat.

As if she could somehow sense how much he was enjoying his coffee, a faint smile played on her lips. Feeling uncomfortable under her watchful gaze, he put the cup down and tore into one of the thick fluffy pieces of bread the footman had given him.

She did that delicate clearing of her throat again and he looked up to find her pointedly staring at the porcelain bowl of jam.

'The strawberry jam was made here from the plants grown in the kitchen gardens this year. It was an exceptional batch of berries. The jam goes very well with the bread.'

'I'm not very fond of sweet things.' When one frequently didn't have sugar available, one did not acquire a taste for it.

'The jam is not overly sweet. You might want to try it to see. The taste reminds me of summer.' She picked up her cup and took a small sip of what might be tea.

How did one woman have so many opinions on what one consumed for breakfast?

He tore another piece of bread and put it in his mouth. She stole a glance at him before she looked out the window, apparently losing interest in him and his dining habits. The porcelain bowl with the jam was a few inches from his plate and the faint fragrance of the berries drifted his way. It did smell of summer and warm days. He remembered picking strawberries behind his Uncle Peter and Aunt Henrietta's house the summer after he turned twelve, five months before a fire burned down the house, killing his mother's brother and his wife. It had been years since he'd thought about that farm.

Simon eyed the jam and glanced at the Duchess, who was concentrating on refilling her teacup. Slowly, he pulled the bowl over and spread a thin layer of the jam on the bread. As the taste exploded on his tongue, he closed his eyes to savour it.

'Does it not remind you of summer?' she asked.

He nodded without opening his eyes. The idea that she would have a satisfied smile on her face was keeping him from opening them.

'The kitchen also has raspberry and blackberry jam, as well. I happen to prefer the strawberry. The blackberry jam is very good and not as sweet. You might prefer that one above all the others.'

He opened his eyes and found her looking off to the distance with concern as if she were truly considering which type of jam he would like best. He took another drink of coffee and cut into his bacon, trying to recall when anyone had ever paid this much attention to his dining preferences. 'I didn't know there were blackberry bushes in the grounds.'

'There are. They grow wild in the wood on the west border of the property. My youngest sister, Juliet, enjoys them so I had the kitchen make some jam each year for when she came to visit. I suppose there are quite a number of jars still sitting on a shelf somewhere downstairs.' She eyed his plate. 'What do you think of the bread?'

'It's very good. I don't think the kitchen has made this bread before for me.'

'It has been my favourite for the last few years. I asked Mrs Moggs to have Cook make a few loaves. Since our journey to Bath may take some time, I thought having a loaf for the trip would be wise in the event the inns are too crowded to stop for luncheon.' As if it had just occurred to her that his servants were not her servants any longer, she paused and bit her lip before continuing. 'I hope you don't mind?' It might have been the first time she'd sounded unsure about anything. 'I am certain there will be plenty left for you to enjoy,' she said as if to offer him something to appease his disapproval.

The fact that she was ordering his staff around, and they were listening to her, was something he should probably discuss with Simpkins or Mrs Moggs. But all of her directions to his servants, so far, were to his benefit.

'Then asking you to stay the night has its advantages,' he said, leaning back in his chair and watching her.

It appeared as if she was trying to hold back a grin. 'It did. It's a shame you hadn't agreed to allow us to stay a fortnight. Just imagine how well fed you would be.'

It surprised him to find he was actually smiling along with her. He knew she was teasing, but it had him wondering how she would have managed the house and the staff if she had stayed that long. For the past two Mondays, Mrs Moggs had approached him about deciding on a menu for the week. Each time she asked, he would tell her to serve him the type of dishes they served down at the tavern in the village. Whatever she had picked so far had been good. Seeing how interested the Duchess was with choosing the perfect accompaniment to his bread, he imagined she would have some definite preferences when it came to working on the menus with his housekeeper. And she would probably be appalled to find out what her old cook had been preparing for him.

Within minutes, he was picturing her sitting at the

dining-room table as a line of footmen brought in dish after delicious dish. He silently cursed himself. Musings like that weren't helpful.

'How is your wrist?' he asked, glancing over at the graceful hand wrapped around her teacup.

She lowered her cup and looked at the thin scab before turning her wrist and showing it to him. The area around the scab was black and blue. 'It's fine, thank you. I had my maid fetch some ointment for me from Mrs Moggs last night.'

'Does it hurt?'

'No,' she replied, shaking her head. 'I'd forgotten it was there until you mentioned it.'

He nodded, unsure if he should apologise for injuring her. They had agreed to fight until one of them drew blood, after all. Someone getting cut was the point of the duel.

'I have presents for the staff for Christmas,' she blurted out rather suddenly. 'Each year I have given each of them something. There is a basket with them that Simpkins has. Would you permit him to hand them out after I leave? I think it best if he does it for me this year.'

'Of course.'

Without a doubt she was the most unusual woman he had ever met. One minute she was practically demanding he turn over this house to her, the next minute she was lifting up her skirts so she could lunge at him with a sword and now this morning she appeared to be behaving like the perfect hostess and proper Duchess. Which one was the real woman?

His gaze slid over her form, lingering on the swell of her breasts with the white lace resting against them.

Her skin looked so smooth and soft, and he found himself watching her breathe—captivated by the movement. His heart hammered in his chest while he was fighting this need to touch her. Realising he must have been staring and wondering why she had not issued him a strong setdown, he lifted his gaze and found her looking into her teacup, apparently lost in thought. There was melancholy about her now that hadn't been there earlier.

'Is your aunt still abed?' he asked, scraping jam on to another slice of bread and feeling an unexplained need to distract her from her thoughts.

'No, she will be in shortly. I think she wanted to take one final walk through the conservatory before we depart since she has always loved the selection of roses that are grown in there.'

'I don't think I've been in the conservatory yet,' he replied before taking a bite of bread.

She looked at him as if he had just issued her another insult. 'Certainly that can't be true. That conservatory is one of the finest in all of Dorset.'

He resisted the urge to roll his eyes. 'Surely that's an exaggeration.'

'No. It isn't. There are over two hundred different species of plants in there. The Duke of Devonshire himself had given me some of his cuttings for various flowering plants and it is well known that he is very proficient in horticulture. If you have an opportunity to meet him while you are in England, I think you might find you have some things in common. He is a bachelor duke, as well. Come to think about it, he is the only other eligible bachelor Duke in Britain.

Surely that alone would give the both of you something to discuss.'

'You mean ways to avoid fortune hunters.'

She narrowed her eyes at him and for a moment he thought she might stick her tongue out. 'If you are so inclined. He might be able to offer you a perspective on all the unmarried women that are fit to be a duchess. I would think you would appreciate a male perspective instead of my opinions.'

This might be the only thing he could think of that she wasn't offering her opinion on. It didn't matter, though. Years ago when he was on leave in Brighton, a number of women from English Society had turned their noses up at him because he had been a naval officer who wasn't the son of a titled peer. He would not be choosing a wife from the ranks of English Society now.

His thoughts strayed to the night he confessed his affection to Miss Frederica Shaw and how she laughed at the very notion of considering his proposal. Evidently it was one thing to happily listen to an untitled gentleman fawn over you, but it was quite another when he expected you to admit that you felt the same way about him.

Surely you don't expect me to marry you. My father is a viscount. And your father was what exactly?

His father had been the distant cousin to the Duke of Skeffington. He was a man who had no title or land, who fell in love with a woman and because she was a French Huguenot his family disowned him. He was a man who joined the navy and worked his way to Sailing Master of the HMS *Conquest*, dying at sea when Simon was twenty-four. None of that had been good enough for Freddy.

'I will not be staying in England long enough to find a wife.'

She tilted her head and quite openly studied him. 'Why are you so eager to leave? You could be living very well here as the Duke of Skeffington.' She put her cup down, leaned forward and lowered her voice to a whisper. 'What is it you do after you leave these shores?'

He matched her movement and lowered his voice, as well. 'I uncover ancient artefacts for museums and private collectors.'

She sat back on the blue-velvet cushion of her chair and let out a breath. 'You do not have to lie about what you do. I only asked to be polite.'

If there was one thing he had learned over the years, it was that there were times that even when you told the truth, people wouldn't believe you. He didn't even try to hide his smile as he concentrated on cutting more of his bacon. Placing his knife down, he looked up at her. 'I knew you were coming to this house, you know.'

'How could you know that? I hadn't even contacted Mrs Moggs or Simpkins to notify them of my plan to stay. I had been with my aunt in Kent, attending my younger sister's wedding, and thought it would be lovely for us to stop here for a short while before travelling on to my aunt's home in Bath.'

He didn't believe the decision to stop here was made as spontaneously as she made it sound. 'But you did tell someone besides your aunt that you would be coming here.'

He watched as she looked as if she was trying to appear innocent of his accusation. While he was eyeing her, he took out the sealed missive from his pocket and slid it across the table. With a perplexed expression, she picked it up and turned it over.

'That arrived for you two days ago. I was going to have it sent to you in London, but it slipped my mind.'

'It's from Mr Sherman,' she said, looking at the penmanship. 'I believe you've been in contact with him regarding my stay at the London town house. He handles all my affairs.'

Chapter Nine

Holding the unexpected letter in her hand, Lizzy said a silent prayer of thanks. There was only one thing that would have made Mr Sherman send a letter to her here. Lady Wallingford's house must finally be for sale. This was an odd time of year for that to occur, but she would not question her bit of good fortune.

She had been so lucky to find Mr Sherman. He had done a fine job negotiating on her behalf with Mr Alexander for an extension to the amount of time she could live in Skeffington House in London while she searched for another home. And he was able to discreetly search for any appropriate London town houses for her at a reasonable price.

Unable to wait until she got into her carriage with Aunt Clara, she immediately broke the seal and skimmed the letter, excited for the first time at the prospect of living somewhere aside from Stonehaven. But as she read his words, her stomach dropped and her hand began to shake so much it was becoming difficult to read the words on the page. In her wildest imaginings, she'd never thought this could happen.

'You don't look well. I'm going to fetch your aunt.'

Not looking well was probably an understatement. She wanted to be sick and pressed her hand into her stomach. How would she be able to show her face in London after word of this got out? How would she be able to live?

Her aunt came running into the room with Mr Alexander following close behind while Lizzy was attempting to try to calm down enough so she would not break down and cry. When he motioned for the servants to leave, she was grateful for his consideration.

'Lizzy, my dear, what is it?' Aunt Clara knelt beside Lizzy's chair. 'His Grace said you had received some distressing news.'

'This is much more than distressing,' Lizzy replied, waving the paper at Aunt Clara. 'This is beyond distressing. I am ruined. My money is gone.'

'Gone? How could it be gone?'

'Mr Sherman has written to inform me that someone has broken into the safe in Skeffington House and all the money that I had in there is now gone.' She threw the letter on the table and stared up at the ceiling, afraid to think what was to become of her.

Mr Alexander stepped forward and reached his hand out to her in a silent request to read the letter. Without thinking she handed it to him with an unsteady hand. The tremors that had started in her hands now moved throughout her body and she wrapped her arms around herself to try to calm down.

Aunt Clara looked up at Simon. 'Is it truly all gone?

He finished reading the letter and held it out for Lizzy to take back. Anger was etched across his face and there was a visible tic in his jaw. It wasn't his money that was stolen. Why was he so angry? She wouldn't be appealing to him for support. She'd had enough of being beholden to a Duke of Skeffington to last a lifetime.

'It appears a substantial portion of her fortune was in it,' he replied to her aunt while keeping his eyes on Lizzy. 'Why were you keeping so much in the safe?' There was bridled anger in his voice that was unmistakable.

Because I am a fool.

'Because I was planning on buying a town house soon in London,' she tried to explain, sounding much more composed than she felt. 'It was easier to have the money in the safe for when the time came to make the purchase.'

Mr Sherman was not happy about the idea, but Lizzy needed to see the money with her own eyes. If there was one thing that Skeffington's death had taught her, it was that she could not assume anything was as she was told. She needed proof that she had enough money to buy a fashionable, if small, town house on a sought-after street in Mayfair. It was her stupid idea to store all of the money in the safe and now she would be forced to live in Clivemoore away from everyone she held dear because of it. There wasn't enough income from Clivemoore for her to rent a London town house indefinitely and sustain her expected style of living. Oh, heavens, she only received the income from Clivemoore on an annual basis. The additional money that was in there to pay her staff and her other expenses was gone, as well. Her throat was beginning to close up and soon it would be impossible to speak.

The tic to his jaw was moving faster and he looked as if he wanted to hit something.

'I don't understand why you are angry with me,' she shouted, standing up with her hands fisted at her sides. 'This isn't your money and I won't be asking you for additional funds. This is my fault and I will deal with the consequences.'

She would have to live in Clivemoore House now. This was to be her fate. She was to be hidden away in the remote old home and that is where she would be until the end of her days. She could never let the *ton* know she no longer had her fortune. She would rather live in that dark, old house with no money to decorate it to her liking than have those people whisper about her and laugh behind her back. They had laughed enough when her father had sold her off to Skeffington at seventeen for his personal gain. Every ball and assembly she went to, every dinner party she had to endure, and every Sunday in church, she heard the girls she thought were her friends giggle and whisper snide comments about her and her marriage to the ancient Duke of Skeffington. It had been horrible, but she had learned to hold her head high. She'd learned to use her position and her wealth so that everyone wanted an invitation to one of her events. She made herself into someone that Society said was important and she was not going to go back to be the girl who silently cried herself to sleep at night over being tormented by the *ton*.

Teardrops were pooling in her eyes and she was afraid to blink—afraid that if she did, they would come streaming down and would not stop.

'I'm not angry with you,' he replied in a softer tone even though he looked as if he could take one of the chairs and throw it across the room. 'I'm angry at whoever it was who thought that they could go into *my* house and steal money out of *my* safe. This is as much a violation to me as it is to you. I am angry for both of us.'

While she was relieved to hear he wasn't angry with her, he still had his money. He still was able to pay the staff that he employed. She didn't even know how she would be able to do that.

Lizzy needed to find out the state of her finances right now. She could not wait. 'I need to go to London. I need to speak with Mr Sherman.'

She headed for the door, but Mr Alexander pulled her gently back by her arm. 'In this letter Mr Sherman asked if you would require him to contact Bow Street. If you'd like, you can send him your reply from here. The letter will arrive before you will. I am accustomed to handling my own affairs and, although it is my house they broke into, it is your money that was stolen. I will leave the decision to you.'

The very mention of Bow Street made her stomach drop. 'I cannot have him contact Bow Street.' She tried to say it with conviction, knowing that he could contact them on his own and she wouldn't be able to stop him.

'Why not?' Simon was watching her as if he was trying to determine her reasoning without her saying a word.

'Because if we do, people will find out. The *ton* will know that I have lost my fortune. I cannot have that.' The trembling that had been racking her body had finally stopped, but just the thought of them finding out brought the shakes back and she crossed her arms again to prevent him from seeing.

'But they can help,' Aunt Clara said, coming to his

side. 'They are trained in such matters. They found His Grace for Mr Nesbit. They can find your thief and bring him to justice.'

'And if they can't, what then? I will not be a social outcast because of this. I will not have those people mock me any more than they already have. I will not have Bow Street involved. It is my money and therefore it is my decision. Perhaps Mr Sherman will have some thoughts on who stole it and how I can get it back.' It was the only hope she had. 'I've made up my mind. I'm going to London.'

'If this is truly what you wish, then I'll go with you,' Aunt Clara said, taking her hand. 'There is no need for you to do this by yourself.'

There were times that her family meant more to her than she could ever say. This was one of those times.

'That isn't necessary,' he said, surprising them both. 'I will go to London to find out who did this. I'm good at finding things.' Mr Alexander looked into her eyes and she could see the determination in them. 'I'll find the person who broke into the safe and, in turn, find your money.'

The confidence in his voice and demeanour made her legs grow weak with relief, but she managed to stand tall and not give away how his offer of help had affected her. She never liked to show weakness. It was something she had learned living with Skeffington.

Aunt Clara was watching both of them closely as he continued to eye Lizzy as if he were waiting for her agreement. Her life had been tossed upside down and, truth be told, she had no idea if Mr Sherman would be able to find out who took her money. He hadn't indicated in his letter that he had any idea who might have it. Mr Alexander's help was something she didn't want to turn down.

'His Grace seems sure that he can help. I think you should let him go with you,' Aunt Clara said unnecessarily.

'You mean with us?' Lizzy clarified.

'I meant I'd go alone,' he stated.

'No, he should go with you,' her aunt said before turning to His Grace. 'Having Lizzy with you will be helpful. Mr Sherman works for her. He will probably be more forthcoming with her because of that.'

'But certainly you don't believe His Grace and I should go alone?'

'I will just slow you down. You know how I like to get out and stretch my legs on long journeys. If you travel with me, it will take you longer than three days to get to London. I'll follow along in a day or so after I stop at my home in Bath. You don't need me as much as you do His Grace. Do not look at me like that. You know what I'm saying is true, Elizabeth.'

Her aunt made it sound as if she were ancient. The woman had more life in her than Lizzy ever had. Nothing slowed her down and yet by the way she'd just described herself, one would think she took two naps a day. It hadn't escaped Lizzy's notice that her aunt had been watching her and Mr Alexander closely since they had arrived at Stonehaven. It was just like this woman to think she was somehow orchestrating an opportunity for romance to grow between the two of them.

'It would be a scandal should word get out that we are travelling alone together.'

'Well, which scandal are you concerned about more,

my dear, your fortune or your virtue?' her aunt replied impatiently. 'The faster you reach London, the better chance you have at finding whoever stole your money and hopefully you will be able to get it back. I'm sure you two will find a way to be discreet. There will be no scandal if both of you are careful.' Aunt Clara turned to him with an expectant expression. 'Your Grace, do you swear you will be a perfect gentleman to my niece during your journey?'

'I assure you, I have no designs on your niece.'

Words every woman would want a handsome gentleman to say about them.

Aunt Clara smiled up at him as if he had promised to keep her safe from a band of plundering pirates.

They would be travelling together with one shared goal and that goal was to find the person who had broken into the safe and retrieve Lizzy's money. Spending more time with the man who had sent her pulse racing last night just by holding her hand was not going to be good for her composure, but she knew he wasn't attracted to her which made her determined to hide the effect his presence had on her.

She looked at him, trying to determine how annoyed he was with the idea of travelling together. 'We can travel separately to London. If people were to find out we were travelling together—'

'We are travelling together, Duchess. You and I. It is safer for you this way. And no one is going to find out. I'll make certain of it. I'm sure we can arrange it so that we do not call attention of ourselves. And we can stay in inns so small that the people there will have never even heard of the Duke and Duchess of

Skeffington. There will be little chance of being recognised.'

How accommodating would these small inns be? Did he have any notion of the standard of rooms a duchess required when she stayed overnight?

'Perhaps you can stay at the smaller inns and I can stay in the ones I normally visit on my way back to London from here.'

'That will never work. I will not have you staying overnight in an establishment without being accompanied by a man to protect you from the riff-raff that would be more than happy to prey upon a beautiful woman travelling alone. It makes more sense if we travel together.'

He'd just said she was beautiful. Had he even realised he'd said it?

Her heart flipped over in her chest as she thought back to the image of him in his shirtsleeves with his neck exposed. She could not let herself fall for him. It would only lead to disappointment and heartache. Of that, she was certain.

Chapter Ten

Two hours later, Simon was pulling up the collar on his brown-wool greatcoat on the front steps of Stonehaven, missing the warmth of the Mediterranean sun and wondering why the two ladies beside him couldn't have said their goodbyes inside the house. He had moved around so much in his life that he never gave much thought or effort to saying goodbye to anyone. There were always new adventures and challenges down the road so it wasn't ever necessary to look back. But watching the Duchess say goodbye to her aunt was mind-numbing.

And they would be seeing one another again in a week.

Did all women behave this way? What should have been a five-minute wish of a safe journey was taking much too long. There were hugs and baskets of food for the journey that had to have the contents of which reviewed and commented on. There were more hugs. Promises of safe travels from both women. A debate about which road would be the best this time of year and more hugs. And just when he thought that Mrs Sommersby would be heading towards her carriage, she reached inside her reticule and held out a folded piece of paper to the Duchess.

'Until this thief is found, I want you to stay at my town house. I will feel that you are safer there. Give this letter to Brent at my home,' she instructed her niece, who tucked the missive into the lavender-embroidered reticule that hung from her wrist. 'I've advised him that if you decide to stay in my home, he is to make certain any needs you have are met. I should arrive in London a few days after you.' She took a step back and gave both of them an encouraging smile. 'Find out what you can and if I can be of any assistance to either of you in this matter, please do not hesitate to let me know.' She took the Duchess's hand in hers and gave it a squeeze. 'All will be well, Elizabeth. You will always have me.'

Simon had no brothers or sisters. Both of his parents were dead and he never formed any type of attachment to any of the various relatives he lived with after his mother died. He did have friends who he knew he could turn to for support, but Mrs Sommersby's last statement, said with such caring, made him glance away at the very intimate nature of her reassurance.

Then she sought out Simon's attention with a warm smile. 'Thank you for your assistance with this matter. We will always be grateful you took it upon yourself to help.'

He gave her a nod and she led him aside by his elbow. When they were far enough away from the Duchess, Mrs Sommersby lowered her voice and tilted her head his way. 'As you know my niece can be headstrong and impulsive at times. I would be eternally grateful if you would look out for her while you are travelling to London.'

'I will do my best,' he assured her, wondering if there was anything that could stop the Duchess from doing what she wanted when she put her mind to it.

Mrs Sommersby's suggestion that he should travel alone to London with her niece had been a surprising one. It wasn't at all proper and it hadn't escaped his notice that she had been studying them. He had heard of matchmaking mothers. It appeared the Duchess had a matchmaking aunt. If she were trying to promote a match between them, Mrs Sommersby would be sorely disappointed when she learned he was returning to Sicily—without a wife on his arm, especially one from the ranks of the British aristocracy.

Three days travelling with Elizabeth, the Duchess of Skeffington, would probably feel like three years. She could be quite exasperating at times—but she also had the ability to keep him awake at night thinking about taking her in any number of ways. He honestly didn't know which was worse for the close confines of the journey ahead.

Finally, the Duchess walked her aunt to her carriage and saw to it that she was comfortably settled inside with hot coals in the box resting on the floor and warm blankets for her aunt and her aunt's maid. When she stepped back on the snowy drive and waved as the carriage rolled away, Simon almost sighed with relief. It might have been faster to have her aunt come along with them after all.

The air was crisp and the sunlight glistened on the snow on the ground and on the trees as she turned and walked back to him in her black fur-trimmed cloak. She painted a dramatic picture that suited her personality.

Just as she reached his side, two carriages rolled up in the drive that was already packed with her trunks and his valise.

She turned to him with a furrowed brow visible under her lavender and black bonnet. 'What are these? Where is my carriage? Where is yours?'

'These *are* my carriages.'

'No, they're not.' Her confusion was written on her face. 'Your carriages have the Skeffington crest on them, as do mine.'

'My carriages *had* the Skeffington crest on them. I had them painted over.'

She appeared to be in shock. 'Why ever would you do such a thing? You are the Duke of Skeffington, no matter how hard you pretend that you are not. A duke travels with his crest on his door to announce to everyone that he is an important person and commands respect.'

'Can I not command respect without the crest? Can I not command respect even if I am not a duke?'

She appeared flustered by his questions. 'I suppose one can, but why would you want to try when the symbol on your door will do it for you?'

'Perhaps commanding respect comes more naturally to some of us than it does to others,' he couldn't help saying with a wry smile.

She raised her chin and looked down at him in that superior manner of hers. 'I can command respect without my title.'

'Are you certain of that, because a few moments ago you said you would need your title and a crest on your carriage to do it?'

'If you are trying to instigate a challenge, sir, I will not back down.'

'If you'd like to see travelling in unmarked carriages as a challenge, so be it. I like to think of it as travelling under the cover of anonymity. This way we lessen our chances of being set upon by highwaymen and we don't have to concern ourselves that someone might see the Duke and Duchess of Skeffington travelling together.'

The Duchess visibly shivered when he mentioned their names.

'If you are cold, we can step inside the carriage to warm up.'

'I'm not cold. This cloak is very warm.'

Something had made her shiver. If it wasn't the temperature, what could it have been? He took note of the reflection of the sun on her gold earrings and necklace. 'We can send your driver on ahead with your carriage to meet us in London. Travelling in these unmarked carriages is a wise choice. And while we are discussing our travels, did you really need to adorn yourself with all those glittering gems? We are journeying on roads where there have been highwaymen.'

'Yes, but now we are travelling like members of the gentry with those carriages you have defaced and we look unimportant.' Her face fell and he could see she was remembering her reduced financial condition.

'Members of the gentry, as you well know, have money,' he said shaking his head, 'so just because we are travelling in unmarked carriages does not mean we are not a target for theft. We've already had one robbery this week. We do not need another.'

'Oh, very well, I will place my earrings in my reticule.'

'And your necklace.'

Her gloved fingers moved to cover the emerald. 'I wasn't aware you had an overly cautious nature. My fichu covers most of it. And how will we get the finest table to dine at in the posting houses and the best rooms to sleep in if we do not show them we deserve those things?'

'The wealth that I have now does not mean I deserve those things. I deserved them even before I had money to spare. Now it just means I can afford to purchase them. I think this undercover journey will benefit you in more ways than you know. Now put them away.'

She let out a small huff and handed him her reticule while she took off her gloves and removed her jewellery. It was the first time he had held such a thing and wondered for the first time what women kept inside of them. She motioned for him to return it to her as they walked side by side to the carriages in two inches of snow. When they got about ten feet from the conveyances she stopped walking and looked between the two shiny black carriages. 'Which one would you like me to take? I have no preference.'

'For now, you and I will ride together in the first carriage and your maid and my valet will take the second one.'

She looked at him from the corner of her eye. 'Why would you and I ride together when there are two carriages?'

'Why would we not? I believe we have things to discuss regarding the purpose of this trip and I doubt you want that information shared with anyone else. It would be best to discuss these things in a moving vehicle when no one else is about and can hear us.'

'I'm sure we can discuss things over dinner.'

'What if we are not afforded privacy in the inn that we stop at?'

There was a distinct hesitation on her part before she pursed her lips together and walked past him to the first carriage. As she took the footman's hand and allowed him to assist her up the step, she looked longingly at the second carriage. Was her reluctance to travel with him solely because she feared for her reputation or was it something else?

He would make certain that news of them travelling together did not get out. His reasoning had nothing to do with hers. He wanted to make certain that whoever broke into his safe was not privy to the news that they were heading to London. The element of surprise was always an advantage.

She might believe it was a random break-in, but Simon was not convinced. He had been granted permission by the Italian government for his excavation with the stipulation that he could keep 25 percent of what he uncovered. When he had unearthed the two small gold statues, he knew the British Museum would be interested in one of them. It was made of solid gold and worth a small fortune. There already had been an attempt to steal it on his journey back to England. If someone wasn't aware he was staying in Dorset, they might logically assume that he was at his London residence and a safe would be an ideal place to store such a valuable item.

He settled into the green-velvet bench across from

her, allowing her the courtesy of facing forward without having him sit beside her. He would face backwards if it would ensure that he had no chance of touching her tempting body while they were alone in such close confines.

'I had two foot warmers placed in the carriage for us.' He grabbed one of the heavy travel blankets and draped it over his legs. 'I know you can be particular.'

She paused from tucking a heavy velvet blanket around her own legs to look up at him as the carriage jerked forward and began to move. 'I am not particular. Although I confess the heat feels heavenly on such a cold day. Thank you. It was very considerate of you.'

'It's selfish on my part, I suppose. I've lived so long in temperate climates that I no longer have a tolerance for the cold.'

'So where exactly do you live, Mr Alexander, when you are not in England?'

Even now that he was heading to London to help her get her money back, she had to remind him that he was not her social equal. No matter the title that was conveyed on him, to her, he would always remain a mere mister.

On some level he liked hearing his real name on her lips. It was how he thought of himself anyway. He had never been told he was in line to inherit the title of Duke of Skeffington, even if a number of people had to die for him to do it. He didn't feel like the Duke of Skeffington and didn't want the responsibility that came along with it. He missed being just Mr Alexander—except when she called him by that name. When she did, even though there was no sneer in her voice, he knew she had an ulterior motive.

He adjusted the brim of his hat and crossed his arms. 'Why is it that you still call me by that name? I would think that a duchess who has informed me I should boldly display my crest on my carriage door would be referring to me by my title.'

She looked down and slowly brushed at the velvet blanket on her lap, visibly uncomfortable with his question.

'Why is that, Duchess?' He tilted his head and caught her eye. 'Do you find you need to constantly remind me that you are above me?'

Her eyes widened and she brought her hand to her chest. 'Is that what you thought every time I called you that?'

'It did occur to me. There seems to be no other reasonable explanation as to why you are the only person of my acquaintance here in England that does it.'

It was apparent that the direct questioning about her actions made her uncomfortable and he found satisfaction in that he could rattle her cool composure.

'My husband has been dead for less than a year, sir. I am still, in some ways, adjusting to that fact. I keep expecting him to pop up at an unexpected time like he used to. To me he is and always will be Skeffington. Just the mere name conjures up the image of him and the sound of his voice. You are not the same man—far from it from what I have observed. Maybe if I saw similar qualities in you, it would be easier for me to refer to you by that name, but there is so much that is different in you that it is too incongruous for me to call you by that name. I don't know if any of that makes sense to you. I just know that the times that I've tried to call you Skeffington, my lips couldn't seem to form the name. I know that you are no longer Mr Alexander, but there is no other name I can use.'

It never occurred to him that her marriage might have been a love match. He'd just assumed by the little he had been told about the old Duke and what he perceived to be the character of his Duchess that she had hunted the man for his fortune and for her title. As he thought back to the reading of the will he tried to remember what was said about the amount of money she was given and why she was granted Clivemoore, but it had been months ago and at the time he hadn't cared to pay that close attention. Now he just felt like an ass for bringing up reminders of her heartache.

'You may call me Simon,' he offered. 'Since we are going to be spending a considerable amount of time together during the next three days, I think we could place the formalities aside…and we are like family of sorts. And Simon is still my name.' It was an intimate gesture and he knew the minute he said it that he had shocked her from the expression on her face. But they were two people who were tied together by circumstance. There was no reason they needed to be so formal.

She looked remarkably uncomfortable which was not a state he was familiar seeing her in. He waited to see if she was going to return the courtesy.

Chapter Eleven

Lizzy wanted to tell him to call her Elizabeth or Lizzy, but the words got stuck in her throat. Simon, as he wanted to be called, looked over at her as if he was waiting for her to offer her Christian name to him, as well. The idea was making her uncomfortable. No man had ever asked her to call him by his first name. Her own husband had never granted her that permission and they had been married for twelve years. Just the idea of calling Skeffington by his Christian name had her nerves on edge as she pictured the rant that would have definitely followed.

First names were too intimate, especially with the handsome gentleman sitting across from her. It was bad enough she would be spending a considerable amount of time alone with him. There was no denying there was something about him that had set her aflame with just a touch of his hand. She couldn't even imagine how her body would react if she heard him say her name.

A flash of humour crossed his face. 'I see the idea does not appeal to you. I know how much you enjoy your title whereas I am not very fond of mine. So you may call me Simon, or Mr Alexander. I will answer to both. And I will continue to refer to you by your title, as I always have. Do not fear I will overstep and call you Elizabeth.'

The sound of her name on his lips was like a caress that made her whole body tingle and that made her want to ask him to say it again. She was in trouble. There was something about him that affected her and she knew, from her experience with Lord Andrew, those feelings would not be shared.

'What is it you wanted to discuss that we needed to be alone in a carriage to do so?' she asked, placing her reticule beside her to give her hands something to do.

He took a small leather-bound book out of his pocket and tossed it beside him on the bench, then settled further into his seat. 'Can you think of anyone besides you and Mr Sherman who you've given the combination of the safe to?'

'No, there is no one else. Who else would I give that information to? For what purpose?'

'What do you know about Mr Sherman? What of his family? How comfortably off is he? Does he gamble?'

'Mr Sherman is a trustworthy gentleman who, to my knowledge, is not fond of cards. I believe he has a wife and one small child. He is an honourable man and was referred to me by Lady Jersey.'

When Simon gave no reaction to the lady's name, the Duchess leaned closer.

'Lady Jersey—you do know who Lady Jersey is, do you not?'

He couldn't keep track of all the women he had been introduced to when he had first arrived back in

England. The name sounded familiar, but after a while all the names of the *ton* blended together. He chose to ignore her question.

'I would think that if Mr Sherman was the one to steal your money, he would not be foolish enough to remain in your employ and would be far away from here by now.' He rubbed his chin. 'However, you do realise there is a chance that Mr Sherman has run off and we will discover he is gone when we reach London. Or it is entirely possible that he is working with the person who broke into the house for a portion of the money.'

'No. I refuse to believe that.' The idea that a man who she trusted with her future could be so cold and calculating as to do this to her was making her stomach roll. This entire episode felt like such a violation. She could not believe that about Mr Sherman. She would not believe it. Not until they had proof. 'I have known him for the past three years and he has been invaluable to me since my husband's death. And I don't see why he would notify me of the theft if he were the one who stole the money in the first place. It must be someone else.'

'A man's motivation isn't always clear to those on the outside. You may rule him out as a suspect, but I will not.' He sat back in his seat and eyed her. 'Is there anyone who you can think of who might want to steal your money? Are there any friends or acquaintances who seem in particular need of funds at the moment?'

'Not that I am aware of, but having difficulties with one's circumstance is not something people are very forthcoming about. It does tend to alter the numbers of invitations you receive.' She looked out the window, thinking of all the balls, garden parties and routs that she would not be invited to.

'Anyone in particular you might have insulted recently? I can take notes if you think the list is particularly long.' He actually had the nerve to take out a small ivory notepad from the pocket of his coat and remove the pencil that was secured to the side of it. He was actually waiting for her to give him a list of names.

'I have not insulted anyone.'

'Are you thinking of the past week or month?'

She clenched her fist in frustration. 'Month. Two months. I don't recall insulting anyone.'

He let out a groan and put the notepad back in his pocket. 'Then anyone could have done it. I can pretty well guarantee you've insulted someone in the past month if not in the past week. If you can't recall, it does us no good.'

She crossed her arms and glared at him. 'You seem to think I am far worse than I actually am.'

'And you seem to be unaware when you are being insulting.'

'I am not being insulting.'

'Not now you aren't—however, I assure you that you have been.'

'You don't have to help me. I didn't ask for your help and I certainly didn't want to be stuck in a carriage with you all alone for hours.' Her voice was rising with every statement she made. 'You seem to forget, sir, that this is my problem, not yours. I am the one who is to suffer because of this act. I am the one whose circumstances have been greatly reduced, unlike you who can travel anywhere on a whim with the substantial funds you now have at your disposal.'

'I'll give you the money,' he replied sharply. 'It is probably my fault it was stolen.'

'I don't want your money.' She didn't want anything from any Duke of Skeffington ever again. 'I am trying to find my way without anyone's help.' It came out forceful and strong and was spoken with all the determination she could muster. She wanted nothing more to do with men. He would never understand that. Lizzy took a deep steadying breath. 'I think we should alter our plan. It is clear that this arrangement we've made will not work. We can part ways at the next posting house. I will take one of the carriages and you can take the other. I will be sure it is returned to you in London when I arrive. I will have my things brought to my aunt's where I will stay while I try to find my money.'

'So you are going to give up and not try to settle this between us?'

'There is nothing to settle. You and I do not get on.'

He tilted his head and studied her. 'If you truly want to part company, I will not force you to remain with me for this journey. I do feel it is safer for you, however, to travel with me and not travel alone, but I will leave the decision to you.'

Why was he leaving all the decisions to her? First he let her decide if Mr Sherman should contact Bow Street and now he was leaving it up to her if they should part ways and not work together. Skeffington would have charged through and done what he pleased without asking her opinion. He was making her head ache. She closed her eyes and pinched the bridge of her nose. What he said was true. She would be safer travelling with him.

'I know you don't like me very much,' she said, 'and I know you are only helping me because it was your house that was broken into and you feel that this is an attack on you, but is there any reason why we cannot be civil with one another?'

She opened her eyes and found him watching her.

Slowly he shook his head. 'Forgive me if I offended you.'

His apology was unprecedented. No man had ever apologised to her before and she found it took her a minute to come out of her state of surprise and accept his apology.

'Would you still like to stop so that we can go our separate ways?' he asked.

Turning towards the window, she gave a longing look out to the fields and houses they were passing. 'What I would like is for this all to be one bad dream that I will wake up from, but I suppose that will not be happening.' With her finger, she lazily traced a circle on to the foggy glass window.

'I dream of bacon.'

His absurd comment made her look at him and laugh.

'It's true,' he continued with a hint of merriment in his eyes. 'I have since I was a child.'

They both laughed this time. She thought he might have said it to try to improve her mood. As the gravity of her situation hit her once more, her smile fell and she leaned her head on the window to watch the snow-covered trees and houses go by, thankful he seemed to understand her need for silence.

The world that she knew was crumbling around her. With each mile that the carriages rolled over she was getting closer and closer to the disaster awaiting her in London. For all she knew, word had already got out that her fortune was gone and someone had stolen it. Servants were known to talk. Had Mr Sherman been able to keep the theft a secret? It might be in the papers. There might be cartoons of her in her reduced state of fortune in the printing-shop windows right now. She felt ill, imagining all the women of the *ton* making their morning calls and laughing about her circumstances and saying that the Earl of Crawford's middle daughter had the worst luck of any woman to walk through the door of Almack's. First, she married a horrible old man and now she was practically penniless—and *penniless* was a way they would love to describe her financial woes.

If you were tormented by the whispers and sharp comments at one time in your life, you should not be forced to endure it for a second time. She had suffered much being the Duchess of Skeffington, but her wealth and privilege had eventually made her virtually untouchable—until now.

'I just can't imagine why someone would do this to me,' she muttered with her head pounding.

'Perhaps it's not you they did this to.' His voice was soft and reassuring, and it made her turn to look at him. 'Perhaps it's me.' His brow furrowed as he sat forward with his forearms resting on his thighs and rubbed his palms together.

'You? Why would you think someone did this to you? You have not been in London save for the short time you were there after the will was read. You've been in Sicily. I'm sure this was about hurting me.'

'I'm not so sure…' He looked into her eyes and she saw what appeared to be true sympathy there. 'It is much too early for us to know that for certain and we have yet to get the details of what exactly was done. I know you think this seems impossible, but we will find the person who did this. I promise you that.'

'How can you be so certain? They may have already left London or England, for that matter.' She rested her head on the window, her bonnet the only thing between her and the cold glass pane.

'Because, as I said, I am good at finding things and if our quest takes us outside of England, all the better. I only hope it is to a warmer climate.'

'I feel as if I don't even know where to begin.'

'Then you are fortunate that you have me beside you.'

'You're across from me, not beside me.' The teasing comment slipped out before she even realised it. Hearing she was not alone in trying to track down the robber made her entire body soften and she had to turn to look out the window again to hide her relief at his words.

'Will you be contrary the entire way to London?' There had been an accompanying teasing lilt to his voice that was settling some of her nerves.

'If you are lucky—otherwise you might grow bored.'

'We have three days. That should give us sufficient time to mull this over in our heads. Hopefully, we will devise a small list of suspects before we get to Town. Has the house ever been broken into before?'

'Not to my knowledge. Not while I have lived there.'

She wished she were as confident as he was that this would all be settled and hopefully they would be able to retrieve the money that was stolen from her.

They had been travelling for miles with only two stops along the way, making Lizzy grateful she'd had only one cup of tea with breakfast this morning and had the forethought to have the kitchen pack baskets of bread and cheese for both of the carriages. Simon was determined to reach London as quickly as possible, which was beginning to suit her just fine since the faster they could begin searching for the thief, the faster her heart would return to its normal rhythm and she could breathe again.

His calm composure as they travelled was settling and while she kept occupied by looking out the window, he was content to sit quietly across from her and read from his leather-bound book, ignoring her.

She was accustomed to being ignored by men. That was her husband's usual state of behaviour when they were together. When she was growing up, her father had been no better. In both cases she had never sought to engage them but now, with this man, Lizzy found she wanted his focus on her, not on that book of his.

She cleared her throat in a polite and soft manner.

He kept reading.

She let out a faint sigh and stretched her legs out a bit, putting her new black-leather walking boots within what she believed to be his line of vision, since she could not see his eyes with his head lowered the way it was.

He turned a page and didn't look up.

How could one person be so absorbed in a book

that they had no notion of what was going on around them? What was more interesting in that book than having a conversation with the woman he shared a carriage with to pass the time?

Lizzy took the opportunity to study him. His shiny dark hair was a bit longer than was considered fashionable and rested near the collar of his deep brown coat. The white cravat he wore was tied neatly, but not in an elaborate fashion like some men of the *ton* preferred. This was more of an efficient knot that did what it was supposed to do without calling attention to itself. Under that cravat was hidden the smooth, tanned skin of his neck that had a vein that ran from under his ear to the hollow of his neck that would become more pronounced when he exerted himself. She didn't know why it had grabbed her attention yesterday when she saw it in the armoury and why she had the oddest urge to run the tip of her fingers along it.

She raised her gaze to try to see if he had caught her looking at him, but his eyes were shaded by his dark lashes. She hoped he hadn't noticed her staring. There was no sense in making him think she had designs on him and heaven forbid he should think she was eyeing him in a flirtatious manner.

When his tongue touched his upper lip as he turned another page, butterflies swooped low in her stomach. It was just a small gesture. Many people had done the same thing in her presence before now without it affecting her in any way, but for some reason watching Simon was completely different. She began to wonder what his tongue would have felt like gliding across her lips. Before she realised what she was doing, Lizzy found herself brushing her gloved fingers over her own lips.

Startled by her subconscious reaction, she quickly clasped her hands together on her lap and jerked her gaze back to the window. After a few minutes, she stole another glance at him.

'Do you not read while travelling, Duchess?' He flipped a page of his book without looking up at her.

Wonderful, he must have seen her staring at him.

'No,' she said, keeping her eyes focused on his reflection in the window so as not to embarrass herself. She could just pretend she hadn't been staring at him. If she pretended long enough, he might think he was mistaken. 'Reading in a moving carriage has always made me queasy.'

'What about a stationary carriage?' His head tipped to the side as if he had begun reading the opposite page.

'Well, since we are in a moving carriage, I don't see how that is a relevant question.'

As if he needed to be reminded of their circumstances, the carriage dipped as it went through a rut in the road and her stomach dropped with it. Even then he continued to keep his eyes on his book.

'Well, we do stop from time to time,' he said, still occupied. 'You could read then.'

'I suppose.'

'Do you do needlework? I imagine some women bring needlework with them when they travel.' His cool impersonal tone hung in the air.

'I do, but it is not a keen enough interest of mine to hold my attention that long. My maid, Emilie, brings needlework with her. She seems to enjoy it.'

He went back to reading in silence and she went back to staring out the window, trying not to think of the fact her financial circumstances were reduced and the only comfort she was finding was stealing glances at his reflection every now and then.

Finally, he broke the silence and her boredom.

'We need to find some type of diversion for you during the next few days,' he said, continuing to look down at his book while he ran his finger under the page and flicked the paper over.

'Why do you say that?'

'Because if you had something to occupy yourself with, you might stop staring at my reflection in the window.' He lifted his lashes and caught her eye in the reflection on the glass pane.

It was becoming glaringly obvious to Lizzy that Mr Simon Alexander knew that he was an attractive man. Well, not every woman would fall at his feet because of his looks. She certainly never would. She was simply bored and he was more interesting to look at than the squirrels running through the snow. But just as she was about to shift her bottom to relieve the numbness, the carriage jerked, sending her hurtling out of her seat and into the circle of his arms.

One of his hands was holding the small of her back and the pressure brought a sensation of pleasure down over her bottom and along her thighs—which didn't make sense since he wasn't touching her there. What if he had been touching her there? Would it have felt just as good to feel his fingers run up her thighs and over her bottom?

She looked into his dark eyes and her gaze dropped to his lips—lips that were very close to her own and looked firm and sensual. The urgent need to stroke her fingertip across them to feel how soft they were overtook her and she fought to resist the need, curling her hand into the fabric of his wool coat that was covering his strong back.

He wet his lips and swallowed hard, and she could feel the even tempo of his breathing change to something more erratic. Those lips of his should not be holding her attention this way. They were just lips. Everyone had them. But it was tempting to think of the feel of his lips against hers and against her skin.

His soft breath was blowing across her mouth and she wanted to raise her head a few inches and press her lips against his. Looking up into his eyes, she saw a passion in them that was startling. No one had ever looked at her that way before. It was as if he was a wolf and wanted to devour her.

A wave of heat was spreading through her body that felt nothing like the warm heat she would feel when she blushed. This was a different kind of heat. It was hotter and seemed to consume every part of her. Lizzy tried to take a deep steadying breath to calm her body down, but when she attempted to do so, she was reminded that his arms were still firmly around her. He shifted and something poked into her back through her cloak. She turned to look at what it was.

'You are still holding that book?' It came out more cross than she intended.

'You didn't give me time to put it down—and I caught you, didn't I?'

She pushed against his firm chest and he released her. The carriage continued to rock, but she managed to steady herself enough to make her way back to the upholstered bench across from him. She picked up the heavy blanket that had fallen to the floor and smoothed the soft velvet out over her legs.

His gaze followed her movement before he shifted in his seat and looked out the window himself. 'The sun will be going down soon. I think it best if we end this part of our travels and find an inn for the night.' Without waiting for her to agree, he tapped on the roof of the carriage with the carved ivory handle of his walking stick.

The sound of 'ho' could be heard outside, signalling to the carriage behind them that they would be stopping. When the carriage rolled to a halt, the door opened and a cold gust of air made the lavender-satin ribbon on her bonnet move. The wind-burned face of a young groom appeared in the doorway as he looked eagerly at Simon for instruction.

'Keep your eyes out for the nearest inn on your map,' the man across from her said, adjusting the brim of his hat. 'We will be stopping for the night.'

'Aye, sir. I heard about some good ones back at the last posting house. I asked around like you told me to and know which ones to look out for. One's coming up in a few miles.'

'Excellent,' Simon said, smiling at the boy who was bundled up with a thick wool scarf and his brown hat pulled down low to his eyes. 'I'd say you've earned an extra tankard of ale tonight, Tom.'

The boy, who appeared to be all of sixteen, smiled broadly as he gave a quick tip of his cap and closed the door.

'You are trusting our accommodations to that boy?'

Her voice rang out and she wished she had sounded more composed.

'He did as I asked and, yes, I am trusting our accommodations to Tom.' He sat back, appearing confident he had made an excellent decision.

'I've never seen him before. Have you replaced some of the staff since you've been at Stonehaven?'

'I've only added Tom and my valet, of course. Tom is a fine lad. Good with horses. He'd been working down at the docks in Liverpool, but was injured when a crate fell on his foot. His father served alongside me in the Royal Navy and sent word, asking if I knew of anyone who might hire Tom. After meeting him at the house, I decided to hire him myself. I was told one of the grooms at Stonehaven had left recently and it made sense to see if he could do the job. So far, I think, it's working out very well.'

'I didn't know you were in the navy.' It was the one thing that stood out from all that he had said.

'I was.'

'When did you join?'

'When I was fifteen.'

'Fifteen? My heavens, that's young.' Her eyes narrowed on him as she tried to imagine him in a naval uniform. 'I attended Lord Nelson's funeral. It was such a sad day. Were you there?'

'No.'

'Is that what you were doing when they found you? Were you still in the navy?' She would have thought Mr Nesbit or Lord Liverpool would have mentioned that to her if he was.

'No, I left when I was five and twenty.'

His short answers were driving her mad. She

wanted him to elaborate. Instead it was obvious this
was not something he wished to discuss any further. It
was the first real thing he had revealed about himself
and there was an ache in her heart for the boy who was
sent out alone in the world to travel the seas in what
she imagined was not an easy life. Fifteen was much
too young for him to have left his family. Could boys
that young enlist? How had his parents allowed him
to do such a thing? And why did he want to go? And
where had he sailed? And what did he see?

The questions were swirling around in her head.
She knew she had an inquisitive nature. But the far-
away look in his eyes told her he didn't want to discuss
it further. She pressed her lips together to stop herself
from prying into his past and it was taking considerable restraint. She was not a woman who was content
to know only half of a story. She should have asked
Mr Nesbit, her late husband's attorney, more details
about him, but all she knew was that he was the great
great-grandson of Skeffington's uncle.

She desperately needed him to be open to converse
with her over the next few days or she would expire
out of boredom. If it meant holding her tongue now
and not asking him too many questions, she would do
her best to do just that. Besides, she had bigger issues
to deal with right now.

'While it is commendable that you have found employment for that boy, it still doesn't instil confidence
in me that he knows how to select the right establishment for us to spend the night in.' She rubbed her
brow, not even sure she could make him understand.
'You are a duke now. I am a duchess. There are certain establishments we frequent and there are others

that we do not. I do not believe that boy is qualified to determine the difference.'

'Tom is a smart lad and, I assure you, he has no desire to sleep anywhere where he thinks he will not be fed well or wake up to find bugs crawling on him.'

'Oh, dear heavens.' She covered her mouth to hold in her bile and shuddered at the image that popped into her head. 'I should certainly hope not,' she responded in a matter-of-fact manner. 'But there is more to a fine establishment than that. There is the clientele that frequents the inn. You don't want to have drunken brawls going on when you are trying to dine. At least I do not.'

'I agree. However, I assure you that even in the finest establishments, men will drink more than they should. And most inns will have a private parlour that we can use to dine in if it is available.'

'Most?'

'I'm not certain all do, however the ones I have been to have them.'

She chewed on her lip as she considered dining in a public room instead of a private parlour.

'Do not fear,' he said. 'I will be there to come to your aid should you be exposed to any inappropriate comments or actions.'

His offer to protect and shield her like that touched something inside her. Something that again reminded her of Lord Andrew's assistance at that ball many years ago. She knew the act had meant nothing to him and she quickly told herself not to think it meant Simon found her special in any way. 'While I appreciate that, what about the state of the rooms, the quality of the food and the efficiency of the staff?'

'It is one night. Even if the inn is not to your stan-dards—it—is—only—one—night. You worry too much. You know that, don't you?'

'I worry that your boy will have us in an establish-ment when the water will be brought up barely warm and cockfights are being held in the courtyard under my window.'

'It is winter, Duchess. So even with an efficient staff, having hot water brought up to your room might be a challenge. And if there are cockfights going on under your window, it might be wise to place a few wagers to improve that coffer of yours.'

She sucked in a breath of the cold air in indigna-tion at his reference to her financial hardship and was just about to issue him a setdown, when she caught the twinkle of amusement in his eyes.

'I see one of us finds this amusing and that one of us is not me.' She let out a huff and turned her entire head and shoulders so that she was back to facing the window and made sure this time not to glance at his reflection in the glass.

She felt something settle against her thigh and turned to find he had stretched his legs across the carriage and put his feet up on the bench beside her. When she looked up at him in shock, she found him reclining back on his bench, focusing on that infernal book of his. The leather from his boot should not have generated heat through her clothes, but the pressure against her leg created delicious warmth that spread up her thigh. She didn't want to give him the satisfac-tion of moving away so she forced herself to sit still and pretend his leg pressed against her thigh was hav-ing no effect on her.

They should be stopping soon at the inn. What was taking them so long? She needed to clear her head from the thoughts she was having about him and his leg. At this point it didn't even matter that the inn would not be up to her standards.

Chapter Twelve

He'd almost kissed her.

And Simon knew if he had, she would have probably hit him. She might still be grieving for her husband. What was he thinking?

When the carriage jolted and she was launched into his arms, he was stunned at first. But then he felt her soft body pressed up against his. As his fingers stroked the small dip in her lower back he knew it would have been the perfect spot for his hand if they were having sex. He would be able to hold her steady at that soft spot while he thrust himself inside her.

Elizabeth, the Duchess of Skeffington, could be so exasperating at times that he should have wanted to scrub the image from his mind, but it just wouldn't go away. It stayed there. And as he looked into her big brown eyes and pressed his hand into that dip in her back and his fingers skimmed her bottom, he knew spending three days on the road with her was going to play havoc with his body. The tightening of his buckskin breeches was proof.

He should have moved her off him the minute she

landed in his arms, but within an instant he was fighting the urge to lower his mouth and kiss her. Just the idea of tasting her lips and imagining her responding back was making his heart race.

There was a very proper demeanour about her that he had a driving need to shatter and see what was underneath. It had taken considerable effort not to kiss her and see if that single-mindedness about her could be directed to pleasure. While travelling together over the next few days it would be easy to have a brief, secret, passionate affair. It would be a stimulating way to pass the time and when she wasn't driving him mad, she did have a keen sense of humour. Perhaps there was a way to bring that out in her more.

However, when he looked up from his book, his gaze landed on her black cloak and lavender bonnet, reminding him she had been widowed less than a year—and it might have been a love match. She was a grieving widow and he was an ass.

It was just as well. A passionate tryst with her while they were on the road to London would have been a pleasurable diversion, but eventually it would have to end. In a few weeks he would be returning to Sicily to resume doing what he loved. He had no desire to fulfil the duties of his new rank. He didn't know the first thing about being a duke and had no interest in finding out. Life was lived best when you moved from place to place. If you stayed too long, people would grow tired of you. That was a lesson he learned at a very young age. Moreover, there was too much to see in the world and he knew having sex with her would only complicate his leaving. She would expect him to stay.

He could tell that about her. Elizabeth, the Duchess of Skeffington, was not one to enter into a casual affair.

It didn't take long before the rocking of the carriage slowed and the sound of the clopping of horses' hooves over the snow-covered road was replaced by carriage wheels rolling over cobblestones and good-natured shouts coming from the courtyard of the small inn that Tom had found for them. The building was old, at least two hundred years old, if Simon had to guess. From the outside it appeared well maintained. There was a warm glow coming from inside the building and all the windows on the ground floor were casting yellow-gold squares on the ground.

Stepping down, Simon looked up and took note that the sun was beginning to change the winter-white sky to a soft pink. They had arrived at the inn just in time. In another half an hour, or so, the sky would be inky black without the moon to light their way.

He held his hand out for the Duchess and when she put her hand in his, their eyes held for a few extra heartbeats before he made sure she stepped to the ground without falling or tripping. She gave the building a critical eye before leaving his side to walk over to the other carriage where her maid was just emerging with his valet. From what Simon could tell, she was giving the woman some instructions on her trunks, which were tied to the roof of the carriage. This woman with her fondness for overpacking would never be able to travel around Europe the way he did. She would never be able to fit all that luggage in the rooms he was currently renting in Sicily that overlooked the harbour.

As he waited in the courtyard for the Duchess, he

rubbed his gloved hands together to keep warm and told himself that in the future he would spend all of his winters in sunny climates. There was no reason to come to England and suffer through the cold. From the corner of his eye he spied Tom approaching him with a sense of uncertainty and he turned to face him.

'I hope this is to your liking, Your Grace?'

'We'll know once we get inside, now won't we, Tom?'

He let his gaze settle on the snow-covered roof of the timber structure that had smoke rising from the chimneys and considered entering the establishment to wait for Elizabeth when the front door opened and the light from inside spilled on to the ground. The sounds of boisterous conversations and laughter from inside grew louder and two gentlemen, younger than Simon, walked outside, laughing with one another and buttoning up their coats to the cold evening air.

As they walked past Elizabeth, they eyed her up and down in an appraising fashion. The one on the left with the green greatcoat and red hair arched his brow in approval and elbowed his friend. She was still speaking with her maid and it appeared she hadn't noticed them.

Some primal instinct had Simon striding forward to place himself between the men and the Duchess, but by the time he reached her side, the two men had already walked out of the courtyard.

'Well?' he asked, sweeping his hand out towards the building. 'What do you think?'

She scanned the timber-framed inn and paused on the sign hanging over the door. 'The Stuffed Pig?' She looked back at him in despair. 'That is not helping.'

Going around him, she headed back towards their

carriage with a determined stride, but Simon pulled her back, gently.

'It looks very old,' she commented with a pout.

'So are many things in this country. Old things are interesting.'

'Maybe for you. I, however, am not fond of old things.'

Did she truly mean that or was she just saying that in order to stay somewhere else? He adored old things. His life's work was acquiring them.

'Maybe you have not been exposed to the right old things. Let's go warm up,' he coaxed her away from the carriage. 'If we don't even go inside, how will we know how bad it is? You'll never be able to remind me that I was wrong and you were right if we don't even see it.'

The last sentence he spoke had done the trick. Her nose went up in that way of hers and she sailed past him and into the inn. Simon had a feeling it was going to be a long night in more ways than one.

He followed her into the wood-panelled entrance hall, with a noisy tavern to the right and what might be an unoccupied parlour to the left. The warmth from the fire in both rooms could be felt where they stood and the mouth-watering smells of ale and beef filled his nostrils. It was not a large establishment, but it did appear clean for which he was relieved.

As she stood next to him, the Duchess removed her bonnet and a few tendrils of her black hair came loose from the upsweep of her hair. When she turned to look around, the strands of hair skimmed across her neck. Casting a critical eye, she walked to the doorway of the unoccupied room and took a peek inside.

The door that they had just walked through opened

and the two young gentlemen from the courtyard stepped inside and without a break in their conversation they moved past them and into the tavern. Simon kept an eye on them as he took off his gloves and began to unbutton his coat.

'I don't think this was a wise idea,' the Duchess said, coming up to his side.

'It is growing late. We don't have much of a choice. I take full responsibility for arriving here at such a late hour. I had not been paying close enough attention to the time.' He was too busy enjoying her watching him. 'We don't have much daylight left before it will be too dark to travel safely.'

'I confess, it does feel wonderful to stretch my legs after being in that carriage for so long. But...' She looked around the space once more. 'Do you suppose it is safe with the people who frequent an inn such as this?' Her attention had shifted and was now fixed on the large doorway to the tavern where one could see it was crowded with men and women.

'You are completely safe as long as you are with me.'

'That wasn't a yes.'

'One is never completely safe anywhere. It's best to remember that.' He gave a carefree lift to his shoulder.

With an arch of her brow she swept her gaze from his boots to his hat and then turned without a word to look into the parlour again. From the doorway of the tavern, a small round man with spectacles and grey hair came hurrying out, eyeing them up and down quickly. He greeted them and introduced himself as the innkeeper, Mr Finch. From the way he was eyeing their clothes, Simon knew he was clearly taking stock of the value of his guests. What would the man have done if they had arrived in carriages, displaying their ducal crest?

'Are you here to dine as you continue on your journey or are you seeking rooms tonight?'

'We are looking for both,' Simon replied.

'As you can see, sir, we are quite busy. I'm afraid I can provide you with a good meal, but I have no rooms to offer you tonight.' He looked between Simon and the Duchess to see if they were planning on having dinner, before he glanced over his shoulder at the tavern, silently reminding them how busy he was.

'Oh, that is a pity,' the Duchess said with what Simon knew to be false sincerity.

She turned towards the door, with what appeared to be a relieved smile on her face, when it suddenly opened and Tom walked in, bringing the cold air in with him.

His groom gave a quick bow and caught Simon's eye as he took off his hat. 'Your Grace, would you like us to bring in your bag and Her Grace's trunk? Another carriage has turned into the courtyard and they are asking us to make way for them.'

At the mention of their titles, Mr Finch's eyes widened considerably and Simon didn't have to look over to know the Duchess was wishing it were proper to roll her eyes at the sudden change in Mr Finch's demeanour. The innkeeper would know that having people of such a notable rank staying at his inn would have its benefits.

'Your Grace,' Mr Finch uttered reverently as he pasted on a bright smile. ''Tis an honour to have you here. My wife's an excellent cook. I'm certain we have something that will satisfy your appetites.' The tempting smells drifting around them were more convincing than the unsure tone of Mr Finch's voice.

Simon assumed The Stuffed Pig did not get many members of the upper echelons of Society, if they got any members at all, and he knew that being able to boast he had served a duke and a duchess would be something the man would brag about for years to come to road-weary travellers who stopped at his inn.

The Duchess opened her mouth to reply, but Simon cut her off, afraid of what she might say.

'I'd wager your food is very good if the smells from your kitchen are any indication. Unfortunately, the sun will be setting soon and before it becomes too dark to travel safely we will need to move on to the next inn to see about accommodations for the night.'

Mr Finch's expression fell.

'Those are my thoughts exactly,' the Duchess said, putting her bonnet back on with a much-improved demeanour. 'Tom,' she called out, summoning the groom to her side. 'Do you have that list of inns on your person?'

He nodded, stuffing his hands in his pockets.

She raised her brows expectantly. 'May I see it?'

Quickly, he handed her the folded piece of paper from his greatcoat pocket and shuffled his feet by her side. 'The Lonely Knight is the next one,' he offered. 'It shouldn't be no more than half an hour down the road.'

Even without uttering a distinguishable sigh, Simon could tell she wasn't happy. 'Why don't you go outside and let the coachmen know we will be leaving? His Grace and I will be out shortly.' She waited until the groom had closed the door behind him to turn around and look at Simon. 'It is a shame we have to leave this fine establishment with such wonderful smells stimulating our appetites. Had we but stopped sooner, we might have had a meal and room by now.' Her voice was too sweet and he could tell she was being sarcastic. 'And now I'm sure you will want to move on to The Lonely Knight. I hear Lord Lichtenstein speaks highly of it.' She pursed her unhappy lips together and spun on her heels towards to the door.

Lord Lichtenstein? Her sarcasm at his decision to find lesser-known accommodations should have annoyed him with her inflexibility, but instead he found himself holding back a smile.

Mr Finch glanced back towards the tavern and wrung his hands on his apron before turning back to them and scratching his neck. 'The thing is, Your Grace, with it being Twelfth Night and all, well… all our rooms are occupied.' He took a step towards the Duchess and lowered his voice. 'However, there is one room that we reserve for special guests, like yourselves.'

The Duchess stopped walking and when she turned around she looked at Simon with alarm.

Simon shifted his attention to Mr Finch. 'One room, you say?'

'Aye, only one, but seeing as you and Her Grace are married, it solves your problem and now you don't have to go to The Lonely Knight.'

The Duchess hurried to Simon's side. 'But we're not—'

'We don't sleep in the same room,' Simon replied before she could announce they were not married.

'You see, Mr Finch, members of Society, like ourselves, don't sleep in the same room. It's not done.'

'Simon!' It was the first time she'd said his name and it was uttered with surprised indignation. Her brown eyes widened even more. 'I am not—'

He tapped her thigh lightly through the folded fabric of her gown with the back of his hand in a subtle gesture that Mr Finch couldn't see. Thankfully, she didn't continue. The Lonely Knight might not have rooms either and the longer they stayed on the road looking for available rooms, the darker it would get and the hungrier he'd become. If they had any chance of remaining in this inn for the night and sampling whatever was cooking in the kitchen and making his mouth water, they would have to be creative with the truth. It was a small establishment that did not entertain members of the *ton*, but Mr Finch might take umbrage with an unmarried couple sharing a bed at his inn.

The innkeeper's face wrinkled as if he couldn't understand why Simon would not want to sleep with his beautiful wife. And if they were truly married, Simon knew he would have been an idiot not to.

The Duchess looked down at her hands, which were clasped firmly in front of her. 'Is there a chance that you might have two rooms that are reserved for special guests, sir?'

Mr Finch shook his head. 'No, Your Grace, we just have the one, but seeing as how you are husband and wife, I'm sure you wouldn't mind sharing a room for this one night. I would hate for you to miss my wife's beef pie. They don't make anything nearly as good at The Lonely Knight. I'm sure Lord Lichtenstein would have agreed if we had room the night that he stopped here, as well.' He raised both brows hopefully and shifted his gaze between his distinguished guests.

The Duchess gave him the polite false smile that Simon had seen on her face before and he wasn't surprised when she suggested they discuss the matter in private before giving Mr Finch an answer. Simon followed her to the corner of the hallway near the parlour and stood blocking Mr Finch's view of her. From the look on her face, he could tell she was not pleased.

'Are you mad? We are not sharing a room,' she whispered furiously. 'It is bad enough that man thinks I am married to you. Sharing a room with you is not for consideration.'

'You know we cannot drive much further. The inn appears clean and the food smells good,' he tried to explain the advantages in a low voice.

'And that is all you have to say to entice me to spend the night with you?'

There were many more ways he could entice her to spend the night. Each one involved the bed that was waiting for them in that room that Mr Finch suddenly realised he had. 'I assure you nothing will happen between us. On my honour, I will not lay a hand on you.'

She rubbed her brow and looked past him towards Mr Finch. When she did look Simon in the eye she still did not look at all pleased. 'We don't have much of a choice, do we?' Her gaze shifted to the ceiling as if she was deciding what was her best option.

Simon folded his arms and waited.

'No one is to know we have to share a room,' she said, pointing a finger at him. 'No. One. Not even the servants, so you need to think of a way to make certain of that.'

'I have an idea. I just need you to trust me. I'm certain most of the inns that you do not frequent resemble this type of establishment. If you want to travel to London without anyone you know seeing us together, I suggest we spend the night here.'

'Very well, since it appears I have little choice. But you will need to give me time alone in the room.'

'I understand.' A relieved sigh almost escaped out of his mouth. If he'd had to leave the inn after smelling that food, it would have been a travesty.

'And do not assume I am at all agreeable to this arrangement. I am agreeing to this simply out of necessity.' She folded her arms and glared at him. 'I will handle our accommodations tomorrow night. I will not leave it to chance again.'

'That is fair. You may arrange tomorrow night's accommodations. Will it be in another inn that Lord Lichtenstein enjoys?' He didn't even bother hiding the sarcastic smile from her.

'No, and do not mock me. You should be happy. Lord Lichtenstein got us a room here, didn't he?'

'You are lucky Mr Finch is not well versed in geography.'

'If I have to spend the night with you in a room in this inn, I am not certain that's true.'

He didn't try to hide his smile as he turned and walked to Mr Finch. 'Beef pie, a good tankard of ale, and wine for Her Grace sound like a perfect end to our long journey. We'll stay.'

'Sherry, if you please, Mr Finch. And I'd like a bath with hot water. We have our own towels and soap so there is no need to trouble yourself with those and my maid will take care of placing our own linens on the bed.'

A dazed look came over Mr Finch. The poor man had probably never heard of such requests in his small inn. 'A bath?'

'Yes,' the Duchess replied, looking weary. 'The journey was long and I'd like a nice hot bath.'

The image of her bare skin glistening with water as she lounged in a tub by the fire slipped into Simon's mind. He assumed her plan was to have him leave her alone for that portion of the evening and he wished he could persuade her to change her mind. If he offered to wash her back for her, would she walk away from him in a huff or slap his face?

'We don't have a bathtub, Your Grace.'

And the image of her breasts in the water popped out of his mind like a soap bubble.

Her brow wrinkled. 'You mean in the room I will be staying in.'

'No, I mean in the inn. We have no bathtub to bring to your room.'

Simon tried his hardest to hold back a smile at her stunned expression.

'I can offer you a washbowl and pitcher?' Mr Finch said with a hopeful expression.

The long stare she gave Simon said just how much she was regretting going anywhere with him. 'If that is all you can furnish me with, then that will do,' she replied politely.

'Well, now the problem is all solved, isn't it?' Mr Finch appeared very pleased with his handling of the situation. 'It is a real honour, it is, having a duke and duchess here. You can dine in the parlour if you like.

The tavern there is crowded tonight,' he said, gesturing over his shoulder, 'and you might find yourselves more comfortable in our parlour.'

Simon stepped forward and shook Mr Finch's hand. 'The parlour would do very well. Thank you.'

'My pleasure, Your Grace. Let me go tell my wife we will have more guests for dinner and I'll have my daughter go and freshen up our room. This way you won't have to wait too long for your meal and a nice bed for the night. Who should I tell Mrs Finch we have the honour of hosting tonight?' His gaze darted between Simon and the Duchess.

Before Simon could think how to answer, Elizabeth spoke up. 'We are the Duke and Duchess of Barham. We were visiting friends for Christmas and now we are travelling home.'

'We are honoured to have you with us,' he said, backing out into the tavern before turning and hurrying out of sight.

When they were alone, she turned to face Simon and lowered her voice so only he could hear. 'You shook his hand? A duke would not have shaken the hand of an innkeeper. At least Skeffington would not have. He would have seen the gesture as beneath him.'

'That is preposterous. It was the polite thing to do.'

'Maybe if you are Mr Alexander, but not when you are the Duke of Skeffington.'

'Well, according to you I am not the Duke of Skeffington but the Duke of Barham.' He crossed his arms and almost began tapping his foot. 'Do you care to tell me why we are the Duke and Duchess of Barham?'

'Because we can't let word spread that we are travelling together and no one…' she leaned closer '…no one can find out that we stayed here and heaven knows no one can find out we shared a room together tonight.'

'But where did Barham come from?'

'I don't like the Duchess of Barham. She has never been nice to me and he is an arrogant man. If anyone should be rumoured to have stayed at The Stuffed Pig, it should be the two of them.'

'Very well, I will go outside and have Tom inform the coachmen we will be staying here under an alias for safety reasons. You get the pleasure of informing your maid why she needs to address you as such. Wait for me in the parlour. I'll be but a minute.'

His life as Mr Alexander could be complicated at times, but it had been nowhere near as complicated as his life was now as the Duke of Skeffington.

Chapter Thirteen

If six months ago someone had told Lizzy that some day she would be dining with the new Duke of Skeffington in the parlour of The Stuffed Pig, she would have told them that they were mad.

The room they were in was small with whitewashed walls and wooden beams that crossed the ceiling. Now that the door was closed, it proved to be a quiet and restful spot in the busy inn. The round table with four chairs and the three plump upholstered wingback chairs that were near the roaring fire were old, but appeared clean and softly broken in with use. It was a surprisingly comfortable room. However, her favourite feature of the parlour by far was the delicious meat pie that had been placed on the table for them to enjoy. It had to be one of the finest pies she had ever tasted. Not that she would ever admit that to the likes of Mr Alexander.

If this had been a typical evening while on a journey, she would have freshened up in her room before dinner and changed out of her travelling clothes, but since the food was ready before the room was and Lizzy could feel her stomach rumbling, she had little choice but to eat in her carriage dress.

The silence that stretched between them during dinner was not an unusual experience for her. She was accustomed to sitting in silence with someone while she ate. She had done it throughout her marriage to Skeffington. Tonight's silence was a different kind, though. This silence was brought on by the shared contentment of two tired travellers, enjoying the delicious food and drink that was brought out for them. While Simon savoured his large tankard of ale, Lizzy was surprised to find the sherry adequate and when dinner ended, she felt quite satisfied and ready to retire to her room—their room—for the night.

Just the thought of being alone with him in their shared room was making her body hum with anticipation. That wasn't a good thing. She knew he didn't think of her in that way. He had reassured her that he would not be inappropriate with her, which was his polite way of telling her that he did not find her the least bit attractive. What was it about her that made her so unappealing to men?

Mr Finch's daughter, Mary, cleared their plates from the table as Simon sat back in his chair and stretched his legs out in front of him. 'That was a very good meal. Please send our compliments to your mother.'

The young girl, who was probably no more than twelve, nodded shyly at him. 'Papa says I am to show you to your room when you are ready. If you like, I can take these plates away and then take you upstairs.'

'That would suit us very well,' he said with an easy grin that made the girl start to smile before glancing quickly back down at the plates on the table.

'Her Grace and I have a few things to discuss before we retire for the night,' he continued. 'Why don't you come back at half past and leave the ale and the sherry?'

She bobbed a quick curtsy, finished clearing the plates and Simon closed the door behind her when she left, shutting out the sounds of revelry in the tavern.

The flames in the hearth gave his skin a warm glow as he walked back to the table, looking pleased and content in his brown tailcoat and buckskin breeches. 'Well, I must say, that was an exceptional meal. I hadn't anticipated fare that tasty when we rolled up. Did you enjoy it?'

It would have given her great pleasure to tell him she wasn't pleased with the food and that his idea of staying in smaller inns so they were not seen together by members of the *ton* was folly. However, there was no denying Mrs Finch was a fine cook. 'I did enjoy it. I find my disposition is much improved by that meal.'

'I am glad to hear that since we need to discuss how we are to spend the remainder of the night.' He took a seat across from her and glanced inside his tankard.

'You said you had a plan. That you knew what we should do about this…this…' she fluttered her hand between them '…unacceptable situation.'

He raised the tankard and took a slow sip. 'I do have a plan. One I think you will find acceptable. I have this parlour reserved until we leave tomorrow morning. It will be an ideal place for me to spend the night.'

How was this an ideal place to sleep? The room didn't even have a bed in it. This was her life. She was an unmarried woman and this man would rather sleep in a room without a bed than share a bedchamber with her. She couldn't show how him insulted she was. He would know immediately that she found him desirable. So, she clutched her fists under the table and fought the urge to dump the contents of his tankard over his head.

Without knowing the danger he was in, Mr Alexander looked her in the eye. 'I will go up with you to your room and make certain everything is well. Once you are settled, I'll make my way back down here without anyone seeing and sleep here tonight with the door closed. In the morning, I'll use your room to wash up and change my clothes for the next stretch of our journey.'

Lizzy felt her mouth open in disbelief. 'You intend to walk through this inn in your nightshirt?'

'Of course not,' he replied, letting out a snort. 'I'll be sleeping in my clothes and keep my valise in your room.'

He would sleep in his clothes? Did people actually do that?

'I don't understand. Why don't we just ask Mr Finch to make up this parlour as a bedchamber for you? He can bring in a bed. You would be much more comfortable in a bed than sleeping on...' She looked around. 'What will you sleep on?'

'Well, Duchess, first, I don't believe The Stuffed Pig is the type of establishment that has another bed to spare that they would be willing to move into this room for me to use, so I will be sleeping on those upholstered chairs by the fire. And second, I will not have it known in this inn that you are upstairs alone in that room. As annoying as you can be at times, you are much too fetching and men have already eyed you much too closely for my liking. Earlier tonight, when we were outside, two men took note of you. You will not be assaulted in that room because I am not with you.'

'Assaulted?' The very word sent panic racing through Lizzy. But then his other statement pushed through her fear. He thought she was fetching? Annoying, but fetching. Men didn't look at her twice. The only reason a man would look at her was if he was in need of marrying a wealthy widow with an impressive title. She wasn't wealthy any more. The very reminder made her stomach turn. Now all that she could offer a man was a title that he could not share. Simon was wrong about other men finding her fetching. He was just giving her false flattery to make her more agreeable.

'I will not be alone in my room. I will have Emilie stay with me.'

'It doesn't matter. Your maid cannot protect you the way I can. No one is to know that I am not with you. As it stands, I am not at all comfortable with having to spend the night apart from you here, but I did give you my word that we would not share the same room. So, if you do not wish for me to spend the night on the floor in that room, I suggest you agree to my plan.'

The idea of having him in her room all night should have shocked Lizzy. However, she really did want to know what spending the night with him would be like. If they slept in the same bed, would his body feel warm against hers? Would she have wrapped her body around his in her sleep and listened to his heartbeat? Or would she have spent most of the night lying awake and curled up on her side in bed while she stared down at his sleeping form, lying on the pallet on the floor beside her. The very notion of them sleeping in the same room together was making her heart race.

'Do you agree this is the best course of action?' he asked, breaking into her contemplation.

No, this was not the best course of action! 'Very well, I agree. However, tomorrow night we should begin our quest for a suitable inn earlier in the day. Then hopefully we will not have to resort to such unusual arrangements to have a good night's sleep.' She didn't need to get rejected yet again. 'How will you sleep in here? There is nothing for you to lie down on.'

'I can push two of those chairs together, as I said.' He pointed towards the upholstered chairs with his tankard. 'They will suit me just fine.'

'That doesn't sound very comfortable.'

'I've slept in worse places.'

Where could he have slept that was worse than on two chairs in the public parlour of an inn?

There was a soft knock at the door. Mary had returned and escorted them up the narrow wooden staircase to the first door on the right. Upon entering, Lizzy's maid Emilie bobbed a curtsy and then went back to arranging various items of Lizzy's toilette on the dressing table near the window. There was steam coming out from the pitcher on the washstand and a fire was blazing in the hearth, making the room feel wonderfully warm.

A pang of guilt moved through Lizzy as she imagined Mr Alexander sleeping downstairs in the public parlour on those chairs. He had spent an entire day riding in a carriage, just as she had. Only now she was the only one who would have a good night's sleep. Part of her wanted to offer him the use of her room to share.

'We moved a pallet into my parents' room for your maid,' Mary said, motioning with her hand to the area near the fire that would serve as Emilie's bed for the night. 'I hope that is acceptable.'

'Your parents' room?' Lizzy looked around and now took note of the small personal touches in the room that an ordinary guest room in an inn would not have had.

'Yes, this is their bedchamber.' Her eyes grew wide and she covered her mouth as if she had revealed something she knew she shouldn't have. Lizzy suspected, if they were to leave the inn due to something the girl did, Mary would suffer for it.

'But where will your parents sleep?'

'They are staying tonight in the room I share with my two brothers.'

'But I didn't mean for your parents to give up their room for us. We had no intention to inconvenience them so.'

''Tis no inconvenience, I assure you.' Mary looked at if she would burst into tears if Lizzy said she didn't want to spend the night in the room.

The very notion that Mr and Mrs Finch would give them their own bedchamber revealed to her how very different she was from the husband and his wife. She couldn't imagine letting a stranger stay in her bedchamber and sleep in her bed. But she knew their sacrifice was not done out of the pure kindness of their hearts, but as a practical way to put income in their pockets.

Who knew what the full ramifications of Lizzy's own financial predicament was? It wouldn't be good. That she knew. Very soon she, too, would also have to consider what she would have to give up to respectably survive.

Her grip on her reticule tightened as she thought of the emerald necklace, bracelet and earrings that she had taken off at the insistence of Simon and stashed inside her bag. The set had once belonged to her grandmother and Lizzy thought back to the night before her wedding when her grandmother had taken her aside after dinner and given it to her. She had explained how she had also been forced to marry a much older man to satisfy a marriage contract arranged by her own father and when she handed the jewellery box over to Lizzy, she instructed her to sell the jewels and use the money to run away, if Skeffington was ever physically abusive towards her. The set was a constant reminder of that support she was given on a night when she had wanted desperately to leave and never look back.

This was the first time Lizzy had been conscious of her expenses. This journey back to London was costing money. Each time they visited a posting inn to change horses they had to pay for that. That included her empty carriage that Simon had sent back to London without her in it. The food they had eaten today cost money. And this room was costing money, as well.

She knew Mr Alexander was heading into London because he had taken a personal affront at being robbed, but he should not have to pay for their entire trip himself. Looking at the plump mattress on the bed that he would not be sleeping in made it all seem wrong. She felt beholden to him and didn't like the feeling.

'Is there anything else you need?' Mary asked, looking between them.

Lizzy shook her head. 'No, you've been most help-ful. Thank your parents for allowing us the use of their room this evening.'

The girl gave her a bright smile and a quick curtsy.

'Oh, and, Mary, would you be so kind as to take my maid downstairs and see that she has something to eat in an area of the inn where she will not be both-ered by any of the men staying the night.'

'Aye. Your maid can sit in the kitchen if she cares to. No one will bother her there.' She bobbed one last time before she left with Emilie.

Once more today she was alone with Mr Alexander and this time he was watching her intently as he leaned against one of the bedposts. No matter how tempting he looked standing beside that bed, she needed to re-mind herself that he had no desire to share it with her.

'Thank you for offering to stay in the parlour to-night.'

'I believe you would say it was the ducal thing to do.'

'Actually, it's not. My husband would have never offered to spend the night on a chair in the parlour of a small country inn.'

'Your husband wouldn't have needed to. He would have slept in that bed with you tonight.'

A shudder ran through her body at the unpleas-ant thought.

'If you are still cold, I can put another log on the fire for you. It should warm up the room rather quickly.'

She crossed her arms and rubbed her biceps, more to keep her hands busy than to warm herself. 'That is very kind of you, but it is not necessary.'

'I must say, this morning I would have predicted that you would have spun on your heels and walked right out of this inn the moment you discovered you would be sleeping in an innkeeper's bed. Yet you are adapting rather well and were very nice to that girl just now. You have surprised me through this. You are facing all of this head-on and you are showing... great resilience.'

'Is that one word you would use to describe me now? Aunt Clara has always said I was the *resilient* Sommersby sister, so I know of at least one other person who would agree with you.'

'And how many Sommersby sisters are there?'

'Three. Charlotte is my older sister and she is the most maternal. Juliet, my younger sister, is the most competitive.'

'And you, the middle sister, are resilient.'

'So I've been told. It appears I am known to accept what life has brought my way without complaints.'

A soft laugh escaped those smooth lips. 'You are the Duchess of Skeffington. I don't know how much resilience you need to live with that title. You seem to enjoy your prominent position in Society, so many would not exactly see it as a hardship.'

'No. I suppose they would not and I am fortunate in many ways. I am aware of that.'

He would never understand what it was like to live the life of a woman legally bound to a man who had no use for her other than to bear him an heir. He would never understand what it was like to witness people around you fall in love and be cherished by someone when no one bothered to see anything worthy of such feelings in the person you were.

'Do you have any brothers that you'd care to describe?'

He shook his head. 'I am my parents' only child. From what I've heard from Mr Nesbit there are no other males left in my father's family. If it weren't for me, the Skeffington title would have died out.'

The popping of the logs in the fireplace and the whistling of the wind outside made the room feel intimate and cosy. Even though the inn was busy downstairs, in this room—at this moment—it felt as if they were the only two people in the building. She had been alone with him for most of the day but somehow, in this bedchamber, their being alone felt different.

He pushed off the bedpost and came within two feet of her. It seemed as if the room had suddenly got smaller as he searched her eyes before slowly and seductively his gaze dropped to her lips. All his focus was on her mouth and she pulled in her bottom lip and gently bit it to stop it from aching for his touch. There was an invisible web of attraction wrapping around them that was making her very warm. She needed a distraction before she made a fool of herself and reached out to touch his chest, which thanks to falling into his arms earlier today, she now knew felt hard and strong.

'And if someone were to describe you with one word, what word would they use?'

The bed beside them suddenly held his interest. *'Desperate.'*

There was a catch to her breath because for a moment she thought there was a chance he was feeling this attraction between them, too. At least she thought so. It was possible he was desperate to crawl into that bed to go to sleep.

As if he could sense her uncertainty, he slowly

raised his hand and caressed her cheek. Instinctively her head jerked at the unexpected contact for a fraction of a second before she leaned into his hand. A warm flush of heat was spreading throughout her body and she wasn't sure if that was from the fire in the hearth or from his touch.

'Why did you do that?' she asked, her voice sounding husky to her own ears.

'I wanted to see if you were still cold.' He trailed the fingertips of his right hand under her chin and raised her lips closer to his. 'I've never kissed a tall woman,' he said in a low whisper.

'Neither have I.'

Oh, dear God, what did she just say?

As if he hadn't heard her, he slid his fingers across her jaw and cupped her cheek. Slowly he lowered his head—and kissed her. His lips were soft and wonderful. She closed her eyes, wanting to experience every sensation. It was her first kiss—her very first kiss. And it was wonderful.

The hair that grazed the back of his collar felt soft through her fingers as she held his head gently to hers so that he would not back away too soon, ending this sensual haze she was in. He didn't appear to mind since he was pulling her lower back closer to his hard body. He tasted faintly of ale and when he glided his tongue over hers, she mirrored his action, quickly seeing how to get more from their kiss. Too soon, he moved his hands to her waist and the pressure of his lips on hers was gone.

She didn't want to open her eyes. She didn't want her first kiss to end. Now she knew why scandalous couples risked being caught at balls to do it. It was heavenly.

As if he sensed her reluctance to stop, his warm lips touched her closed eyelids and he kissed them, as well. That unexpected sensation sent a wave of flutters low in her stomach and she let out a soft gasp. When she opened her eyes, she found he was staring at her with a sensual smile playing on those lips that had been pressed against her own. If she thought he had been watching her closely before, that was nothing like the way he was watching her now. There was a hunger in his eyes that awakened a feeling of need inside her.

And for the first time in her life, Lizzy felt beautiful.

His thumb traced her lower lip and then he kissed her once more. It was soft and slow and over much too quickly.

A sense of nervousness was starting to build up inside of her. Why had he kissed her? Maybe he was the type of man who just liked to collect kisses from various women to feed his own self-worth. Or maybe he thought if he kissed her, she would allow him into her bed so he didn't have to sleep on chairs in the parlour? Or maybe…just maybe…he wanted to kiss her just as much as she wanted to kiss him.

She really was horrible at understanding men.

'Emilie will be back soon.' She couldn't let him know that she was desperate to have him stay and kiss her again. It was too embarrassing.

'And this room would be too crowded with three of us in here,' he said, with an understanding nod of his head. He stepped away from her, taking with him the warmth of his body, and gestured to the wash-stand with his head. 'I will leave you now before that pitcher of water becomes too cold for your liking. Do not let anyone into your room unless it is your maid and latch the door when I leave.'

'You need not worry. Emilie and I will slide that chair in front of the door when she returns.'

His concern for her safety was stirring those feelings inside her that she had no use for. Men did not want her and it was best to keep reminding herself of that. It would save her from any crushing disappointment.

One kiss would not change her world. One kiss did not mean he wanted her as a *real* wife. He was a handsome man. He probably had been travelling all around the Continent kissing women. This was her first kiss. And it was heavenly. Unfortunately, she knew their kiss would not have had the same effect on him as it had had on her.

Realistic was a word she would use to describe herself.

Simon gave her a tip of his head and headed for the door. He was Simon to her now. She knew the taste of his lips.

When he reached the handle, he paused and rested his hand on the wooden surface before turning back and letting his eyes meet hers. 'Until the morning, Duchess. I'll knock three times when I return so that you'll know it's me. In the meantime, I am downstairs should you need me.'

Chapter Fourteen

He'd kissed her. It was the very thing he'd promised himself he wouldn't do.

Being beside that bed with her only a few feet away had muddled his logic. It had reminded him of her long legs wrapped in white sheets that he had been thinking about all last night.

When she asked Mr Finch to arrange a bath, Simon envisioned those long legs glistening with water and draped over the edge of the tub. It was an image that was still firmly planted in his brain and, if he had to guess, it was an image that was probably going to stay with him until he left England.

Walking down the stairs, he could tell by his tightened breeches that this was going to be another long night—and sleeping on the chairs in the parlour was only one of the reasons for that. The other was the woman who he had just left, the one who had sparked a fire in his body with just a simple kiss. For a man who never had any trouble sleeping before he met the Duchess of Skeffington, now it appeared he wouldn't be having a good night's rest until he left her.

By the time he walked into the empty parlour and shut the door, he was still reliving the way her body felt against his and the way something inside of him leapt when she began to kiss him back. Her kiss had surprised him. She was tentative at first and it took her a minute or two before she parted her lips for him to deepen their kiss.

It had been apparent that she was not overly fond of him but when he had caught her watching his reflection in the window of the carriage earlier in the day, he found he liked the idea that he intrigued her. As much as it would pain her to admit it, he knew she found him attractive and, when they looked at each other at times, he could see desire in her eyes.

She had passionately kissed him back and watching her stand there with her eyes closed after they had kissed was like watching an awakening of sorts. He knew she had been married. She must have had sex with her husband. But the stillness of her body and her softened expression had made it appear that she was savouring the passionate kiss they had shared. One could almost believe she was a woman who had never been kissed. Even though she did not have any children, that couldn't possibly be true. How he wished he could remember what was said at the reading of the will. It might give him a clue about what kind of relationship she'd had with the man.

For all her strength and assertiveness, there was a sense of innocence about her that didn't quite make sense. But the last thing he wanted to do was picture her sexual awakening at the hands of the old Duke. It made his muscles tighten in anger and brought bile to his mouth.

There was still a half-bottle of sherry left on the table and her empty glass. Her lips had touched that glass. He'd never thought about a kiss this much before. Hell, he'd never thought about any kiss before now.

Inheriting this title was beginning to alter his way of thinking and he didn't like it. Kisses were just a prelude to sex, nothing more. You did it because you knew it would lead to other more stimulating activities for you and the woman you were with. But this kiss was different. He knew he wouldn't be having sex with Elizabeth, but he needed to kiss her anyway. More than anything he had wanted to feel her lips against his and hold her in his arms—and it was better than he had anticipated.

He downed the sherry in one gulp and poured himself another glass while staring at the chairs that would be his bed for the night. What was happening to him? Each day he spent in England he found himself drifting further and further away from who he really was. This new title was not who he was. He was not brought up and educated to be an English duke and go to Parliament and to fancy parties. He was brought up knowing that he didn't have very much to offer anyone and that was why his family shuffled him off from relative to relative when they thought he had stayed too long. The navy had given him a sense of belonging. Finding and negotiating for treasured objects for museums and collectors gave him a sense of accomplishment.

That was who he was. That was his purpose in life. It wasn't riding around in plush carriages and not being able to shake the hand of a man who worked hard to put a roof over his family's head. And he certainly shouldn't be kissing a duchess.

He needed to remember that. Especially now when

he knew that Elizabeth's kisses and their stimulating sparring could make him believe he could want a life here.

Tugging the chairs closer to the fire, Simon set up his bed for the night and hoped his body and brain would settle down and he could get just a few hours' sleep before they were once again on the road to find out who had broken into his house. It was his house. It was his safe. And he was determined to find them.

By morning, Simon's muscles were stiff and sore and he wasn't looking forward to getting back into his carriage for another long ride. If only he could have taken a long, hot bath… Hopefully tonight, at a different inn, taking a bath would be an option.

After he put on his boots and gathered his coat in his arms, he quietly opened the parlour door and was met with the mouth-watering smells coming from the kitchen. At least he would eat well before they headed back out on the road. He might even be able to see if Mrs Finch had some extra meat pies they could take with them.

There were distant sounds of low voices coming from somewhere deep within the tavern, but the rest of the inn appeared to still be asleep. He took care to measure his steps so as not to make any noise as he crept up the stairs to Elizabeth's room. He was almost at the top of the staircase when down from the bottom Mr Finch called up to him.

'Good morning, Your Grace.'

Simon froze. How was he to explain the fact that he had not slept with his wife? He turned and walked down a few steps. 'Good morning, Mr Finch. I was just going to go into the parlour when I realised I'd forgotten my book. I was going back to get it.' He walked down a few more steps so he wouldn't need to shout.

The innkeeper gave him a sly smile. 'You don't have to explain anything to me. I walked in on you last night while you were asleep by the fire. I went in the parlour to make certain my daughter had tidied up after you and your wife left, and I spied your legs stretched across the chairs.'

Had anyone else walked in while he was asleep? Simon was relieved to find his coin purse was still in his pocket.

'Wives are strange creatures, I always say.' Mr Finch nodded sagely.

'Pardon?'

'There's no need to be embarrassed. It's happened to me, too. The wife has got angry and out I've been sent to sleep in the parlour. At least it's warm and quiet in there. Could be worse. There've been nights when the parlour is taken and I've been up with the servants. Not something a man wants to share with those he pays.'

'No, I imagine not,' Simon said, trying to sound as if he empathised with the man's experience.

'Nothing like a feisty woman, though, to make the perfect wife. Your Duchess can give as good as she gets like my Martha. I saw that about her.'

'Does your Martha keep you at sixes and sevens, as well, Mr Finch?'

'Aye, that she does. But truth be told, sir, I wouldn't want it any other way. I think I'd grow bored of a woman who didn't challenge me at times. Keeps it interesting, I say. And there always are those times after you've had a good row that pleases a man's soul, if you know what I mean?'

Simon had been trying most of the night not to think of how Elizabeth could please his soul—as well as other parts of him. 'Yes, I know what you mean, Mr Finch.'

'How long have you and Her Grace been married?'

'We have not been together long.' That wasn't exactly a lie. They just didn't happen to be married during their short time together.

'I thought so. I saw it in the way you look at one another.'

The analysis of his relationship with Elizabeth by the innkeeper was intriguing since he'd never had anyone talk to him about his *wife* before. 'And how do we look at one another?'

'Like you wasn't sure if you should kiss or argue. That's always the sign of a newly married couple from what I've seen over the years.'

'And you think my wife couldn't decide that either?'

'Oh, aye. I saw the way she watches you when you aren't looking. You're a lucky man. Now, go on up and tell her how beautiful she looks when she's sleeping. That always does the trick with my Martha. It slips you right into their good graces again.' He winked and made a skimming gesture with his hand in the event Simon missed his meaning. 'Why don't you send her maid down to us in the kitchen? We'll fix her with a good breakfast so you and Her Grace can have time alone.'

If they had stayed at a more respectable inn, he probably wouldn't have got such advice. It appeared

Mr Finch was unaware that there were topics you did not discuss with someone who possessed a lofty title. At least Simon thought that might be the case from the way he had been treated since being summoned back to England. It was refreshing to have an unguarded discussion. He'd missed them.

'Thank you, Mr Finch, for giving up your room last night to accommodate my wife and me. We were not eager to return to the road to go to another inn after being in our carriage all day.' He opened his coin purse and took out a few guineas. 'Here's something extra for your pains. I hope you had a more restful night than I did.'

Mr Finch caught the coins that Simon flipped to him and gave a quick bow. 'My pleasure, Your Grace. I'll wager I did.' The man grinned at him with open camaraderie. 'We'll set the parlour up for breakfast. Just ring for us when you come down and we will bring in something to keep you feeling full for the first part of your journey.'

'I'm looking forward to it. I'm sure we will be in there shortly.'

'Now, you take all the time you need. Take all the time you need.' He gave Simon another wink as he bowed before he disappeared into the tavern.

When Simon reached the bedchamber door, he pressed his ear against it to listen for any stirring inside. He didn't hear a thing. It was distinctly possible that Elizabeth and Emilie were still asleep. The wise words of Mr Finch came back to him. Was it possible that he would be walking in and finding her asleep in bed just as Mr Finch had probably walked in on his wife on a number of occasions? Is that what married people did?

He knocked three times in rapid succession and didn't have to wait long before Emilie opened the door. She was already dressed and, although she had been very respectful towards him, he did get a sense that he made her nervous. It wasn't the kind of nervous a woman was when she was taken with you. This kind of nervous was different and not the kind he had experienced with a woman before. It felt more like nervous trepidation.

Silently, she let him in. When he stepped into the room, Simon's gaze landed on the rumpled bed and was disappointed to find it empty. As if she sensed his perplexity at where her mistress was, Emilie pointed to the dressing screen in the corner before she walked to the trunk near the window and appeared to resume packing. Simon could barely see Elizabeth's head behind the screen.

She peeked over the top and the corner of her eyes crinkled as if she was smiling. How he wanted to kiss her again and might have if it weren't for her maid. Elizabeth stepped out from behind the screen with her attention now on pulling up her lavender gloves. She was already dressed in a grey-and-white-striped gown with a white fichu obstructing his view of the top swells of her breasts. There was a slight blush about her now when she looked up at him and smiled. It made her appear a bit vulnerable and more beautiful than she had been before.

'I hope I am not disturbing you,' he said. 'I came to wash and get dressed. It would be best if we go back on the road while it's still early.'

'Of course, the more miles we can cover while the sun is out, the better it will be.' She turned to her maid who was just closing the trunk. 'Is everything packed, Emilie?'

'I just need to pack the sheets and His Grace's towel and I will be finished.'

His towel? The idea that she had a towel for him from her own linens made this marriage feel much too real. His discussion with Mr Finch this morning had muddled his brain. She was not his wife. She would never want to be permanently attached to him. His father had proved that by staying in the navy after Simon's mother died and his relatives had reinforced that when he became too much of a bother to have around. And even though they had shared a kiss, in her eyes he would never measure up to her husband. He would always be Mr Alexander. It was best that he remembered that.

Chapter Fifteen

Lizzy stepped out into the courtyard of the inn after breakfast and was happy to see it wasn't a blustery day. The sun was out and birds were chirping in a pine tree nearby. Under normal circumstances this would have been an excellent day for a drive. But since she had been in a carriage for so long yesterday and had two more full days to sit in one until they reached London, she almost wished that they could remain at the inn—almost.

Not sure which carriage to go to, she was silently debating between the two when Tom opened the door to the first carriage with an expectant expression. She and Emilie climbed inside and found Simon stretched out on the velvet bench across from them. They did not need to travel together in the same carriage today and it should not have pleased her to find him inside. But she couldn't deny that just the sight of him, with his head bowed over a book, made her want to smile.

She was wise to have Emilie sit beside her today. With her maid in the carriage with them it would be impossible for Simon to kiss her again and now Lizzy would not spend today's entire ride wondering if he would try to. Those yearnings for him were best left at the inn. Thinking that she was somehow special to him would only lead to heartache.

'What is it you are reading so intently?' she asked, settling in on the green-velvet bench across from him.

He looked over at Emilie and the slight furrow of his brow told her he was wondering why they weren't alone.

'This morning I am reading a book of poetry by Mr Wordsworth,' he replied, holding up his brown leather-bound book as if she wouldn't believe him. 'Yesterday it was a book on the principles of British law.'

When Mr Nesbit first introduced her to him, she had taken note that the cut of his coat wasn't in the latest fashion and his dark brown hair was cut a bit longer than the gentlemen in London favoured. He didn't resemble any of the other English Dukes. There was a carefree yet mysterious demeanour to him the others didn't possess. And while sitting across from him in these close quarters for an extended amount of time, she was coming to appreciate buckskin breeches and brown coats—and men who read poetry.

'I didn't think you were the type of gentleman to read verse.'

'And what did you think I had been reading?'

That was what she found so unsettling. She didn't really know anything about him to make a reasonable guess. Mr Nesbit hadn't appeared to know much about him either and she had found Simon was not very forthcoming when talking about himself or his past.

'I haven't really given it much thought.' Which was a lie. She had tried to see the title of the book a number of times yesterday in the carriage, but he had kept it on his lap and been so engrossed in reading that she had felt foolish thinking of interrupting him to ask. 'Your preference for poetry surprises me, that's all.'

'I'm glad that after spending an entire day together in this carriage yesterday, I can still surprise you.'

He had surprised her—with that kiss. And from the look in his eyes, she thought he might be recalling it, as well. She was thankful that Emilie was riding in the carriage with her today. No good could come from being alone any more with Simon for an extended amount of time.

The carriage jerked forward to begin their journey. They had another day of travel ahead of them and, while Simon went back to reading his book and Emilie took out her embroidery, Lizzy was left with just her thoughts. Thinking too much was never good. It made you dwell on things you could not change. And one of the things that she wasn't able to change was the fact that someone had stolen the majority of her fortune and she was no longer a rich woman.

All day yesterday she had attempted to breathe past the humiliation and fear that made her want to break down and cry. Her legs still felt like jelly just worrying what would become of her. She was too proud to live with her sisters or her aunt, so now she knew her future was at Clivemoore, far away from the people she knew and loved. And even if she stayed with Aunt Clara in London during the Season, her reduced circumstances would see that her invitations would dry up faster than a riverbed in the middle of summer.

How she wished they were in London already so she could meet with Mr Sherman and have him explain the financial ramifications of the theft and what it would mean to how she would be able to live her life going forward. They would have to work out some kind of budget for her. She had never had to live on one before. The one good thing—the only good thing—about Skeffington was that he had let her spend as much money as she had wanted with impunity. Her extravagance informed Society that he was a very wealthy man and she knew he revelled in that.

Last night as she lay awake in the innkeeper's bed, she couldn't help but feel an unprecedented connection with the couple who had rented out their own bedchamber to make certain they had food on the table. Life was made up of sacrifices. In marrying Skeffington she had sacrificed her heart. What would she need to sacrifice now to lead a respectable life?

She let her gaze settle on the man across from her, absorbed in his book, before she looked out the window and watched the farms and villages go by. There was no telling how many hours they had been travelling when Emilie caught her eye and arched her brow towards Simon.

'You don't think he is dead, do you?' she whispered.

Simon's eyes were closed and he was sitting back on the bench with his hands folded on his stomach. After years of sitting across carriages and tables from her husband, it was a nice change to have someone who was handsome to look at.

'No, he is not dead,' she whispered back, admiring how well his shoulders filled out his brown coat.

'He fell asleep rather quickly,' Emilie added quietly, 'and he hasn't moved at all.'

Skeffington had died during dinner from choking on a chicken bone. Lizzy was there when he began to turn blue and the footmen tried to get it out. Did Emilie think all of Lizzy's husbands would die unexpectedly on her—even the fake ones?

'I can see him breathing,' she tried to reassure her maid. 'He is alive.'

'You're certain?'

'Yes, I am quite certain.'

'And if I were dead,' Simon said without moving, 'all the noise the two of you are making would have roused me.'

The comment had been said with such a dry delivery that it made Emilie laugh before she covered her mouth and then shared a smile with Lizzy. It was the first time Lizzy had witnessed her maid relax in Simon's presence. Emilie and Mrs Thacker, her housekeeper in London, were the two people who had witnessed the horrid ways Skeffington would treat her. It was no wonder Emilie was leery of the new Duke. But this Duke was nothing like the old one and it seemed Emilie was coming to realise that.

Suddenly, the sound of their coachman signalling to the carriage behind them that they were about to stop caught her attention and she looked over at Simon with concern. He had warned her about highwaymen and she placed her reticule with her grandmother's jewellery under the folded blanket beside her and looked out the window to try to see the reason why they were stopping.

Meanwhile, Simon rapped on the ceiling with the tip of his walking stick and a small door opened above him. Tom's smiling face appeared through the trapdoor and he notified them that they were coming up on a posting inn. Finally, she would be able to get out, stretch her legs and stop sneaking glances at the man across from her.

The posting inn was a stone structure that was larger than The Stuffed Pig. It had people milling about and horses were being hitched to a nearby carriage in the courtyard. It was situated close to a small village and Lizzy thought a stroll would do her body and her mind some good. The sun had melted most of the snow on the ground and the country lane that led to the village was beckoning her, so she left Emilie and Simon and took a leisurely stroll.

In the past, she would have stopped in the shops and bought a trinket or two. Gloves and stockings were usually good purchases no matter what town you were in. Her gowns were always made by Madame Legiere in London to make certain she was at the forefront of the latest fashion trend so she would never shop outside of London for her gowns, but she did allow herself to have more options when it came to her accessories. Today she found the idea of spending money without a true need was making her stomach churn and, although she would look in the shop windows, she would not venture inside. It would be too tempting.

When she reached the end of High Street, she spied the small stone church with a square bell tower reaching up to the sky. It was a quaint country church, not like the vast cathedrals one would see riding through a large town. With the intention of going inside to have a look around, she adjusted her cloak and walked up the small hill and into the graveyard that surrounded the building. But instead of going directly inside, she found herself walking among the gravestones, reading the names and dates of the people who at one time had lived in the area.

The grave of Lucinda Riddell gave her pause and she stopped to study the gravestone that had an angel's face with wings carved at the top of the arched stone. It wasn't the carving that had caught her eye. Many stones had that image. It was the age of the woman and that of her husband. Lucinda had died when she was twenty-seven and she was buried beside her husband, Mark, who had died the year after, at the age of eighty. Had Lucinda's father sold her off to her husband at a very young age, as well? The stone did not indicate how long they were married or if they had any children.

Lizzy traced the angel's face with her gloved finger, needing to feel some connection to this woman who came before her—needing to feel less alone. Had Lucinda been miserable in her marriage, as well? Had she learnt to put on a brave face to the world to hide her pain the way Lizzy had? And, had she stood, year after year, outside this church and watched as one happy bride after another left the building on the arm of a loving husband and wondered why fate had determined that she did not deserve that kind of life?

For years Lizzy had endured the snide comments about her marriage from women who said they were her friends. She wasn't the only woman of the *ton* who was married off to a man old enough to be her grandfather and didn't know what it was like to feel cherished by a man, but most of the time it felt that way.

The sound of someone coming up behind her sent a chill up her spine and she pulled her black cloak tightly around her.

'We're ready to leave now.'

The deep sound of Simon's smooth voice had the ability to calm her while at the same time to make her heart ache. It wasn't until she turned to look at him that she felt hot teardrops roll down her cheek.

Deep concern etched his brow and he took a step closer. 'Did something happen? Did you know that woman?'

It wasn't until he asked her that question that Lizzy thought to pay attention to the date that Lucinda had died. It was only two years ago. They would have been the same age.

She scrubbed the tears from her cheeks and tried to paste a smile on her face, but then—in that cemetery— at that moment, she didn't want to hide behind the mask she had got so good at showing to the world. At that moment, she was grieving for the life she and Lucinda had been denied and she was tired of pretending everything was fine. No husband would mourn her passing when her time on this earth ended, just as she was certain Mark hadn't mourned Lucinda.

Simon came up next to her. With new tears streaming down her face, they stood side by side in silence, staring at the gravestones in front of them. Wind whispered through the bare branches of the trees, bringing the smell of cold winter air with it and brushing against Lizzy's cheeks.

It took some time but she was able to find her voice. 'Why do we get dealt the cards in life we do? Why are some people given everything and others are given nothing?'

He kept his gaze on the gravestones. 'Some of us just get passed by. There is no rhyme or reason to it.'

Those words, spoken softly and sincerely, took her by surprise.

'I'm tired of playing the grieving widow to the world. I'm tired of wearing black and grey and seeming to mourn a man who was a monster to me. My life was taken from me at seventeen and the life I wanted went to my sister. For twelve years I lived my life under clouds of worry that I would inadvertently make a mistake that would send him into a rage. That's not the life I dreamed of when I was a girl. That's not the life I deserved.'

He moved his hand and his fingers curled tightly through hers as if in holding her hand he was stopping himself from committing some act. 'None of us deserves a life like that.'

There was a strain of anger in his voice and she waited for him to verbally explode the way Skeffington had a habit of doing at the oddest provocation. She held her breath and waited.

'I thought… That is to say, what would he do…in his moments of rage?'

She looked over at him, but his attention was fixed on Mr Riddell's tombstone. In fact, he was so focused on that stone that she wasn't certain that he had spoken to her at all.

'Did he ever beat you?' he asked before she was even able to answer his first question.

She closed her eyes and let out a breath. 'No. No, he never did. But the things he'd say…' They were things she would rather forget. He was a man. How could he understand how words could make you sometimes feel as if your life was worthless? As if you were worthless.

'There are times the things people say can cut just as deeply as those swords on the wall at Stonehaven.'

Their eyes met and all at once she knew. She knew that he had faced someone in his life who had been a monster to him, as well.

'Who did that to you?'

'When I was a small boy my mother died and I was carted off to one relative after another whom I never knew and who didn't know me. You see my father, in his infinite love and understanding, decided he would not give up his naval career to come home and raise the only child he had. He thought nothing of foisting me on my mother's family to have them care for me, but I was nothing but a burden. From the time my mother died, I lived with all seven of my aunts and uncles. I've had monsters in my life, as well. More than I'd care to remember.'

She squeezed his hand, wishing she could have comforted him as a child. 'I'm sorry.'

'Maybe you are not the only one in this world who learnt to be resilient to survive.'

'I thought I was finally free. I thought when he died that I was leaving my broken life behind me. But even in his death my life is still covered in darkness. Even now I cannot have the life I've always wanted to live.'

'We will find your money and get it back for you. I promise that you will get to live the kind of life you wanted to live.'

He was talking about her fortune and being able to live the life of a wealthy duchess. She did want those things, all of them, but she also wanted someone to love her. There would be no man to light a candle to mourn her passing. No husband to love her completely to her dying day.

'And what of you?' she asked. 'Are all your monsters behind you?'

'There will always be monsters, only now that I am older, I can usually escape them. I can leave England and my responsibilities and go back to Sicily or anywhere else I want. When I became Duke, I lost my freedom here. So much of my life here is now directed by protocol and I am expected to surround myself with people who will never see me as anything but a man who does not belong with such a lofty title. I never wanted this life. I tried to give it up, but was told that I cannot relinquish the title. It is a shackle around my neck that is preventing me from living the life *I* want.'

At that moment, he appeared to be a man who was at a crossroads—unsure of what path to take. He always seemed so at ease and confident in his actions. This was a side of him she had not seen before.

'What kind of life do you want?'

'One where I can decide for myself what is best for me, without the world having a say.' The intensity of his emotion was evident in his eyes and his grip on her hand tightened, but not painfully so. 'My life belongs to me and I don't want to have to spend it in one place. There is too much to see of the world for me to remain here. And being a duke is not something I was trained to do. I don't know the first thing about how to be one. I don't know the first thing about sitting in the House of Lords, or managing all those estates. People shouldn't have to rely on me to take care of their interests. I can barely take care of my own.'

Wanting to find a way to comfort him, she gave

him a reassuring smile. 'I don't think you can get out of it. But you'll find your own way. You'll be the kind of Duke you were meant to be.'

'Suppose I run the estates into the ground?' There was a flash of concern in his eyes before he rubbed his forehead. 'What about the tenants who are relying on me to know what I am doing?'

He had help. Had no one told him that he would have help and did not have to do it all on his own?

'You have stewards. From what I have observed over the years they are all exceptionally competent in what they do and trustworthy. Learn from them. Trust them.'

He released her hand and shoved his own into his pockets. Her palm felt suddenly cold and she curled her hand into a fist in an attempt to hold on to the last bits of his warmth. Silence stretched between them as Lizzy looked once more at Lucinda's gravestone. As she rested her head on Simon's shoulder, she wondered if Lucinda was at all happy married to her husband.

'No one should feel obligated to mourn someone who was a monster,' he said, as if he suddenly remembered what had prompted his confession.

'No, they shouldn't,' she said quietly. It was time to tie her emotions back into that neat bow that she was accustomed to and leave for London. She would visit those feelings again. Although next time, she'd be all alone when she did.

They made their way through the cemetery and walked side by side through the village, lost in their own thoughts. As they approached the posting inn, Lizzy felt the need to be alone with Simon, even if they travelled the entire rest of the day without saying two words to one another. She just needed him beside her. They had shared their bleak lives with each other—something she had never done with any other man—and at that moment, she felt less alone.

She looked for Emilie and just as she went to walk towards her to instruct her to ride in the second carriage, Simon walked past her and over to that very carriage. Lizzy caught up with him just before he stepped inside.

'Will you not ride with me?' There was a hint of desperation in her voice even though she had tried to sound unaffected.

There was melancholy in his eyes back in the graveyard and it had not gone away. 'I need time alone.'

'I promise I will not overtax your ears with my voice. I will just be watching the world go by.'

'I'm sorry, Elizabeth. I think we should ride separately.'

It was the first time he had ever used her Christian name. The sound of it should have made her giddy. Instead, he had used it to push her away.

Chapter Sixteen

Simon never opened up to anyone—ever. As he rested his head on the back cushion of the bench in the carriage, he didn't want to think about why he had opened up to Elizabeth now. All he wanted to do was sit beside her and feel her head on his shoulder—because back in the graveyard, for just a moment, his pain was all gone. At that moment, he hadn't felt alone.

Now he knew Elizabeth had married the Duke when she was just seventeen and that it hadn't been a love match. How could it have been when she was still a child and the man was old enough to be her grandfather? And at such a young age she suffered from his cruelty. Did she now regret marrying the man for his fortune and the title he gave her or would she have told him that it was still worth it?

He had wanted her to see that he could understand her pain, so he started to talk about his childhood and the demons that had plagued him during it, until his father had signed Simon up for the navy. It was only in the navy that he began to feel some stability and kinship with other people in his life. The irony had not been lost on him that the first time he felt safe in years had been on a ship in the middle of a war.

He thought he had moved past the hurt he felt as a child knowing he was unwanted. He thought he had moved past the pain of watching other children being doted on by their loving parents. And he thought he had reached a point of his life where he truly felt certain he didn't need anyone in it to make him feel loved.

But then he had held her hand.

And she had rested her head on his shoulder.

All he wanted was to stay with her and that was impossible. He couldn't stay in one place too long. When he did, people came to realise they didn't want him around. She would come to realise that, too— eventually.

His head and chest hurt. He just wanted to go to sleep and forget. He wanted to find a way to forget the feel of her lips, and the tears in her eyes, and how she had wanted to share a carriage with him. He wanted to forget it all.

When they reached the inn about an hour before the sun was to set, she had barely spoken to him when they stood together in the courtyard and looked up at the small Georgian building. The Centrebridge Inn was newer than The Stuffed Pig by a few hundred years. With its honey-coloured brick and white sash windows it appeared more respectable than quaint. The inn, situated alongside a large stream, appeared well-run from what they could observe when they walked inside.

Although she had told him that she had never visited the inn before, he did notice that Elizabeth kept the brim of her bonnet quite low, almost obscuring her face. When the innkeeper greeted them in the entrance hall, he wore a fine navy tailcoat, black breeches and high polished black Hessians. The man was very well groomed compared to Mr Finch. And thankfully, like The Stuffed Pig, this establishment had some enticing aromas filling the air from the kitchen. It wasn't too grand in scale, but it made up for the size with understated refinement.

'Good evening. I'm Mr Hemmsley, the innkeeper. What can I do for you this evening?'

Simon held out his hand to the man. 'Good evening. I am…' he paused for a heartbeat '…Mr Alexander and this is my wife. We are looking for rooms and a good meal for the night for ourselves and our staff.'

He didn't need to look directly at Elizabeth to see her shoulders stiffen at the name he used and he wasn't certain if her reaction was because he had taken away her title or because he had used his real name.

'At this time of year it's unusual for us to have vacancies. However, we were closed due to a death in the family. We returned yesterday and opened our doors this morning. All five of our rooms are vacant. How many do you need?'

'One for me and one for my wife and additional quarters for our servants.'

Mr Hemmsley didn't even blink at the mention of the fact that here was a husband requesting a separate room for his wife. He just gave them a smile and offered to show them the five rooms so they could choose the ones they would prefer. When Mr Hemmsley began to walk up the staircase, Elizabeth pulled Simon back by his arm.

'You could have said we were brother and sister,' she whispered furiously in his ear.

'We have not been brother and sister before. Why now?' he whispered back.

'What if someone arrives and recognises your name or me? And, what makes you believe I want to be Mrs Alexander?' Her hand appeared to be gripping her reticule so tightly that he was convinced she wanted to hit him with it.

'I never said you wanted to be my wife. I am well aware you do not. However, if we intend to have a respectable stay here, we now have no other choice but to continue with this ruse.'

'Are you purposely misunderstanding me?'

What was there to misunderstand? She said she did not want to be Mrs Alexander. There was no misinterpreting that. She let out a huff, spun on her heel and practically stomped up the stairs after Mr Hemmsley.

Each of the rooms was clean and nicely decorated. Simon would have been content to spend the night in any of them. They all had beds with soft blankets and plump pillows. They all had washstands and fireplaces for a warm night. But the minute he stepped foot into the last room, he knew Elizabeth would want it.

The walls were a deep green and the curtains on the comfortable-looking tester bed and on the windows were made out of matching green brocade with brown braiding. The one feature that set this room apart from all the others they had seen was the tub that was placed by the fireplace.

An audible sigh made both men turn around to look at her when Elizabeth entered the room. For a moment, she looked at Simon in what appeared to be relief.

'My wife will take this room. I will take the one across the hall.'

Elizabeth was already skimming her fingertips along the rim of the tub and he could tell she could not wait to have that hot bath she had been longing for.

While keeping her attention on the tub as if it would disappear if she looked away, she addressed the innkeeper. 'Mr Hemmsley, would it be possible to have a bath tonight? We've been travelling for two days and I would like nothing better than to lie in a hot tub.'

'At this time of year it might not be hot by the time you get into it, Mrs Alexander. There are only three men who can carry the water up at a time and the tub takes six buckets.'

Hearing Lizzy referred to as Mrs Alexander made something tighten in Simon's chest. He had been shown her vulnerable side and understood the way she had been treated by her husband. He could try to distance himself from her until he left England or he could enjoy the moments he had with her—with someone who seemed to understand a bit of what his life experiences had been. His heart was telling him to lock himself in his room here at the inn and not come out until it was time to leave in the morning.

'I can carry one.' Apparently, his brain and his heart were not connected at the moment. 'And I have two coachmen who can help. Unless you don't have enough buckets.' He'd let fate decide if he should spend more time with her.

Elizabeth was staring at him as if he had informed them he wanted to eat his hat for dinner.

Mr Hemmsley eyed the tub and then Simon with

uncertainty. 'We have enough buckets, sir. If you are sure you do not mind carrying one?'

'I've carried buckets before. Carrying another one will not break me.'

The image of Elizabeth reclining naked in the tub later that night, however, might.

Since it was apparent that she wished to remain in her room, he left her in there and went downstairs with the innkeeper to make arrangements for dinner and inform the servants of this evening's alias.

He was grateful that tonight he wouldn't be sleeping on two chairs, or inside one of his own carriages. Tonight, he would get to sleep in an actual bed. Although, how much sleep he would be getting was questionable with Elizabeth and that bathtub across the hall.

Chapter Seventeen

There was a distinct possibility that Lizzy would fall asleep before her bathwater arrived. She was emotionally spent from her visit to the cemetery earlier in the day and her body ached from travelling on the rutted winter roads. When she had spotted the tub in the last bedchamber of the inn, she felt as if she could have broken down and cried. A good long soak would help set her body to rights. Her emotions, on the other hand, would not be settling down any time soon with Simon across the hall.

Emilie had put out a towel and some soap for her and then Lizzy had sent her maid to settle herself into her room next door. She was glad she'd had Emilie with her earlier when Simon had decided to remain in the other carriage. When Lizzy needed a distraction from obsessing about him, she could turn to her maid for conversation during the ride.

Now that she was alone, it was not so easy. She did not understand him. One minute he was dismissing her, preferring to spend time by himself in the other carriage. The next he was making her his wife and using his actual surname. When he had informed the innkeeper that they were Mr and Mrs Alexander, it almost felt real. It made her consider what life would have been like if he were still Mr Alexander and she was indeed his wife. It was a horrid tease to her emotions because she knew he truly didn't want her. His request that they ride in separate carriages after she had bared her soul to him in the cemetery proved that.

But then he had offered to bring up one of the buckets of water so she would finally get her hot bath and he confused her all over again. She needed to believe that he would have made the same offer to anyone else he was travelling with. If she didn't, she would eventually face another disappointment when she realised Simon didn't have any special regard for her at all.

She had been pacing her room in front of the fire, practising her nonchalant greeting to him when there was a knock at the door. When she opened it, a stream of servants brought in copper buckets filled with steaming water and filled her tub. Just the sound of the splashing water made her muscles soften. Five servants, including their two coachmen, filed out of her room and then Simon walked in with the final bucket and kicked the door closed behind him.

There was a lot of water in the tub already and he took care to empty his bucket slowly. Moments ago the sound of splashing water had made her relax, but now this sound of water slowly being poured into her tub made her feel as if butterflies were flying around low in her stomach.

'Now you will be able to finally soak in a hot bath.' His voice was sounding even deeper than it usually did.

Just the sight of him without his coat, wearing his

yellow-and-white-striped waistcoat and the sleeves of his white-linen shirt rolled up, was making her mouth dry. 'Thank you. I do appreciate you bringing up one of the buckets for me. You said you've carried them before. Did you do that when you were in the navy?'

'I've carried them on ships. I've also had to carry them when I was living with a number of my relatives.'

'Your relatives made you carry buckets?'

'Among other things. Perhaps they saw it as their duty to train me as a footman or perhaps they just needed an able body that could do the work of a footman.' He looked down at the tub beside him and lowered his hand.

The sight of his fingers trailing through the water had her imagining what they would feel like against her skin if she were lying in that tub at that very moment. The very notion of it brought heat to her cheeks and made her stays feel tighter.

'The water isn't too hot. You should not burn yourself stepping in.' His fingers continued to skim the surface of the water, but now he was looking at her with a penetrating gaze as if he, too, was imagining caressing her skin while she was lying in that tub. Her stays had definitely got tighter because it was becoming impossible to take a deep breath.

Simon walked over to her, reached out and tucked a loose tendril of hair behind her ear, letting his fingertips linger on the skin of her neck. Slowly he trailed them down and caressed her collarbone.

She wished he would kiss her again.

As if he read her thoughts, he cupped her cheek, lowered his head, and kissed her. This kiss was slow and leisurely as if he wanted to spend all night just tasting her lips. His hand slid up her side until he cupped her breast and massaged it gently. How she wished she could feel his palm against her bare skin. If only she were bolder, she might suggest it. When he ended the kiss and lowered his hand, Lizzy felt as if she were in a daze.

'I'll leave you to your bath.'

After he stepped around her and walked out of her room, Lizzy put her hand on her chest to try to steady her heartbeat. On any other night, she would have immediately locked the door before undressing for her bath. Why was she waiting to do so now?

In her head she knew he wasn't coming back tonight. Emilie had already informed her that he had arranged for them to dine in their rooms to avoid the chance of someone Lizzy knew spotting them eating together downstairs. The next time she would see him would be in the morning. The thought was depressing.

She finally decided to lock the door and enjoy her bath before it cooled. A fire was blazing in the hearth, helping to keep the tub and the air around it warm. As she leaned back in the tub and closed her eyes, she was revelling in the relaxing sensation. She recalled the sight of his fingers skimming the surface of the water and trailed her fingers up her arms to her breasts to where his hand had been. This wasn't an area of her body that she had thought much about. She knew there were men who seemed fascinated by women's breasts and would boldly stare at them during social events. She never understood what the appeal was, but now that she was running her own fingers over them, she found she rather liked the sensation.

This might have been the longest bath she had ever

taken and she was in no hurry to get out, but eventually the water started to cool and the pleasurable feeling of being submerged in the water started to dissipate.

She put on another one of her morning dresses since it was more relaxing than an evening gown to wear to dine in her room. Not long after she adjusted the pins in her hair, two footmen arrived with trays of food that they placed on the round table by the window.

She had no idea why there were two trays and assumed one of them was for Emilie. They didn't normally dine together when they were travelling, but they had on a few occasions. There was a knock at the door and she assumed it was her maid. When she opened it and found Simon there, he took her breath away.

'May I come in?' He was in a white shirt, black trousers with polished shoes and a green waistcoat that almost matched the colour of the walls in her room. He wore no jacket and his hair was tousled and slightly damp.

Holding the door open, she stepped aside and he walked past her, smelling of soap.

'I understand my tray of food was brought to your room. Mr Hemmsley must have misunderstood that I wanted our trays brought to our *separate* rooms.'

She narrowed her eyes on him. 'It's a misunderstanding, you say.'

'Quite.' He turned away rather quickly. 'Ah, look, there it is.'

She closed the door behind him although she wasn't sure why. He was just coming into her room for his tray. As she turned the key in the lock, she told herself she did so to prevent Emilie from walking in on them and being flustered by Simon's presence. If he'd heard the turn of the tumbler, he made no indication.

'Have you tried any of it yet?' He picked up a piece of roasted potato and popped it into his mouth. It must have met with his approval since he reached for another.

'The food has just arrived. I haven't sampled it yet.'

'You must try these. They are delicious.'

Instead of piercing the potato with his fork for her, he held the cubed vegetable between his fingers and held it out for her. Had he intended to feed her by hand? Did people actually do that? When her mouth closed around the tasty bite, her lips momentarily captured his fingers. Their eyes met as he very slowly moved his hand away and her lips slid along his skin.

The sensation made her breath catch and, by the expression on his face, she'd had an effect on him, as well. His eyes seemed to darken and his gaze dropped to her lips. He was doing it to her again. He was making her feel desirable and beautiful. This time she was certain that she wasn't imagining his interest. This time she knew he wanted her just as she wanted him. This time she was taking what she wanted.

With a step she took him by the lapels of his waistcoat and crushed her lips to his. The feeling of not wanting the kiss to end was becoming overwhelming. And his eagerness to kiss her back encouraged her to be even bolder and she untied his cravat, needing to feel the bare skin of his neck. She was encouraged when this prompted Simon to unbutton his waistcoat and shrug out of it—all while they continued to kiss.

Passion was rising inside her, hotter than the fire they were standing near. When he began to kiss his way along her jaw and to the area of her neck that was just under her ear, her legs began to feel weak. And when his tongue traced tiny patterns along the shell of her ear, she caressed the warm skin of his neck before sliding her hands under his shirt and up his firm chest to the curves of his shoulders.

This was all new to her—every sensation he was eliciting from her body was like nothing she had ever felt before. And it all felt so right.

His mouth was going lower as his hands were moving from her waist up to her breasts and the gentle pressure on them reminded her of the bath she had just taken. Only this time with *his* hands on her breasts and it felt much better.

'You are so beautiful,' he whispered in her ear. 'So damned beautiful.'

She had never had anyone say that to her before. She had never felt beautiful. But right now with his hands on her breasts and the faint stubble on his cheeks rubbing against her neck, she felt like the most beautiful woman in the world.

He lifted her into his arms and carried her over to the freshly made bed and laid her down on the soft mattress. It was feeling much too warm in the room and it got even warmer when Simon reached over his head and pulled off his shirt. The planes and muscles of his firm chest and arms were like nothing she'd ever imagined. She had seen the statues of naked men in the British Museum, but she never thought they were actually based on what men really could look like.

'Oh, heavens.'

His lips rose in a devilish smile.

The room was getting hot—so hot. And the way

he was looking at her wasn't helping matters. It was a
struggle to catch her breath and Lizzy pulled off her
fichu and dropped it over the side of the bed. A flash
of raw passion crossed Simon's expression before he
lowered his head to kiss the upper swells of her breasts
and tried to remove them from her stays. Becoming
frustrated at not being able to feel his touch on her
bare breasts, she rolled to her stomach and suggested
that he unbutton her gown.

His fingers slid along her spine with each button,
sending a tingling sensation all the way up and down
her back and through to her bottom.

'You're shivering, but this time I know it's not because you are cold. I've thought about this. Thought
about you lying in bed wrapped in only sheets since
the night you slept at Stonehaven. I thought about what
you would look like. What your skin would feel like.
In my dreams I never imagined I would get to find
out,' he whispered into her ear before he tugged the
dress down her body.

Earlier in the day when she'd confessed what her
life had been like and he'd told her of his childhood
she had wanted to be wrapped in his arms. But this
need was different. This need made her nipples harden
and that fluttering feeling kept moving lower than her
stomach. These were the feelings that made her want
to slip out of her dress in front of this man.

As she rolled over and looked up at him in just her
stays and cotton chemise, he watched her with an un-
wavering gaze that was awakening a sexual desire in
her that she hadn't known she possessed. She didn't
know it was possible to want someone the way she
wanted Simon. Tentatively she reached out and slid

her hand back and forth and traced the corded muscles of his chest.

'You have no idea what your touch does to me.' His lips were back on her neck while he was untying the ribbons of her stays. 'I need to touch you. Tell me you want that as much as I do.'

'I do. You have no idea how much I want that.'

'I think I do.' He helped her out of her stays and lowered his mouth to her breast. He sucked on her nipple through the cotton of her chemise and she almost rose off the bed with the sensation. It felt heavenly and she threaded her fingers through his hair to let him know she didn't want him to stop.

Simon was tender and slow in his ministrations and it was making her ache between her legs. As if he knew, he trailed his fingertips up between her thighs.

A faint part of her brain was telling her that what she was doing with the new Duke of Skeffington was wrong. They weren't married. They weren't even engaged.

'Lizzy, I want you.'

He said her name—the one that only the people closest to her called her. It felt so personal and intimate and special. Could it be that he felt this deep connection between them that she had and it went far beyond yearning for this very physical act?

'Lizzy, do you want me?'

'I do. I don't want this to end.'

He sucked on her nipple a bit harder and slid a finger inside her while he moved his hand in a particular fashion that was making her feel as if she were waiting for something important, but she didn't know what that was.

Then it hit her and wave after wave of pleasure filled her body. He kissed her as his hand continued to move and she moaned into his mouth.

When the pleasure had subsided, he kissed her softly on the nose.

'What just happened?' she asked, feeling her heartbeat so strongly that it was pounding in her ears.

He looked down at her first with a puzzled expression and then with a look of understanding. 'The French call it *la petite mort*.'

'The little death? Well, my legs feel dead. I don't think I can move them.'

He kissed her lips softly and smiled down at her. 'If you'd care to continue, then you don't need use of your legs for a while.'

There was no rushing through this, not caring if she wanted to continue. Simon was looking down at her with an arch to his brow—waiting.

'I want to continue.'

'Thank God. I was hoping you'd say that.'

He left the bed and removed his shoes and trousers. Every part of him had well-defined muscles, including his thighs. He climbed back into bed and settled between her legs, giving her a long deep kiss. She had been married and knew what occurred during sex, but for the first time in her life, she was eager for it to happen. She even slipped her hand between them to feel his length as it rested along her stomach. When her fingers brushed along his long hard length, it elicited a groan from Simon that gave her the best feeling, knowing she could move him that way.

'Lizzy, I cannot wait. Put your legs around my back.'

Why should she move her legs around his back?

They needed to be straight down on the mattress for this to work. 'You said I didn't have to move my legs.'

'Trust me.'

That one small statement made her realise how much she really did.

She did as he asked and soon discovered why that was a good thing to do while having sex. His thrusts were deep and steady, as if he was trying to build up an expectation inside of her. And he felt so very hard. Their shared kisses while they were meeting each other thrust for thrust seemed never ending. Under her fingers, his shoulder muscles were tightening and soon his thrusts were getting even deeper. That overwhelming sensation was overtaking her again and she felt as if her body would once more shatter into a million pieces. And this time when she did, she knew that Simon had felt the same when he moved back suddenly and spilled his seed on her stomach.

They were both struggling to breathe. He reached over the side of the bed to clean her with his cravat before lying back down on the bed and tucking her into his side. She placed her head on his chest and the erratic pounding of his heart was matching hers. They just lay there together in a comfortable silence. Neither one seemed in a hurry to speak.

In all her life, she never thought she would feel this way with a man—or about a man. She had trusted him. She did trust him. This moment was perfect. He was perfect.

With him she felt understood and accepted. With him she felt desirable. And being with him made her want to hold on to their time together and never let it go.

Oh, God, she was falling in love with him!

She knew it and now she knew how stupid she had been to let her feelings get away from her.

He could never find out. Years ago, she had thought Lord Andrew Pearce liked her because he had defended her on the dance floor. She had spent years thinking he was pining for her after her marriage. She thought some day she would marry him and her life would be perfect and he would make her happy. But then when she was free to marry, he fell in love with her sister. She had foolishly created a scenario in her head that wasn't real. Andrew hadn't cared about her. And finding out she had been so terribly mistaken had crushed her.

She couldn't allow herself to do that with Simon. She couldn't go through all that pain again. And this time, with all they shared, she knew the pain of believing his feelings were stronger than what they were would be so much worse.

Her head was telling her she should regret having sex with him, but her heart was telling her it was worth it. For this one time in her life she felt cherished and she would take that feeling with her until she died. For this one time, to this one man, she was special.

Chapter Eighteen

Simon had felt the moment Lizzy had stiffened up while lying on his chest. He was caressing her soft skin when he felt her back muscles tighten. It was brief, but it was a sharp contrast to his body that felt like wax melting into the bed after the amazing sex they had shared. He just wanted to lie there with her in his arms. It had felt so perfect and so comfortable.

But that quick tensing of her muscles told him she might not feel the same. It became hard to swallow. No one had rejected him in only a few days. This was a record, even for his family.

'Lizzy?' He tried to catch her eye, but she rubbed her face like a kitten against his chest before moving off him and rolling on her back.

He rolled to his side, propped his head in his hand, and looked down at her. It was as if she didn't want to look at him as she rubbed her hands over her eyes as if she were wiping sleep out of them. He knew he felt sleepy, but something was telling him she didn't feel the same.

'Lizzy, do you regret what just happened between us?' *Damn it!* He knew there was a catch in his voice.

She moved her hands away and looked up at him with surprise before studying his face. Then her features softened and it warmed her expression. 'No, I don't regret a single moment of it.'

The lump in his throat disappeared. He knew he would be remembering this time with her for years to come. He didn't want to think she was already pushing him away.

Then her forehead wrinkled. 'Do *you* regret what just happened?'

He wanted her and she had wanted him. They had time to explore the attraction that was between them and honour the vulnerability they had shared with each other earlier in the day. He caressed the side of her face. 'I never will.' He leaned down and kissed her, hoping the kiss said more than he ever would.

'You'll be leaving England again eventually, won't you?'

It was a roundabout way of asking about any future they had together. She was clever. There were times she could try his patience, but right now he knew she would be the one thing in all of England he would miss when he left. He studied her a bit before answering because he wanted to find a way to answer her without hurting her. He never wanted to hurt her.

'I will be going back abroad. You know why I can't stay here. There are too many bad memories for me here and if I remain in one place too long, I grow restless.' *Because I need to leave first. I need to leave before I am told I'm no longer wanted.* 'I am not ready to leave my life there behind and become the Duke of Skeffington.'

'But you already are the Duke of Skeffington.'

'But I'm not a very good one.'

She let out a soft laugh at his statement and gave him a genuine smile. 'I think that is debatable.'

'You might be biased in light of recent events.' Leaning down, he kissed her neck and took a deep breath of the unique perfume she wore, hoping to sear it into his senses and his memory. Then he looked into her eyes and knew that if he stayed and she pushed him away, it would devastate him more than anything else in his life ever had. Thinking about a future with her was dangerous. It would only lead to pain.

'There is so much of this world I have yet to see,' he tried to explain, 'and I have a life I've built for myself there.' It was the best he could do. He had built a life for himself. It was a life he was good at.

'A life on the road.' She nodded as if she understood why that kind of life was important to him and traced his eyebrow gently with her finger. 'What do you do there?'

'I travel from place to place in search of new sites and new finds. Some countries will contract me to help them arrange an excavation of a site that local townspeople believe contains significant objects from things they have uncovered as they go about their daily lives. I'm granted a percentage of the artefacts to keep. That is how I support myself. The payment for the excavations and the sale of the objects that I keep allow me to live a life where there are new adventures waiting in new cities and towns.' He looked into her sad eyes. 'Just because I need to go back doesn't mean that I will not miss you. I will.'

Her eyes grew glassy before she blinked that away. 'Thank you for saying that.'

'It's true. Please believe me. I shared things with you that I have not shared with anyone. You will be unforgettable.'

'Another word to describe me?'

'Probably the most accurate one.'

'I will never be able to forget you, either.'

With that she pulled him closer for another searing kiss and they spent the remainder of the night creating even more memorable moments.

Chapter Nineteen

Lizzy sat in the carriage the next day beside Simon, travelling with her head on his shoulder as he read poetry. Occasionally, he would find a poem that he felt she would like and he would read it out loud. And there were a number of times during the day he would put his book down and kiss her. They weren't kisses that were filled with passion. They were kisses that made her feel cherished.

She had travelled from Dorset to London on many occasions and this was the first time she'd wished the journey could take much longer. In the close confines of the carriage, with foot-warming boxes to ward off the cold air outside and a basket of food and drinks from the inn to keep them sustained, it felt as if they were the only two people in the world.

When they finally arrived in London that afternoon, Simon's mood turned sombre and Lizzy was having a hard time trying to appear unaffected. Their time together was over and she would now be faced with finding out the full ramifications of the theft. The reality of losing her money and the man beside her was making her physically sick and she only hoped Simon would not notice that she kept rubbing her stomach to settle it.

As the carriage rolled up to Aunt Clara's house, he took her hand in his and held it tight. She knew that he realised their time as Mr and Mrs Alexander and the Duke and Duchess of Barham were over. Taking a deep breath, she squeezed his hand back. Now it was time to face the fact that her money was gone and soon Simon would be, as well.

Resilient. She had always been resilient.

He moved the curtain away from the window and looked out at Aunt Clara's brick town house. 'The knocker is on the door. They must have received word from your aunt that you will be staying with her.'

'Thank you for offering your assistance with the theft. I do feel much better knowing that there is someone else who wants to catch this thief as much as I do.'

'We will work out who did this. We'll review the series of events with Mr Sherman and hopefully develop a list of suspects.'

'I appreciate your optimism, but I am prepared that we may never find out who broke into the safe and that the money is long gone.'

'Remember, you are resilient.'

She had tried to remind herself of that a few minutes ago and it hadn't worked. She didn't feel very resilient. At the moment, she felt like crawling under the bedcovers and not coming out.

'Thank you for being my wife, Lizzy. Even if it was just for three days.'

From his melancholy expression it was apparent that he, too, knew that the moment she stepped out of the carriage things would not be the same between them. The reality of the real world was on the other side of that door.

He leaned over and kissed her softly before she stepped out of the carriage and fought back the tears in her eyes.

She had written a letter informing Mr Sherman that she had arrived in Town and that she would like to meet with him at Skeffington House the next day to discuss the theft. When she received his letter confirming the time, Lizzy wasn't certain if she was relieved to finally be able to find out all the details of how her life had changed or if she would rather go on in ignorance.

Since Aunt Clara had yet to arrive, there was no one in the house to distract her from her worries. Lizzy sent a footman to see if either of her sisters had returned to London, but neither Charlotte nor Juliet had. She was afraid to contact any of her friends for fear that the news of the robbery had got out.

When she arrived at Skeffington House, it felt odd to be announced by a footman who had once been her servant in a house that still held a substantial amount of her wardrobe. He escorted her to the Duke's study where she found Mr Sherman and Simon. Both had been sitting around Skeffington's old desk and stood when she walked in.

'Thank you for coming to speak with me, Mr Sherman, on such short notice,' she said, taking a seat in the chair beside her solicitor.

'You're welcome, Your Grace. I'm sorry I had to interrupt your holiday with such disturbing news.'

'So it really is gone? All of it?' She clasped her fingers tightly together on her lap.

'Not all of it—you still have two thousand pounds in the bank.' He glanced at Simon, who had resumed his seat at the desk. 'And the future income from Clivemoore House.'

How could she pay her servants, maintain her carriages and buy anything fashionable living on that? Was it even enough to live in Clivemoore House until next year's payment? What if it wasn't?

'Does anyone else know that my money is gone? Has word reached the papers or the ballrooms?' She braced herself while holding her breath.

'No,' Mr Sherman said. 'I have not told anyone. I was waiting for instructions from you on how you would prefer to handle the matter.'

She almost cried out in relief. At least she would not find satirical cartoons of herself in print-shop windows. Not yet, anyway.

Simon was watching her intently and she was glad when he shifted his attention to Mr Sherman.

'As you already know, Mr Sherman, Her Grace is interested in handling this matter privately and with discretion, so we have decided not to contact Bow Street about the robbery.'

From the look on Mr Sherman's face it was evident he did not approve of her decision. 'She had indicated that to me in her letter of response.' He turned to face Lizzy. 'I must say, with all due respect, it is not something I agree with. A substantial amount of money has been stolen. They are experts in retrieving such things. It is in your best interest to have them try to find whoever did this.'

'I understand and appreciate your concern, but my mind is made up.' She glanced over at Simon who gave her a supportive nod. At least she did not have to try to convince him it was a good idea.

Simon shifted his attention to the man sitting next to her. 'Who else to your knowledge would know the combination to the safe?'

Mr Sherman adjusted his wire-frame glasses and leaned forward. 'I have been giving this much consideration since I discovered the safe had been broken into. Her Grace gave me the combination of the safe when she retained my services—however, I've not shared it. If anyone else has the combination to it, Her Grace would be the only one to know that.'

'How did you find out the combination to the safe, Elizabeth?' Simon asked.

'My husband's family…your family…has a substantial collection of jewellery. I had access to the pieces during my marriage and would wear a number of them frequently. They are kept in the safe. Skeffington did not want any of the servants knowing the combination since he had kept money and other important papers in there, as well, so he told me the combination.' She turned to Mr Sherman. 'Was any of the jewellery taken?'

He gave a shrug. 'I'm not familiar with the pieces to be able to say.'

Simon folded his hands on his desk and studied Mr Sherman. 'How did you discover the money was stolen?'

'I came in to get money to pay the servants for Her Grace. Nothing appeared amiss when I entered the room that day. It was when I opened the safe that

I saw a large amount of the Duchess's money had
been stolen.'

Lizzy walked over to the bookcase next to the fireplace and pressed in the volume of *The Canterbury
Tales* that released the hinge of the small door that covered the outside of the safe. Whoever stole her money
would have had to know how to access the safe in the
first place. She dialled in the combination and tried to
prepare herself for an empty chamber. But when she
opened it, the stacks of velvet boxes were there. Simon
came up beside her and held out his hand. She handed
him box after box of his family's jewels.

'Is everything there?'

'I'm going to check. Simon, has anyone showed
you this safe before now?'

'Mr Mix showed it to me when he came to collect the snuffboxes your late husband had bequeathed
him.' He arched his brow, which told Lizzy that Simon
had placed the man on his list of suspects already.

Mr Mix had been employed by her husband even
before her marriage. She had known the man almost
half her life and he had always appeared very respectful and kind to her. The thought that this man might
have stolen money from her made her stomach drop.

'I am acquainted with Mr Mix. He has always pre-
sented himself as a gentleman of the finest character.
I do not think it is wise to accuse anyone of a crime if
there is no evidence,' Mr Sherman said with a troubled
look. 'Is there anyone else who might know about the
location of the safe and how to open it?'

Lizzy shook her head. 'We are not accusing him.
We are making a list of possibilities. I wasn't aware

of anyone else aside from myself who had the combination.'

One by one she opened the velvet-covered jewellery boxes, scanned the contents and returned them to the safe. The jewels were all there—every one of them. 'None of the jewellery is missing. If you risked breaking into this house and into that safe, why would you not take everything in it?'

'Money is easy to use,' Simon said with a shrug. 'It cannot be traced the way a piece of jewellery can. There is a chance that whoever broke into the safe was looking for something of mine. When they didn't find it, they took your money as a way to console themselves.'

Lizzy leaned back against the wall for support. 'I'll never get it back.'

'There is still a chance I can find it,' Simon said.

'And if you can't?'

'We could still contact Bow Street,' Mr Sherman offered.

Lizzy rubbed her arms, feeling a chill run through her body. 'No. No Bow Street.' She caught Simon's eye. 'I need to sit down with Mr Sherman and review my finances with him. I imagine my spending habits will need to change going forward.' She was trying to politely tell Simon that she wanted to speak with Mr Sherman alone. It was a small relief when he nodded in understanding.

'Find me when your business concludes. You and I still have matters to discuss.'

After reviewing her finances with Mr Sherman she was despondent and didn't think she would be able to climb out of it. Gone were her carriages pulled by four horses. She would have to make do with two horses and with only one carriage. She couldn't spend nearly as much on clothing as she had been and her elaborate balls and subscriptions to Drury Lane would have to be eliminated. And she did not have enough money to buy a town house in Mayfair. On her income, she would be living up in Clivemoore and if she wanted to remain in London for the Season she would have to stay at Aunt Clara's. The cost even to lease her own London town house was now prohibitive.

If she stayed in London for too long now, people were going to notice her change in behaviour. Within two weeks of living on her new budget, she would be drowning in false pity while those same women who had taunted her about marrying Skeffington would laugh behind her back.

She couldn't do it. She wouldn't endure that again.

While she was walking Mr Sherman to the door, Lizzy was saying a prayer of thanks that she had a solicitor who was trustworthy and one who she could afford to continue to use. After she had closed the door behind him, she turned to find Simon leaning on the doorway that led to the main corridor. He closed the distance between them and lowered his voice, even though they were alone.

'I can tell Mr Sherman did not deliver happy news.'

A sigh slipped out even though she was trying to hold it back. 'There are many things I will need to give up.'

'Let's see if we can find out who broke in.'

'And if we are not able to?'

'Then I will give you the money you need.'

Lizzy felt no relief in her chest. If he gave her money

now, it would almost feel as if he was trying to pay her for the time they spent together. Did he feel a particular sense of obligation to her because they had sex?

'I won't take your money, Simon. If these last three days have shown me anything, it is that I am adaptable. I need to find a way to live in this world without being dependent on your charity'

'Don't think of them as handouts. Think of them as help from one friend to another.'

It would feel too much like payment for their time together in bed. She knew that wasn't what he meant by his offer, but it was how it made her feel. She didn't want to feel as if she had been his kept woman for three days. She would rather remember their time together with her as his Duchess for three days. 'It is too much. I cannot accept your offer. I will rise to the challenge and adapt. I will find a way to make a new life for myself in Clivemoore.' She looked down at her reticule where her grandmother's jewels were kept. She hated to ask for help, but took a breath and met him in the eye. 'Would you do me one favour?'

'Of course.'

'I have some jewellery that belonged to my grandmother. Would you be able to arrange for them to be sold to a buyer outside London? I'd like to have more funds to put into my account and I would prefer not to see them on a woman of my acquaintance.'

'What makes you think I know how to do that?'

'That's what Mr Finley does, is it not? I saw the way he looked at my aunt's bracelet and how he knew where she had purchased it.'

'I will not confirm or deny what he does,' he said with a hint of a smile. 'However, I can get you the money for the jewels if you are certain you wish to sell them. Perhaps you should wait until we see if we can find the thief.'

'You will be leaving England soon and there is no one else I know of who can do this for me that I trust the way I trust you. I know word will not spread that I am selling my jewels if you are the one to do this for me.' She took a deep breath and held the velvet box out to him.

Their fingers touched before he took it from her hand.

'My grandmother told me to sell them if I needed to. I think I need to now. Do you think I will be able to get a reasonable amount for them? I've never sold any jewels before and I imagine it would be easy to have someone swindle you out of the true value of the pieces.'

'I would never allow that to happen.'

As he opened the box to look at them, Lizzy chewed on her lip and told herself that it was for times like this that her grandmother would have wanted her to sell them. It was still breaking her heart that she would have to part with them.

'This is the necklace I've seen you wear quite often. Lizzy, I will give you the money you need. I don't care what the will stipulated.'

'While I am touched by your very kind offer, if I economise and live at Clivemoore, I should be fine.'

'I don't understand why you won't let me help you this way.'

'I need to do this on my own.'

Simon looked down at the jewels once more before closing the box. 'Very well, I will see that you are well compensated for them. In return, allow me to take you to the British Museum tomorrow. Looking at old things, though you say you don't like them, might put a smile of your face, even if it is for only a little while. And there is something there that I want to show you.'

She didn't like old things and his mention of them had her thinking about living in Clivemoore and her head and heart began to ache. It was time she faced the fact that her life, from now on, would be up north away from her family and the people who loved her. And miles upon miles away from Simon.

Chapter Twenty

The next day, when Simon watched Lizzy walk into the drawing room of Mrs Sommersby's town house wearing a long-sleeved pink dress, it felt as if he hadn't seen her in weeks. He wanted to take her in his arms and kiss her and it took a tremendous amount of restraint not to. He would be leaving for Sicily in a few weeks. He had an excavation for the government to finish. And even if he was able to stay, it was only a matter of time before she'd grow weary of having him around. They had no future together and a sharp pain pierced his chest every time he was reminded of that. But before he left, he needed to find out why his house had been targeted and hopefully recover Lizzy's money in the process.

'I have some good news,' he said, hoping to make her smile.

She sat down on the sofa near the fire and patted the cushion beside her. 'Good news is always welcome. I don't feel as if I've had any in the past few months.'

'Well, this might make you feel better. I have found a buyer.'

'For my jewels? Already? But I just gave them to you yesterday.' She didn't appear to be as happy as he would have thought she'd be.

'Have you reconsidered selling them? We don't have to go through with the transaction.'

'No, it's just… I thought it would take some time, that's all. I want to sell them.'

'Well, the set is exceptional. The emeralds are of very fine quality. There is someone who is interested— however, they only want the necklace.'

'I never thought to break the set up. Do you know how much they are willing to offer me for it?'

'Four thousand pounds.'

Her eyes widened. 'For just the necklace? That can't be. Surely you must be mistaken.'

It was difficult to tell if she was pleased by the amount. 'Is that less than you were expecting?'

'No, it's more.' She leaned closer to him. 'You're certain?'

'Yes, I told you the stones are of high quality. I realise it's not all the money you lost, but with the right investments it will add to your yearly income. If you are interested in selling the earrings and bracelet, you will have more.'

'Thank you, Simon. I can't begin to tell you how much I appreciate your seeing to this for me. I think I will keep the earrings and the bracelet for now.'

'Very well. If you change your mind before I leave, let me know and I can see to finding a buyer for them, as well. I wanted to make certain that you were agreeable to the offered amount before I arrange for the exchange so I can have the money delivered here later today if that meets with your approval.'

'Yes, yes, by all means. I can secure the money in Aunt Clara's safe.'

'Let's hope it remains secure here.'

She leaned over and kissed his cheek. No one had ever done that before. It wasn't a sexual gesture. It was one that was done with pure affection and he felt a rush of joy flood his body that lasted until they entered the British Museum an hour later and he knew that wasn't a good thing.

He had been inside the museum a few times since he had been back in England. In fact, he had been meeting with one of the museum's curators right before he had met Lizzy at the reading of her husband's will. She had looked so sad yesterday that he had felt this need to try to find a way to make her happy, if only for a little while. Walking through the exhibitions, surrounded by objects of the past had always made him happy and perhaps he could offer her a few hours away from her troubles.

As they walked up the museum's stone staircase with light streaming in from the high-arched windows and the frescoed ceiling above them, he was also beginning to realise that in taking her here he would be sharing a part of his life with her and he was growing nervous wondering what she would think. For the first time in a very long while what someone thought of him mattered.

Their footsteps echoed as they made their way up towards the gallery that housed some of the ancient treasures he was responsible for bringing to the museum. When they walked through the doorway that began the collection of Greek and Roman ancient objects, he dug his hands into his pockets and looked over at Lizzy out of the corner of his eye. This is where his story began and he tried not to think too much about what she would think.

As they walked slowly along the frieze that once was at the top of the Parthenon in Athens, she studied the images with no expression and it was difficult to determine if she was bored.

'Have you visited the museum before today?' he asked, hoping to sound nonchalant.

'I have,' she replied, stopping at one particular area of the marble reliefs and peering closer at the half-man and half-horse figure in front of her. 'My sister Juliet had an interest in visiting. I took her here about a year ago. She found this place fascinating.'

'And you?'

She gave a slight lift to her shoulder. 'I confess I do not understand the appeal of objects such as this. It is lovely, but it's broken.'

'Broken things can be stunning.'

She didn't appear convinced.

'Think of how old that is. Think of the skill of the craftsman who carved it. It was all done out of one giant rock and now look at it. And that is over two thousand years old. All those years ago someone looked at a giant rock and said, "I am going to make something out of you."'

She leant closer to one particular panel and almost had her nose up against it, she was studying it so closely. 'You seem to enjoy them.'

'But you do not.'

'Maybe you are making me see them in a different way. I confess the day I was here with Juliet, I was more concerned with my dress fitting later that day and speaking with people that I knew here.' She continued to walk along and stopped at another section of the frieze. 'I understand these were attached to a building in Greece.'

'They were part of the Parthenon. It's an ancient temple.'

'It seems wrong that they were cut from the building and brought here.'

Over the years he had heard other people voice the same feeling. Lord Byron was one of them. 'I understand people feeling that way. I would have liked to have seen the Parthenon as it had looked before they removed them.'

'You've seen it?' She turned and looked at him with surprise.

'I have. I have been travelling around that part of the world since I left the navy.'

'Is it very large? This building they are from?'

'It is enormous. Men are dwarfed by the size of it. Think of our great cathedrals. That is the only comparison I can think to make.'

'How long were you in the navy?'

'Ten years. I had had enough of fighting and of war. And I had no desire to die in battle like my father.'

She stopped walking and turned to him. 'You have my condolences. Has he been gone long?'

It was hard enough talking about this without her eyes on him, so Simon continued to walk alongside the frieze. 'He died a year before I decided I no longer wanted a life at sea. I hadn't seen him in more than ten years. Occasionally, I would receive letters from him. I appreciate your condolences, but the sentiment is unnecessary. We were strangers to one another while he lived.'

'How did you find yourself in Greece after your career with the navy ended? I would think most men would have returned to England.'

'There was nothing for me here. I loved being out at sea and found work on a trading ship that sailed the Mediterranean. There is nothing quite like the colour of the water there. It is so clear, the blues and greens mix to create a turquoise sea. I cannot do it justice with my words. I wish I could show it to you.'

She stopped walking and looked over at him as if she were waiting for him to continue. He wasn't sure what she wanted him to say.

When he didn't continue, she left his side and walked to the statue of the horse's head and tilted her head as she studied it with her back to him. 'How did you go from sailing the seas to what you do now?'

'During one voyage in particular, the ship was transporting some ancient artefacts from a site in Sicily. They were all crated up, but the gentleman who was bringing them to the north of Italy allowed two of them to be opened so I could see the contents.'

She looked back at him with surprise. 'This gentleman spoke with you during the journey about these items? I am surprised you had time due to your duties on-board.'

'There is time to have conversations on-board a ship. Have you never crossed the Channel?'

They walked on into the next room where there were two ancient vases that he had uncovered during a dig last year and sold to the museum. The urn-like vases were made out of clay and painted black. Both had white cameo reliefs on them, which depicted various scenes from ancient life, and he was fighting the urge to pull her by her arm to see them.

'No, I've never crossed the Channel,' she replied. 'I've never left England, for that matter. I was not given the opportunity.'

'You've not even seen Scotland?'

She shook her head, appearing uncomfortable with the admission.

'That's a pity. The world beyond this country is a beautiful and wondrous place.'

They walked silently side by side as she looked at each of the items on display. When she reached his vases, she took her time studying the reliefs and he put his hands behind his back while he waited for her impression.

'These remind me of my tea set.' There was a trace of wonder in her voice. 'I mean your tea set now. The blue Wedgwood set that I bought for Stonehaven, although this is black. How astonishing!' She looked back at the vases and studied them closer.

The smile on Simon's face would not go away as much as he tried to appear unaffected by her words and he rocked back on the heels of his boots. 'Mr Wedgwood has based his style on vases such as this one.'

She looked back at him in surprise. 'I had no idea. I suppose I never gave much thought to where his inspiration came from. I thought he made it up on his own.' Her attention was drawn once more to the two vases. 'How do you know that about him?'

'I have friends who were also friends of Sir William Hamilton. His books that contained drawings of items such as these had been studied by Mr Wedgwood, or so I've been told.' He stepped up beside her, and grazed his knuckles gently across hers. He just couldn't help touching her. Heat from that brief contact spread throughout his body.

Their eyes met and he knew she felt it, as well. 'Have you seen objects such as these when you travel?'

'Those vases you were admiring that reminded you of your tea set—I found them.'

'You did? How? Where? How is it that they are in this museum?' Her astonishment was evident in her voice.

'Over the years I have found a group of friends that share my interest in ancient artefacts. We hear about certain areas where people have found remains of ancient objects in the ground and we enter into agreements with local governing bodies to excavate those areas to see if there are additional objects we can bring back to the light of day. Some of the items are sold to private collectors and some, like those vases, are sold to museums. The majority of what is found is given to the local government. It is based on agreements we have with them.'

Her attention was back on the vases. 'How are they not broken? How is it that they are in such pristine condition?'

'They were found in what had been a home that was buried underground. The area they were in was a pocket that had not been completely filled in with dirt so digging them out wasn't as difficult as I've encountered at other times.'

'Are there other things you've found that are in the museum?'

Her interest in what he had collected, in what he did, had him standing a bit taller as he held out his arm for her to take before showing her the small statue of an ancient Roman goddess that was in the next room. After having the childhood he had, it was still surprising when someone took any interest in what he did.

After she had visually inspected that one thoroughly and asked him about how he discovered it, they continued on to various other exhibits.

At one particular display she had asked him about what it symbolised and he went into a probably too-long explanation of the Roman gods and goddesses.

She looked at him over a case of ancient jewellery. 'You truly enjoy digging in the ground.' This seemed to amuse and astonish her because, for the first time since they entered the building, she smiled.

'I think it is valuable to retrieve items that have been buried underground and bring them to people and institutions so that they can be admired and studied. It's important to understand what came before us. How would you get to experience ancient civilizations otherwise? You yourself said you were unable to travel outside England. The objects in this museum help to bring a bit of those countries to you. You might be able to look at drawings, but a drawing cannot compare to seeing the beauty of the real thing in person with your own eyes.'

'You truly do enjoy uncovering these items. I can see your enthusiasm when you talk about them.'

'I always have in the past, but nothing compares to watching your astonishment and pleasure at the realisation that your Wedgwood set really is based on objects people used thousands of years ago. It now feels as if all that time I spent digging in that location was to uncover those vases just for you.'

His spontaneous honest admission took him aback. It would do no good to travel down that road with her. She would never want a future with him. She would never really want to be his Duchess. She would only grow tired of him after a while and leave. The only thing he could offer her was his money and the security it would give her. If he asked her to stay with him and she agreed, that would be the real reason. She had married his predecessor for this title and fortune. He couldn't live his life knowing that the only reason she'd want to marry him would be to regain her fortune.

'You said earlier that you could not stay out too late today,' he said, guiding her through another doorway. 'I assume you've accepted an invitation to a ball or some other grand event.'

'I am to meet Mrs Thacker. You remember the woman who was the housekeeper at Skeffington House? She has finally decided to sell that painting that Skeffington left to her in his will and it will be auctioned off later today. She had asked if I would accompany her to explain the proceedings to her.'

'That is kind of you to do so.'

'I had arranged the appraisal for her. I thought I'd be in Dorset, but now that I am here in London, I sent word to her that I will be available to go with her.'

'A duchess and a housekeeper. That doesn't sound like you.'

'Mrs Thacker was always very helpful to me after I was married to His Grace. She was the lady's maid to Skeffington's first wife. She understood things about him that helped me manoeuvre in the murky waters of his temperament.'

'So you are repaying the favour.'

'In a way. She was hesitant to sell the painting for sentimental reasons. But a woman has to be realistic. I told her that by selling it, she would have a way to provide for herself. I believe that being able to leave her life of service was not something she thought she could ever do.'

'It must have been a substantial amount.'

'Three thousand pounds.'

'No wonder she is selling the painting.'

'What will you be doing this evening?' Her voice was light as she walked beside him—unusually light for Lizzy.

'A friend has invited me to join the Travellers Club. I thought it would be a good idea to have somewhere to go for the times I am in London.'

'I believe you had mentioned to the Prime Minister that you would not be joining White's when we first met. So this means you will be coming back every now and again?' She stopped walking and he could tell she was watching him closely.

'I really don't have a choice, do I? There will be things that will require my attention in the coming years, I would assume.'

'Of course. Over the years you would be needed.'

People were walking past them and the chatter of voices from various conversations was going on around them—but neither Simon nor Lizzy were paying any attention to them as they stood in the middle of the British Museum looking at one another. Simon had booked passage on a ship leaving England in two weeks to return to Sicily. He had commitments to fulfil, but he knew leaving her would be one of the hardest things he had ever had to do. He only hoped that he could see that she was settled well before he left.

Chapter Twenty-One

Simon had spent the next two days working with Mr Sherman trying to locate Mr Mix. It appeared the man had disappeared. Simon had been to the Albany where the gentleman had a suite of rooms, only to be told by the porter that he had not seen the man in almost a fortnight. This didn't seem to concern him since he explained that Mr Mix would often leave London at this time of year to visit his sister. Unfortunately for Simon, the man did not know Mr Mix's sister's name or where she lived.

Later that night he managed to break into the man's set of rooms, only to find that everything appeared undisturbed as if he had gone out for the evening and planned to return by morning. No money was stashed away as far as he could tell. Was it possible that something sinister had happened to the man? Hopefully Mr Sherman was having more luck finding out who Mr Mix was now working for since he had declined to remain as secretary to the Duke of Skeffington.

Simon had spent another evening at the Travellers Club, needing something to get his mind off Lizzy.

He was grateful to be invited to join the gentlemen's club by Captain Jonathan Barry, who he had served under in the navy. He preferred the men here to the ones who frequented the likes of White's and Boodle's. The gentlemen who belonged to the Travellers Club had a broader view of the world beyond the shores of Britain and they had a keen interest in what he did. In fact, a few of them had benefited directly from his excavations.

Upon returning home, all he wanted to do was grab a good book and crawl into bed. Soon he would be spending weeks at sea and even though he could fall asleep easily on a ship, there was nothing like the plush comfort of the beds in the Skeffington homes. He wanted to enjoy them for as long as he could since he didn't know when he would be coming back.

He was just taking off his greatcoat in his entrance hall when he spotted Lizzy step out of one of the drawing-room doorways at the far end of the hall. The sight of her in a crimson gown with her black hair artfully arranged in an upsweep took his breath away. For the past two days he had tried to stop thinking about her, but she had been sending him letters asking if he had any new thoughts on who might have broken into the safe, so she had been making it very hard to do.

Handing his greatcoat to the footman who had opened the door for him, he dismissed the man for the night.

'You haven't answered any of my letters.'

'I have had nothing to write back.'

'Nothing?'

'There has been no progress.' He had promised her

he would help her retrieve her money. Mr Mix was the only lead they had. The fact that he was unable to locate the man was burning a hole in his gut and it was hard to face her. 'I will notify you when we have pertinent information.'

He walked past her to go to his study to fetch the book he had been reading earlier in the day. It was painful to be alone with her, knowing he would be leaving her soon.

But instead of leaving, she ran up to his side. 'What kind of progress has been made so far?'

Her soft floral perfume swirled on the air around them and as much as he didn't want to, he couldn't help taking a deep breath. He stopped in the hallway to face her.

'I have visited his home and he has not been seen for a while. I broke into his suite of rooms and nothing appears amiss. It looks as if he went out in the morning and did not return. However, I have no way to tell if he packed some things and left to visit family or friends.'

'And you couldn't write to me and tell me that in a letter?'

'I didn't see any reason to. It tells us nothing.' He needed to put distance between them. Hoping she would get the hint, he again made for his study.

She continued to follow him. 'Are you purposely avoiding me?'

He stopped again and ran his hand through his hair. When he turned she was directly behind him and they were only two feet apart. Immediately his gaze dropped to her lips. The corridor was dark and deserted—and perfect for stealing a quick kiss.

How he missed kissing her.

He saw her gaze drop to his mouth as she wet her lips. He would be leaving England soon. If he kissed her now, she would be even harder to forget.

Before he had the chance to decide what to do, she closed the distance between them, pulled his head down to hers and kissed him. It started out as a simple kiss, but when she went to pull back, he threaded his fingers through the back of her hair and deepened the kiss. Her response was to slide her arms around his waist so now their bodies were pressed against each other. It was heaven and hell at the same time. He knew he wanted her, but he had to leave her.

Reluctantly he pulled away. In the dim light he could see her watching him with her lips still wet from their kiss. 'We can't do this. Go home, Elizabeth. I promise I will send word when I have news. In the meantime, you can also direct your questions to Mr Sherman.'

Her hand went to her stomach and he saw her chest rise with the deep breath she took. 'Very well. I won't bother you further.' She spun on her heel and stormed off towards the entrance hall.

Simon watched her until she turned the corner. He scrubbed his hand across his mouth, needing to wipe away that kiss and any reminders of what he could not have.

Now, more than ever, he needed that book to keep his mind off of the woman who had turned his life upside down. He went into his study and walked directly to his desk where he had left the leather-bound tome. The faint candlelight in the hallway cast a dim light into the room and his thoughts turned to spending time with her in her bedchamber the last night of their travels. An urge to go after her was growing. They had so little time left to be together that part of him wanted to enjoy every last second that he had with her. His mind, however, was telling him that going after her would be the stupidest thing he had ever done.

As he reached for the book, the top paper on a small stack of bills fluttered. A window was open—and Simon wasn't alone. Slowly he moved his right hand down and opened up the top drawer of the desk. His hand wrapped around the handle of his gun. It wasn't loaded, but he prayed whoever was lurking by the window would not realise that.

He raised the gun quickly and aimed it at the startled expression of the man he had been looking for, standing in the faint moonlight across the room by the heavy blue curtains.

'Mr Mix, how kind of you to call. I've been looking for you.'

'Your Grace, I… I…'

'You can either tell me what you are doing here…' he cocked the gun '…or I can shoot you for trespassing.'

Even in the dim light of the room, Simon could see the man, wearing a dark greatcoat, take a step back.

Just then Lizzy stormed into the room behind him. 'You truly don't want to see me any more, do—'

He hadn't moved from pointing his gun at Mr Mix, afraid if he took his eyes off the man, he would jump out the open window into the bushes below and get away.

Her gasp was loud enough for him to hear and he wasn't sure if her exclamation was because she realised he was holding a gun or because of the presence of the man it was pointed at.

'Elizabeth, look who decided to pay us a call.'

'Mr Mix, where did you come from?'

'The open window is my guess.'

Out of the corner of his eye he could see her step closer to his side.

'You have a gun?'

'Yes, and lucky for us that I do. Mr Mix here was about to tell me what he is doing here. And I suggest you tell us the truth, sir. I have very little patience for people who lie.' He stepped around his desk and walked slowly towards the man.

'I came because I had forgotten something. I knew that Her Grace had left for the country and was told that you were still abroad. I didn't want to inconvenience either of you so I decided to come here when I thought no one was at home.'

'How very considerate of you and, pray tell, what was it that you forgot?'

Mr Mix scanned the room as if he were trying to find something that he could have possibly forgotten.

Once more Lizzy stepped to Simon's side. 'Did you also forget the jewels when you went into the safe recently?' Sarcasm dripped from her voice. 'Is that what you forgot and had to come back to get?'

'No, Your Grace. I don't know what you're talking about.'

'My money was stolen from that safe, Mr Mix,' she stated clearly, pointing to the bookcase where the safe was located. 'You knew that combination. How could you do that to me? How could you steal my future like that? What is it that I did to wrong you?'

Mr Mix rubbed the back of his neck. 'I don't think of it as stealing.'

'What would you call it?' Lizzy demanded.

He started to wring his hands in front of him. 'I would call it *borrowing.* I needed to borrow the money to purchase something, but then I was going to resell the item and put all the money back.'

'What something did you want to purchase?' Simon asked.

'A painting.'

'It must be a very special painting if you went to all this trouble to get it.'

'It is.'

'But you're not keeping it?'

Lizzy rubbed her forehead. 'This doesn't make any sense.'

Mr Mix looked over at Lizzy and nervously licked his lips. 'When the Duke died, I… I had been promised something in the will by your husband, but he did not give it to me.'

'I know what that feels like,' Lizzy mumbled under her breath, but loud enough for Simon to hear.

'I simply wanted to collect what was rightfully mine.'

'The only painting mentioned in the will was Mrs Thacker's.' Simon was just as confused as Lizzy. 'Then if it means so much to you, why are you telling us your plan is to resell it?'

'It's not the painting that has meaning. It's what was hidden in the painting. You see, there was a letter that was written to me by someone I hold very dear. The old Duke had found the letter in my coat pocket a number of years ago when I had been working in just my shirtsleeves.'

'So he took this letter from you and hid it? That sounds like something my husband would have done, but for what purpose?'

'He didn't approve of the contents, but I think he couldn't bring himself to bear the burden of responsibility by turning it in. He also felt it would reflect poorly on him to have employed someone like me.'

Simon shook his head. 'And you believe this letter is hidden behind Mrs Thacker's painting?'

'He told me he would see that the letter was released from his possessions after he died by including it in his will. I assumed this meant he would be returning it to me and I couldn't understand why he gave me his snuffbox collection, but then I thought it might have been hidden in one of the larger boxes. However, all that was inside those boxes were lewd images of men and women. Rimsby received the chess set. No letter could be hidden in those pieces. The only logical conclusion was that the letter was hidden in the frame of Mrs Thacker's painting.'

'Why didn't you try to get the painting months ago?'

'I did try, but each time I attempted to get into the house, I would see a servant or Her Grace. I was afraid I would get caught. I knew if I just waited, eventually Her Grace would leave Town for the holidays and it would be easier to get into the house without someone seeing me. But a few weeks ago I met Mrs Thacker in the park and she informed me her painting was going up for auction and was stored in the vault at the auction house. I knew I would never be able to steal it from Christie's and the only way I would get it is if I purchased it at the auction. I just wanted to borrow the money to get the painting.'

'I was at the auction that day,' Lizzy muttered. 'I saw the person who bought the painting. It was a woman.'

Mr Mix nodded. 'I had someone act as my purchasing agent. I couldn't risk anyone seeing me and wondering how a man of my means could afford to buy a painting like that.'

'And was the letter attached to it?'

'It was behind the painting in the frame.'

'Why would your husband have done that?' Simon asked as he glanced at Lizzy.

'I think he wanted to torture me about it,' said Mr Mix, 'and make certain that I did not live a peaceful day for the remainder of my life.'

'Damn it, man, what is in that letter that would cause you to steal money and risk being hanged to get it back?'

'I can't say.'

'I am pointing a gun at you and if you expect me to believe any of this, I suggest you tell me.'

'If word gets out, I could be hanged.'

'We are not about to run to the papers with the news, are we, Your Grace?' He glanced at Lizzy out of the corner of his eye, while keeping the gun pointed at Mr Mix.

'No, I know what it is like to have my husband exert his powerful position over you. I will not give up your secret, sir.'

Mr Mix looked visibly ill. 'You have my word, sir,' he said, 'on my honour, I am telling you the truth. Is that not enough?'

'Since you broke into my house, Mr Mix, and stole

Her Grace's money, I don't think you can hang your hat on the honour you seem to think you have.'

He rubbed the back of his neck. 'It was a love letter.'

'And the woman is married,' Lizzy said with speculation in her voice.

But then Simon saw the way Mr Mix was reacting. This was a level of nervousness and discomfort that went far beyond a clandestine affair with a married woman. He held Mr Mix's gaze and then he understood.

It wasn't a woman. That was why it was so imperative that Mr Mix get it back. British law forbade a relationship between two men. Mr Mix was right. His life would be in danger if someone found the letter and reported him.

No man in his right mind would admit to a relationship with another man to a virtual stranger and place his future in jeopardy, but he had to be certain.

Mr Mix saw fit to plead his case. 'His Grace did not approve of my relationship, to say the least. When I came to borrow the money out of the safe, I had no idea how much the painting would cost, so I took all of it. I knew Her Grace would be out of London for at least a month based on years past and knew she would not need the money until she returned. I planned to return all the money once I was able to sell the painting. But I saw Her Grace leaving St James's Church after service yesterday and knew I had to return whatever money I had now. I knew she would realise the money was missing. If I returned even a portion of it now, I thought she might not notice. That is why I came back tonight. I put back all the money that I did not need to buy the painting. I swear I will be able to return the rest when I find a way to resell it.'

'Elizabeth, why don't you go see if the money is there?'

A few minutes later she confirmed it was.

Simon lowered his gun. 'Where is the painting now?'

'At a friend's house for safekeeping. Since we had to remove it from the frame, it needs to be reframed before I can arrange to sell it again.'

'I can probably help you with that,' Simon said, letting out a breath.

'You would do that for me?'

'Considering that the money will be going to Her Grace, yes, I would do that. I understand now why you broke in. There is no need to involve Bow Street. You've returned some of the money already and soon, hopefully, the rest will follow. You have your letter now. It is over. But understand me and understand me clearly. If you ever enter my house again without permission, I will shoot you. Maybe not in the heart or in the head, but somewhere you will feel the effects afterwards for a very long time.'

Mr Mix shifted nervously on his feet. 'Will you tell anyone about this?'

'What is written on that page is between you and whoever sent it to you. It is not my concern or anyone else's. I will not be telling anyone about it. Duchess, will you?'

'All of us have secrets, Mr Mix. I will not be sharing yours.'

Simon wasn't certain that she completely understood the extent of Mr Mix's secret, but there was a sombreness to her tone that revealed how sincere she was in her statement.

Mr Mix almost staggered with his relief. 'Thank you. I do not know what to say.' There was a catch in his voice.

'Go home, Mr Mix. I will come to see you tomorrow morning at your residence. And leave through the front door, if you please. There is no need to climb out of my window now.'

When Mr Mix walked out of the room, Simon went over to his desk, placed the gun back in the drawer and lit the oil lamp. His nerves were strung tight after realising there had been an intruder in the room with him and he went to the table by the unlit fireplace and poured himself a glass of port.

'Can I offer you anything? I'm sorry to say I only have port and brandy.'

'No, thank you.' As if she realised she hadn't moved from her spot, she shook her head and went towards the door. 'I should leave. I'll have a nice cup of tea when I get home.'

He recalled how all of this had started when she had stayed at Stonehaven to have some tea. It felt like a bittersweet memory now.

Catching her eye, he gave her a small smile. 'I think I need something a bit stronger than tea after all that.'

The corner of her mouth lifted. 'There might be brandy in my cup, as well.'

She turned and walked out of the room, and Simon went swiftly after her.

'Can I escort you to your aunt's?' he asked, walking up beside her as she headed for the entrance hall.

'No, thank you. My carriage is parked by the

square. It is a short walk and I could use some air after all that.'

When he went to open the door, she put her hand gently on his sleeve to stop him.

'I'm sorry I kissed you. It was a foolish thing to do.'

He raised her chin so she was looking at him. 'Please don't apologise for kissing me. If you were foolish for doing it, then I was foolish for wanting you to.'

When he closed the door behind her, he leaned against it and knew the sooner he left London, the sooner his heart would stop hurting. At least, he hoped so.

Chapter Twenty-Two

Lizzy should have had a restful night's sleep. She had most of her money back and, once they were able to sell the painting, she would have all of it and an additional four thousand pounds that Simon had been able to get for her emerald necklace. There was still a chance Lady Wallingford's town house on Mount Street would be coming up for sale and she would send a letter to Mr Sherman, asking him to enquire about it again. All these were good things. She would be able to remain in London. No one would know she'd had a financial setback and her reputation as a premier hostess in Society was intact. So, why had she only been able to get a few hours of sleep last night?

'Lizzy, I hope you won't be this melancholy when your sister arrives. Juliet should be here shortly,' Aunt Clara commented from beside her on the sofa.

Sunlight was streaming into the morning Drawing Room from the window behind her aunt so Lizzy had to squint her eyes to look at her. 'I am simply tired. That is all.'

Her aunt gave her a sympathetic pat on her leg.

'That is very understandable. You did return very late last night.'

'How do you know what time I returned to the house last night?'

'I asked Brent to inform me of it.'

'Aunt, I am a grown woman.'

'Forgive me if I was concerned for your well-being.'

'Well, as you can see I made it home fine. I am fine.'

'Are you?'

'Of course I am. I have the money that was stolen. No one knows it was taken. My life will go on as it has been. I might even have a ball in a silent celebration once I settle into my new town house.' She tried her best to sound excited at the prospect. 'And soon I will hear if Lady Wallingford's house is up for sale. Everything in my life is wonderful.'

'And yet you don't look happy.'

'I told you. I am just tired.'

Lizzy took a sip of her tea and was saved from having to answer any more of her aunt's questions by the arrival of a footman in the doorway. Thank heavens her sister was here. It would deflect some of the attention off her. But instead of announcing Juliet, the footman announced the Duke of Skeffington.

Her heart flipped over in her chest and for the first time all day she felt like smiling. She touched the back of her hair for any stray tendrils that might have come loose and then froze when he strode into the room. For a man who had helped her catch a thief, he did not look particularly happy.

'Your Grace,' her aunt called out with a warm voice, 'it is so good to see you again.'

Her aunt waited until the footman left the room

and closed the door before she stood and walked up to Simon. 'I am so grateful for the help you've given my niece.' She held her hand out to him and he shook it. 'Can I offer you some tea?' she asked, gesturing to the pot on the table in front of Lizzy.

'Yes, please,' he replied, taking a seat beside Lizzy.

'A nice cup of tea on a cold day like today is just the thing. How do you take it?'

'Without milk or sugar, please.'

He finally looked at Lizzy and she wished he wouldn't leave England, but she knew he didn't want to stay. She wasn't the kind of woman a man would change his life for.

'Why don't I leave your tea here?' Aunt Clara offered. 'I do have a few things to attend to elsewhere in the house. You wouldn't mind if I leave the two of you alone for a bit, would you?'

'No,' they both said in unison.

Lizzy was too busy watching Simon to notice when her aunt left the room. Neither she nor he seemed to be in a hurry to speak.

'I didn't sleep at all last night,' he finally said.

'Neither did I,' she admitted.

'I went with Mr Mix's associate to deliver the painting to Phillips auction house with all the necessary paperwork. They will be reframing it and storing it in their vault until it's auctioned off later this month. You should have all your money back soon.'

She took a deep breath, but that didn't help to make her feel any better. 'Then that is it. I am all settled thanks to you.'

'To me?'

'Yes, you handled yourself very well with Mr Mix.

If I had stumbled upon him like you did, I don't know what I would have done.'

'You would have handled yourself spectacularly well, I have no doubt.'

'When are you returning to Sicily?'

'I'll be leaving London tomorrow to head to the coast. I'm allowing extra time to travel. One snowstorm could delay my journey and I have booked passage on a ship that leaves from Portsmouth on the morning of the fifteenth. I could miss my ship if I don't give myself enough time.'

Why wasn't she enough for him? What was wrong with her that he didn't want to stay? 'How long will you be gone?'

He raked his hand through his hair—hair that she now knew felt like silk to the touch. 'I don't know. I suppose until I find what I am looking for.'

Her eyes met his and she willed herself not to cry. 'What is it you're looking for?'

As if he was avoiding answering her, he leant forward and rested his elbows on his knees. 'I'll know it when I see it,' he replied, looking down at his clasped hands.

She was right beside him. She was right there! But she wasn't what he was looking for. What could she possibly do to make him fall in love with her?

Lizzy reached for her tea to have something to do that did not involve watching him.

'I'll be glad to leave this cold behind.' His gaze was still focused on his hands as he told her how much he was looking forward to leaving her. 'I can't wait to feel the warm sun on my face.'

'I'm sure that will feel heavenly.' She didn't even try to sound the least bit happy for him.

'I wish I could show you the Mediterranean Sea, Lizzy. And I wish you could taste the amazing food in all the small villages and see how wonderful the people are. I wish I could show you what I do so you could feel the excitement that fills you when you uncover something that hasn't seen the light of day for centuries.'

His words hung in the air and she tried to take a sip of tea, but it was impossible to swallow. If he had really wanted her to see all that, he would ask her to go with him. If he really wanted her...

She had made a fool out of herself thinking Lord Andrew had wanted her for his wife. She would not make that mistake again.

He looked over at her hand that was wrapped around her teacup and traced the small scar from where his sword had cut her. 'Forgive me for hurting you.'

'I do,' she managed to say without her voice breaking. 'I wouldn't have had it any other way. Thank you for not treating me as anything other than a worthy opponent that day.'

'You are a worthy opponent, Lizzy. You were fearless.'

She let out a soft laugh. 'Your final word to describe me?'

'I suppose so.'

He needed to leave. He really did or she was bound to start sobbing.

'Lizzy, why did you want Stonehaven so much?' he asked. 'I've been to the other estates and I'm trying to see what it was about that house that made you so determined to have it.'

She looked up at him and she knew it would be impossible to hide the sadness in her eyes. 'It just felt like home.'

She thought his eyes grew glassy for a moment, but it must have been a trick of the light. A small smile played on his lips. 'And I thought it might have been because of the impressive garden and conservatory.'

'When my father first sold me off to Skeffington, the only thing in my life that gave me joy was the time I spent at Stonehaven with my sisters and my aunt. When I was out in the gardens there I felt free again. The cloud that always hung over me when my husband was around did not surface there because he would rarely take the trip out to Dorset. It was my sanctuary and because of that it was the one place in the world that felt like home.'

Simon reached into his pocket and pulled out what appeared to be a letter. 'I want you to have this.' He held it out to her.

As she scanned the words, she couldn't hold back the few tears that slipped down her cheek, making it impossible to read. 'I don't understand.'

'Don't cry on it. You will make the ink run.' Although his voice was teasing, it lacked the lightness and levity that should have been there. 'I had Mr Nesbit draft that up. It gives you the right to live indefinitely in Stonehaven, until your death or should you marry. All you have to do is sign that paper and the one below it, which transfers Clivemoore back to me. Unless you have no desire to—'

'I don't understand. Stonehaven belongs to you. We

even had a duel for it and it was apparent it was destined to be yours. Why are you giving it to me now?'

'Because I am not like your husband and now you will have that house to remind you of that.'

His words brought a sad smile to her lips as she recalled when he asked her why she wouldn't call him Skeffington. She told him then that it was because he was nothing like the previous Duke of Skeffington. She didn't need this house to know that.

'You don't appear to be as happy as I thought you would,' he said, his forehead creasing.

She needed to lie. She would spend every day of her life in that house thinking about him and their brief time together in those rooms. 'I am very happy.'

'If you sign the papers now, I will get them back to Mr Nesbit before I leave for Portsmouth. He will notify you when the filings are complete.'

For so long she had wanted Stonehaven, but now that it was tied to his leaving she was having trouble signing her name on the papers as she sat at the lady's writing desk by the window.

'Thank you,' she said, handing the papers back to him. 'This is very kind of you.'

'I hope you will be happy there.'

This was it. He was leaving. And she didn't know if or when she would ever see him again. The pain in her heart was becoming unbearable. If he stayed much longer, she was bound to start crying.

'I'm sure you have arrangements to make before you leave. I don't want to keep you longer than necessary.'

He tipped his head politely at her. 'Please send me a letter if you need anything. Mr Nesbit will know how to reach me.'

'I will. Please take care of yourself. Do not place yourself in any unnecessary danger.'

He gave a small laugh. 'I shall try not to.'

She reached out and patted his brown coat just above his heart, needing to touch him one last time. He caressed her cheek before lowering his lips to her forehead. When he stepped back, she was proud of herself for being able to hold back her tears.

It would have been acceptable to let him walk out of the room and find his own way to the entrance hall, but she wanted to stay with him until the very last second he would walk out of her life. They made their way slowly down the corridor, not saying a word to each other. They always were good at sharing silence. When they reached the front door of the deserted entrance hall, he turned to face her one last time. 'Be fearless, Duchess, in everything you do.'

The lump in her throat was back and all she could manage was a slight nod of acknowledgement before he turned and walked out of the door and out of her life—leaving her alone. Just like every man before him and just like everyone after him.

'*That* is the new Duke of Skeffington?' It was Juliet's voice that broke the sombre stillness of the hall from where she was standing just outside the drawing room.

Lizzy brushed her cheeks and willed her tears to dry. She had become very good at putting on a mask over the years. If she gave Juliet her undivided attention, she prayed she could stay composed and not crumble from the pain of her broken heart.

'The air is very cold outside today,' Lizzy said, walking towards her sister. 'I didn't realise it until

His Grace opened the door to leave and the cold air stung my eyes.'

They hugged the moment she reached Juliet. That hug meant more to her at that moment than Juliet would ever know. She ran her hands down Juliet's arms and held her hands. Her sister was her anchor and she wasn't even aware of it. 'Look at you. You look like someone's wife.'

Juliet's smile brightened her entire face.

'You are positively radiant. When did you arrive?'

'A few minutes ago. Our aunt pulled me into this drawing room saying you were with the new Duke in the other one and we were not to disturb you.'

Lizzy hooked arms with Juliet and guided her down the hall to the drawing room she had just been sharing with Simon.

'You never mentioned how handsome the new Duke is when you talked about him.' Juliet took a seat on the sofa, pushed Simon's cup across the table, reached for a new one and began to fix herself a cup of tea.

Aunt Clara walked into the room before Lizzy could answer. 'I hope you did not disturb your sister and His Grace, Juliet. I told you I would be but a minute and then, when I returned, I find you in here with your sister.'

'I waited until he left before I came out to greet her.' She looked up from stirring her tea. 'And why did *you* not tell me the new Duke was handsome?'

'I didn't have time to. You just arrived.'

Juliet looked between the two of them. 'Something is going on here and neither one of you is telling me what it is.'

Lizzy looked over at her aunt who was usually

fairly forthcoming when it came to family news, but she was also exceptional at keeping secrets.

'Lizzy had been disappointed we were unable to stay at Stonehaven during Twelfth Night. That is all.' Aunt Clara glanced at Lizzy before she focused her attention on Juliet.

'I'm sorry, Lizzy,' Juliet said with real remorse. 'I know how much you like that house and it was lovely having you so close to Aunt Clara's home in Bath.'

'Oh, heavens, I forgot.' Lizzy turned to Aunt Clara. 'He has given me Stonehaven in exchange for Clivemoore. He came here to tell me.'

Her aunt threw her arms around Lizzy and gave her a tight hug. 'That's wonderful news! I hoped he might.' She stepped back and smiled. 'I am so very happy for you. You have everything you ever wanted. You have a good fortune and you have Stonehaven.' There was a marked look as she held Lizzy's gaze for a few moments longer than necessary.

Was her aunt trying to tell her that she knew what Lizzy really wanted was Simon? Was it so obvious to everyone that she was already missing him? There had to be a way to lock this pain inside and go on with her life as if she had never met the new Duke of Skeffington.

'So tell us, Juliet,' Aunt Clara said, directing her attention to Lizzy's younger sister, 'for someone who on her wedding day didn't look at all happy to be marrying her husband, how is married life?'

Lizzy didn't want to hear about her sister's honeymoon. She didn't want to hear about anyone's marriage for the rest of her life.

Juliet took a sip of tea, put the cup gently down

in the saucer on her lap and then sighed. Her little sister, who wasn't so very little any more at two and twenty, just sighed thinking about her marriage. And it wasn't even the kind of sigh you made when you were disgusted with something. This was the kind of sigh you made when you were in love. Lizzy wanted to push her off the sofa.

'I thought you didn't want to marry Monty,' she reminded her.

'Yes, well, first I did and then I didn't, but now I am happy that I did. It's much better that it happened now. If we had run away together when I wanted to, I don't think we would be as happy as we are now.'

Both Aunt Clara and Lizzy stared at her in shock.

'What do you mean—run away together?' Lizzy asked slowly, not sure if she wanted to hear the explanation.

'Oh, I suppose it doesn't matter now.' She let out a deep breath. 'When your husband refused to allow Monty to marry me all those years ago, I suggested to him that we run away together.'

Lizzy had to blink a couple of times. 'Juliet, do you realise how scandalous that is?'

'Of course, but at the time I didn't care. At the time all I knew was I loved him and I would do anything to be with him.' She looked with sympathetic eyes at Lizzy. 'I know that this might be hard for you to understand, but sometimes when you love someone, you have to be fearless, otherwise you will never be together.'

Chapter Twenty-Three

As if leaving London wasn't painful enough, Simon watched the snow start to fall outside his carriage window. He really did despise English winters. Just the thought of being in the sunshine in Sicily in a few weeks' time should have filled him with happiness. Instead, all he had to comfort him on his journey was the warming box at his feet and a heavy blanket to keep him warm. How he missed snuggling with Lizzy at his side as they rode back to London together.

He wondered if she was sitting by a fire in Mrs Sommersby's town house. He wondered if she missed him—and how soon it would take for her to forget him. Just that thought enlarged the hole in his heart that appeared when he left her.

The snow was starting to come down harder and he cursed himself for staying last night at the Merry Widow on the outskirts of London. They should have left the inn when the sun came up. But it had been difficult to get back on the road this morning. Each mile he travelled was taking him further and further away from London—and from the woman he loved.

When the snowfall became so great that it was difficult to see far into the fields they were passing, he rapped on the carriage roof and Tom's face appeared at the trapdoor. Snowflakes clung to his woollen scarf and to the brim of his hat.

'How much further, Tom? Do you think with the conditions this poor we will be able to make it?'

'Aye, sir, The Centrebridge Inn is not much further up the road. We should reach it in less than half an hour.'

Simon was such a sentimental fool. He should never have told his coachman to go to that inn. He should have told him to find the nearest inn and get them out of the snow—yet he couldn't. He just didn't want to let go of the time he had spent with Lizzy.

Once more he rubbed the stones in the emerald necklace that she had worn and that he now held in his hand. The gold had once lain against her soft skin and he was grateful he had decided to keep it for himself and not have Adam sell it off. It was all he had left of her.

As they approached the inn, it wasn't as quiet as it had been the night he stayed there with Lizzy. One carriage had just rolled out of the courtyard as they pulled in and another one pulled to a stop right behind them.

Bracing for the cold winter air, he shoved the necklace into his pocket and stepped out of his carriage. Swirls of snowflakes blew about and prompted him to pull up his collar as he looked around. It would be wise to go inside before the occupants of the carriage behind disembarked. This way he would have a better chance at getting a room for the night.

The inside of the inn smelled just as good as the last time he had been there. And once again, he was greeted by the impeccably attired Mr Hemmsley. Only this time, the man seemed startled to see him.

'Good afternoon, Mr Alexander. It's a pleasure to see you again.'

'Likewise, Mr Hemmsley. I was wondering if—'

Before he got to finish, Mr Hemmsley leaned in closer and lowered his voice so the two gentlemen behind Simon could not hear their conversation. 'I don't like to involve myself in marital discord and I'd rather not have a dramatic scene unfold at my inn, if you please.'

'Pardon?'

'When last you stayed here, the both of you seemed so in love. But I understand that appearances can be deceiving.'

The cold must have frozen his brain because he had no idea what the man was talking about. Simon shook his head and closed his eyes, trying to grab on to the last threads of his patience.

'Mr Hemmsley. I am cold and hungry and at the moment I just want some brandy.'

'I understand. Would you care to have something in the tavern before you get your wife?'

'My wife?'

The words felt like a blow to his gut. Simon only had one wife. Well, one fake one. But Lizzy was back in London.

Mr Hemmsley nodded and looked apprehensive, as if he wasn't certain if he had overstepped the mark. 'I assume that is why you are here.'

It wasn't uncommon for husbands to drag their

wives back home if they had run away, but Lizzy hadn't run from him. She wasn't even his wife and had no desire to be. He had hinted at showing her the Mediterranean Sea, but instead of telling him that she would love for him to show it to her, she had barely said anything. At that moment, it had confirmed what he feared. Her fortune and Stonehaven meant more to her than he did. He needed to accept that and forget about her. But if she was here in the inn, how could he stay away from her?

'Where is my wife?' he managed to ask through the pain the word was causing him.

'She's in there.' Mr Hemmsley hesitantly gestured to the closed parlour door.

All she had ever wanted from him was Stonehaven. She had to be travelling back there now. That building was the one place she said felt like home. It was the one place she could go to escape his predecessor—the one place she could go after her father had sold her off to Skeffington...

Sold her off?

Those were the words she used. Why had the meaning of that phrase not occurred to him before now?

He headed to the parlour to confront his *wife*.

When he opened the door to the private room, Lizzy turned from where she was seated at the small round table by a roaring fire, having an early dinner. The fork in her hand fell to her plate with a loud clatter. She looked as if she had seen a ghost. He closed the door and stepped further into the room.

Simon needed to know the truth and he needed to hear it from her lips.

'You were forced by your father to marry him, weren't you?'

'What are you doing here?' A sense of disbelief was in her voice.

'Answer my question, Elizabeth. Did you want to marry your husband?'

'You searched me out to ask me that?' Her bewilderment was evident on her face.

'Answer me.'

She stood and threw her napkin down on to the table. 'Of course I never wanted to marry him. What girl of seventeen would have? How could you believe I would have wanted that?'

All this time he had thought her a fortune hunter. All this time he had thought that her title and fortune meant more to her than anything and she had gone to an extreme measure to get them. Now he didn't know what to believe. Now he didn't know what she valued above all else and how he fit into that.

Lizzy had decided to go back to Dorset. Part of her knew that once she stepped foot into Stonehaven, she would never want to leave it again. She could no longer live in London. Since Simon left, it had lost all its appeal. She had no interest in hosting dinner parties and balls any more or in mingling with her Society friends. Before she left she sent a letter to Mr Sherman to discontinue his search for a town house for her. London held too many memories of Simon leaving her and each time she passed Skeffington House, it would be a painful reminder that he was somewhere far away without her and she had no idea if he was safe or even still alive. The empty house, with the doorknocker removed, was just a giant reminder of how her heart felt without him near.

And here he was, demanding that she tell him about her marriage. Acting as if all this time he had believed she had wanted that horrible man for a husband. How could he think that of her?

They stood there, staring at one another as if they both were unsure what to say next. Simon was breathing so hard that one would think he had run all the way from London.

'What are you doing here?' he asked, narrowing his eyes.

He didn't love her and she wanted desperately to forget him. Couldn't he have had the decency to go to another inn so she could at least try? 'I'm on my way to Stonehaven. What are you doing here? You left London days ago.'

'I had some matters to attend to outside of Town before I could leave for Stonehaven to gather my belongings and then head to Portsmouth. I'm headed there now and stopped here for the night.' He glanced back at the door. 'I didn't even ask Mr Hemmsley for a room. When he told me that you were here I had to see you. Now I suppose there are no rooms left.'

Was he blaming her for that? 'I have a room.' And since he was so eager to leave England, he could sleep in this parlour for all she cared.

'You mean we have a room… *Mrs Alexander.*'

'I mean *I* have a room, Mr Alexander.' Their pretend marriage while they travelled together for three days was over. Apparently, it wasn't good enough for him to offer to make it a real marriage. 'I couldn't

exactly tell Mr Hemmsley my real name, now could
I?' she continued. 'He knows me as Mrs Alexander.'

'Why are you staying here and not at one of the
inns you normally frequent?'

'I liked it here.' She crossed her arms and arched
her brow.

He mirrored her stance. 'So did I.'

Had he missed her at all? Had he thought about
their time together at this inn? She needed to stop
being foolish. They both were here together because
of coincidence. It wasn't as if he came after her because he couldn't bear to be apart.

'Are you travelling alone?' he asked, looking
around the room.

'I have my maid with me. She is feeling under the
weather so I sent her up to her room for the night to
get some much-needed rest.'

'Travelling with just your maid does not seem safe.'

'I have my coachman, as well, and my groom. It
is what I have been doing for years before I met you.
Do not concern yourself.'

He seemed taken aback by the way she'd responded
to him. What did he expect? He didn't want her and
she'd be damned if she'd let him know just how much
she wanted him.

He tilted his head. 'Why are you angry with me?'

'I am not angry with you.'

'You appear to be angry with me. I've travelled with
you to London to help you try to catch a thief. I offered
you money when you practically had none. And I gave
you Stonehaven. I'd say you do not have a reason to be
angry with me and yet your nails will be drawing blood
soon if you continue to squeeze your arms like that.'

She uncrossed her arms and lowered them to her sides. But then when she thought about what he'd said, her fingers curled into fists. 'Not everything is about possessions. Not everything is about money and fine houses.'

'Then what is this about?'

'It's about you not wanting me!'

Oh, God, why couldn't she just stop talking?

Simon stood there in his chocolate-brown great-coat, with his dark brown eyes so focused on her that she was certain he hadn't blinked. 'Why would you think I don't want you?'

'Because you are leaving.'

'Because I have to.'

'You could stay. You could find your own way to be the Duke of Skeffington, but you choose not to.'

'I can't stay, Elizabeth. People are expecting me to return to the excavation site. The Sicilian government expects me to return and finish what I have started for them. I have to leave, but it doesn't mean that I won't miss you.'

'But not enough to ask me to go with you.' She turned away from him, not wanting him to see the pain she was in.

When he came up behind her she wanted to lean back into his strength and warmth.

'Lizzy, I can't just take you with me. You know the kind of scandal that would cause. I won't do that to you.'

What he meant was as an unmarried couple her reputation would be in tatters. He wouldn't consider marrying her first. He didn't want to spend the rest of his life with her. And, like the fool she was, all she wanted was him.

She spun around to face him and all those years of knowing that she was destined to be alone exploded out of her.

'What is it about me? Is it something I do? Is it something I say? Is it because you think I can't have children since Skeffington and I never had one? The man was over eighty years old. Perhaps I was not the one to blame for our childless state. Tell me what it is! Tell me why you don't want me!' She covered her mouth to try to hold in the sob she felt in her throat. Tears ran down her face and she just wanted the floor to open up. It was surprising her outburst hadn't prompted him to run from the room. Everything she vowed never to say to him had just come spilling out of her and she wished with all her heart she could take it back.

Simon closed the distance between them and cupped her cheeks and kissed her. 'Lizzy, having children is not something I ever thought I would have in my life. So it doesn't matter to me if you can have them or not. It certainly wouldn't stop me from asking you to marry me. I do want you. Please don't doubt that I do.'

'But not enough to make me your wife.'

He froze. She wasn't even certain he was breathing.

'You never said you wanted to go with me. And marrying me is not what you truly want, trust me.'

'Why would I not want that?'

'People don't stay with me very long, Lizzy. You know that. Even my own family could not stand to have me around for longer than a year or two. Some, after only a few months. This isn't about me not wanting you, Lizzy. It's about you growing tired of me and then wanting to leave me.' He lowered his hands from where they had been cupping her cheeks and it looked as if he was going to walk away—until she stopped him with the touch of her hand on his sleeve.

'So you are doing me a favour by not asking me to marry you?'

'Something like that.'

'Do not dare to presume to know how I feel about you, when you've never asked. I'm in love with you. And as much as I want to forget you and go on with my life, I know I never will.'

'You don't know that. You may change your mind.'

'I won't. I feel it deep inside. It is like nothing I have ever felt before. So you can get on that boat and I will stay here. But my love for you will not change.'

He took her hand in his. 'Lizzy, more than anything I want you in my life. I didn't want our three days together to end and you've become everything to me in such a short time. Spending time with you in our false marriage felt more real to me than anything else in my life. I'm afraid I'll ruin that.'

'How could you possibly ruin what we have together?'

'I don't know. I just seem to do that.'

'Simon, I am not your family—not the one you spent time with as a little boy. But I would like to be a family with you now. You are a good man and there isn't anyone else in the world I want to be with. When I was with you, no matter where we were, it felt right. We felt right. How can you ruin that?'

'I don't want to. I don't want to ruin anything we have between us.'

'Well, don't you think leaving me ruins everything? If you return to Sicily without me, there is no us.'

He took her in his arms and kissed her. And from that one long, slow kiss, Lizzy knew that he loved her, too. It was a kiss that conveyed how much he cherished her and how important she was to him. When the kiss ended, the wrinkles through his brows were gone. And he lowered his head so their foreheads were touching.

'I love you. I don't know how. It's been such a short time, but I know I do. I want you with me. I want to show you the warmth of the Sicilian sun.'

'Then you know what you have to do.'

'It's not what I have to do. It's what I want to do. I want to marry you, Lizzy. I want you to be my Duchess of Skeffington.'

They were words she never thought she would hear him say and it made her heart flip over in her chest. And when he kissed her neck and then whispered his proposal in her ear, she was certain that both of them finding themselves at this inn on this night was no mere coincidence.

This was all she had ever wanted. He was all she ever wanted. He was a man who loved her not for her title or her money or what things she could give him. He was a man who loved her just for the woman she was. And that felt amazing.

Epilogue

Stonehaven—three years later

Simon tilted his face up to the warm summer sun and closed his eyes while he lounged back in the rowboat with his wife tucked between his legs. The slow lapping of the water against the boat had lulled Lizzy to sleep and he felt as if he could soon follow. Her head rested on his chest and he felt her rhythmic breathing as his hand rose and fell as it rested on her back. While he wasn't enjoying the briny smell of the sea, he had become fond of the smell of honeysuckle mixed with grass that hung in the air around this particular bank of the lake. The boat had been a wedding gift from Lizzy's sister Juliet and her husband, Monty. Simon couldn't recall ever receiving a gift from his family, but now that he was part of this family he was growing accustomed to kind gestures and feeling loved. However, there were times when having family around could be so inconvenient.

Just as he felt himself drifting off to sleep, there was a splash in the water beside the boat. Simon thought it might be a fish that flicked its tail too close to the surface, until it happened again, making Lizzy stir. The third time a big plonk sound accompanied the splash along with the faint sound of laughter.

'What is that?' Lizzy mumbled.

'It has to be the children. I think they are throwing pebbles at us from the shoreline.'

'Edgar is three and Henry is two. They can't throw that far.' Lizzy rubbed her eyes but didn't move from his chest, which suited him very well.

'I wasn't referring to Andrew and Charlotte's children. I was referring to Juliet and Monty.'

'Oh, those children,' she said with a laugh. 'It was your idea to invite them for the week.'

'Because normally I enjoy their company.'

Another pebble was thrown from the shoreline and this one landed in the water near Simon's head, splashing the warm water on to his face. This was followed by loud laughter from the shore.

'That's more than just Juliet and Monty.'

She looked up at him and gracefully wiped some of the water away from his eyes with her finger. 'I'm sure Charlotte and Andrew are there, as well.' She picked her head up and looked over at their guests. She had untied her bonnet and left it on the bottom of the boat when she had decided to snuggle up with Simon. Now some of her hairpins must have shifted because long wavy black tendrils of her hair blew in the soft breeze. 'What are you lot up to? Can't you see we are trying to nap?'

'We didn't know you two were in there,' Juliet called back. 'Monty and Andrew were having a contest to see who could hit the boat the most.'

'Do not bring me into this,' Andrew shouted over. 'This was all your idea, Juliet. Your sister is telling a Banbury tale, Elizabeth. Do not listen to her. She was throwing those pebbles with that poorly aiming husband of hers.'

'I hit more times that she did.'

'Neither of you hit the boat once,' Lizzy's older sister, Charlotte, said.

'And you can do better,' Juliet taunted back.

Charlotte raised her brow at her husband and he nodded. 'Challenge accepted,' he shouted to the younger couple.

'We are still in this boat!' Simon pinched the bridge of his nose and then reached slowly for one of the oars that was lying beside them.

'And you wanted to have brothers or sisters,' Lizzy mumbled.

'Yes, but ones that would let us nap in the middle of a Sunday and not throw rocks at us.'

'I don't know of any brothers or sisters who are like that. That sounds wonderful, though. I think they only exist in books.'

A hard pebble landed on Simon's booted foot.

'Ow!'

'Sorry. I'm so sorry. I was trying to hit the side of the boat.'

'Charlotte!' Lizzy raised her head again and glared at her older sister, who bore a striking resemblance to Lizzy. When Simon first met her, Lizzy had described Charlotte as the responsible Sommersby sister. Well, throwing pebbles at people in boats did not seem very responsible.

'Do we need to remind you that you're someone's mother, Charlotte?' Simon called out to her.

'They are taking their naps. They will never know,' she replied.

This time Juliet and Monty simultaneously threw pebbles that landed near Lizzy and seemed quite pleased with themselves for how wet they got her.

'That's it. I'm finished being the nice sister.'

'Has anyone ever referred to you that way?' Simon asked.

'I'm sure at one time…maybe? Oh, just give me something hard to throw.'

'I have a better idea, my love.' And with that he sat up and scooped the tip of the oar through the surface of the water, splashing water far enough that he got Juliet and Monty very wet from where they were standing.

Charlotte let out a laugh, until Andrew turned to her and pulled off his boots.

'Andrew, you wouldn't.'

He took a step towards her and she backed away a few steps.

'Andrew…' Her voice was lilting with a warning.

Unfortunately for Charlotte, her large, broad husband had no problem catching her and lifting her into his arms and carrying her into the lake.

After a few more rounds of splashing they all agreed to call a truce and head back to the house to change and have ale for the gentlemen and lemonade for the ladies out on the terrace.

As they walked back through the woods, Andrew kept pace with Simon. Charlotte and Juliet had married two men who were the Duke of Winterbourne's brothers. It had been a helpful connection for Simon because he found the Duke to be a trusted gentleman to go to for advice on ducal matters and now counted him as one of his friends.

When they reached a particularly narrow part of the path, Andrew graciously allowed Simon to go first.

'You were able to splash that water very far with that oar. It was impressive.'

'It's an old sailor's trick.'

'Perhaps you might show me how to do it before we leave Stonehaven.'

'Perhaps.'

After walking further on, Andrew went ahead to walk beside his wife and Lizzy. As soon as he left Simon's side, Juliet dropped back next to him.

'He wanted to know how you did that trick with the oar, didn't he?'

'What makes you believe that?'

'Because I know how competitive he can be.'

This coming from the one Sommersby sister who everyone agreed was the most competitive.

'You know you are my favourite brother, Simon.' She hooked her arm through his and gave him a playful bump into his shoulder.

'I'm sure you say the same thing to Andrew.'

'Only when I want something from him.' Her cheeky smile brightened her face.

'Do you want me to show you how it's done?'

'Only if you'd like to show me. I would never be so bold as to ask.'

'Of course not.'

They grinned at each other as she squeezed his arm. Lizzy had stopped walking and was waiting for them to make their way to where she was standing beside the path.

'And what are you two discussing back here?'

'Just that Simon is my favourite brother.'

'I thought that was me,' Andrew called back.

'Today it is Simon. You can have your turn to-morrow.'

When they reached the terrace behind the house, Simon held Lizzy back by the arm while the others went inside.

'I'm sorry your nap was interrupted. I should have done a better job of defending you,' he said with a teasing voice.

She leaned in and kissed his cheek. 'You were per-fect. I only wish we had more time in the boat.'

'So do I...without your family there to torture us.'

'We could sneak back to the boat later tonight.'

'You'd like a moonlit boat ride around the lake?'

Tilting her head, she smiled at him and then whis-pered exactly what she wanted to do in that boat—on the lake. And now Simon was counting the hours until she could.

* * * * *

*If you enjoyed this story
check out the other books in
The Sommersby Brides miniseries*

One Week to Wed
*'One Night Under the Mistletoe'
in* Convenient Christmas Brides

*And be sure to check out
Laurie Benson's miniseries
The Secret Lives of the Ton*

An Unsuitable Duchess
An Uncommon Duke
An Unexpected Countess